D1115022

rough
waters

rough waters

S. L. ROTTMAN

PEACHTREE
ATLANTA

a freestone publication

Published by
PEACHTREE PUBLISHERS, LTD.
494 Armour Circle NE
Atlanta, Georgia 30324

Text © 1997 by S. L. Rottman
Cover illustration © 1997 by Suzy Schultz

Book design by Loraine M. Balcsik
Composition by Dana Celentano and Dana L. Laurent

Manufactured in the United States of America

10 9 8 7 6 5 4 3 2

Library of Congress Cataloging-in-Publication Data
Rottman, S. L.
   Rough waters / S. L. Rottman. —1st ed.
      p. cm.
   Summary: After their parents' death in an automobile accident, two teenage
brothers are sent to Colorado to live with an estranged uncle, owner of a white
water rafting outfit.
   ISBN 1-56145-172-X
   [1. Grief—Fiction. 2. Brothers—Fiction. 3. Orphans—Fiction. 4. Uncles—Fiction.
5. Rafting (Sports)—Fiction.] I. Title.
   PZ7.R7534Ro 1998
   [Fic]—dc21
                                                              97-39434
                                                              CIP
                                                              AC

to my uncles Joe and Tom, who made me a
"river rat wannabe,"
and to Barb, who became a river rat.

.

Thanks again to Art, Grandma, and Russ
for their editing advice.

Special thanks also to Eric, who believed in
my first book enough to ask for a second.

—s. l. r.

Chapter One

Boxes were everywhere. And the sight of them just made me sick to my stomach. I couldn't believe that I was just calmly packing up my life, calmly sorting through the last ten years in this house, calmly making "sell," "donate," and "keep" piles.

Nancy came into the living room. "How're you doing, kid?" She reached out and ruffled my hair. I let her, but only because I knew it was for her reassurance too. Nancy had been our neighbor since we moved in when I was three. She had become an adopted aunt; we didn't have any of our own. I didn't even know we had an uncle until we were told our parents had left us in his custody.

I heard the shattering of glass from the kitchen, and "Dammit" close on its heels. Nancy gave me a weird combination of smile and frown as I started to leave the room. "He's having a hard time," she said softly.

I tried not to roll my eyes. "So am I," I said as I left the living room, "but at least I'm willing to admit it."

When I walked into the kitchen, Gregg raised the dustpan and broom in self defense. "I don't want to hear it," he snapped.

"Gregg," I began.

"No, Scott, I don't want to hear it. I'll get it cleaned up. Just go get the living room done."

"Gregg, we don't have to do all of this today."

"Yeah, we do, Scott. We've got to get the house cleaned out so we can get it sold."

"It will sell," I said, barely keeping my patience. He was my older brother; he was the one who was supposed to do the comforting.

He bit his lower lip, and I saw the tears start to form in his eyes. He dropped the broom and dustpan with a clatter. "I think I'll go take a bike ride."

I shook my head. "Why don't you go take a nap?" His blue eyes had a haunted look, enhanced by the black smudges under them. "I know you haven't been sleeping much." I had been getting just barely five hours a night myself, and he was awake every time I went to sleep and again when I woke up.

"I feel fine. I just need some fresh air."

I sighed and picked up the broom. He left without looking back. I heard him argue with Donna, the social worker, and then the back door slammed. A few minutes later, Donna came into the kitchen.

"How are you?"

"I'm fine," I said, wishing people would quit asking such a stupid question. I wasn't fine and I wasn't going to be fine for a long time, but they didn't want to hear that.

"Your brother went for another bike ride."

"I know."

"He should be sleeping."

"I know."

"So should you."

I swept the last bits of my mother's favorite vase into the dustpan and dropped them into the trash.

"Scott?"

"I heard you."

"But you don't have anything to say?"

"No," I said, "I have things to do, but nothing to say."

"Holding it in like this isn't healthy for either of you."

"Well, you all know Gregg's having a hard time, so why don't you just track him down and make him get healthy first?"

"We know you're having a hard time, too," she said quickly.

"Whatever," I said, heading back to the living room.

She followed me. "It's okay to feel this way."

I looked at her for the first time in the conversation. "Feel what way?"

"Well..." she hedged.

"I haven't told you how I feel, so how do you know it's okay?"

Nancy stepped in. "Scott, it is okay."

"No," I said. "It's not okay. My parents are dead. It is definitely not okay, and neither is Gregg, and neither am I. Just leave us alone so we can finish packing up our lives."

I turned and climbed the stairs two at a time. I walked down to my parents' room, ignoring the boxes lining the hallway. I forced myself to enter their room. I hadn't been in it since we had been taken to the social worker's office two weeks ago and told that our parents had both been killed in a car accident.

I sat down on their bed, and felt the hot tears trying to escape. I knew why Gregg kept going for bike rides instead of sleeping. It's when you curl up to sleep that you really realize what's wrong, what's missing. That's the time your mind starts to remember, and when it becomes impossible not to cry. I knew that Donna and Nancy were bothered because Gregg and I weren't crying in front of them, but that just wasn't our style. I knew he had cried himself to sleep that first night, just like I had. I didn't know if he had cried since. No matter what I was doing, the tears just kept sneaking up on me, but I had become better at keeping them hidden. All through the funeral, Donna kept telling us it was okay to cry. And I kind of think that the more she told us that we should cry, the more convinced we became that we shouldn't.

Who was she to come in and tell us what to feel? Just some social worker hired by the courts. She didn't know us from a hill of beans. Nancy had been one of the few friendly and familiar faces at the funeral. Out of the seventy or so people that showed up, I think I knew maybe fifteen. We didn't have any family, other than our parents. It had never seemed to be a problem before.

But the courts saw it as a problem now, to have a fifteen and seventeen year old without other family members. They were going to place us in a home. That's really where I thought we were going to have to go.

Then, five days ago, we got a phone call from Uncle Dave. I never even knew we had an Uncle Dave. Gregg remembered some stories about an uncle, but he wasn't sure if it was Dave or Dan. Apparently the last will my parents had drawn up placed us in his custody. The will was almost fifteen years old, but it was the only one they had ever done. So now we were leaving for Buena Vista, Colorado, in two days—leaving behind the house we grew up in, our neighborhood, all our friends. I tried not to think about it.

When I stretched out on the bed, I could smell my mother's perfume in the bedspread. This was the only room in the house that hadn't been touched, the only one that still looked like it was our home. Neither Gregg nor I had been willing to come in and sort through our parents' personal belongings. But we weren't willing to let Nancy do it either. I thought Gregg was going to hit her when she suggested it. He didn't, but from the way she flinched, I think she had the same thoughts.

"We'll do it," he had snarled. "We're just not going to do it today."

I looked around the room, confused for a moment because it seemed blurry. Impatiently, I wiped my hand across my eyes, drying them. There really wasn't much of a reason not to let Nancy help us in here, I thought. It wasn't like we were going to keep any of their clothes or furniture or linens. We could barely take anything with us as it was. Uncle Dave had made it clear that he was willing to take us in, but that it was a very small house and most of it was already full of his stuff.

"Hey."

I jumped. Gregg was standing in the doorway.

"What do you think you're doing?"

"Just sitting here," I said. "You went for a ride, so I thought I'd take a break too."

For a minute, it looked like he might actually come into the room, but then he just let himself slide down the door frame so he was sitting on the floor, leaning against it and propping his feet on the other side. He let out a big sigh. "This sucks."

I stared at him in disbelief. "Well, yeah, I guess you could say that."

He went on as if he hadn't heard me. "I'm almost an adult. I'm going to college in three months. What do I need with a guardian I've never met for a lousy three months?"

I looked at him. "What do you mean?"

"I know you need a guardian; you're only fifteen, but I'm an adult. I can be legally responsible for myself. Why do I have to go to Colorado? I've never been there. It's a stupid hick state and I'm going to be stuck with a stupid hick uncle who doesn't know us or even want us there."

I ignored the implication that he was willing to let me go alone.

"How do you know he doesn't want us?"

Gregg snorted. "You heard him on the phone. 'Your parents were under the delusion that I'd be a good guardian for you.' That doesn't sound like he wants us. And then all the talk about how small his house is and how we can't bring much. And how he's been living alone for eight years and he's not sure how easy it will be for him to adjust." Gregg shook his head. "He was just waiting for one of us to say we didn't want to go so he could back out of it."

"So why didn't you?" I countered. "If that's all it would have taken, and you don't want to go anyway, why didn't you just tell him that?"

Gregg didn't answer, and I knew he wouldn't. When Uncle Dave had called, he had sounded as spooked and unsure of himself as we were.

Gregg closed his eyes and leaned his head back against the door frame. Without opening his eyes, he said, "What do you miss about them the most?"

I was surprised. This was the first time he had brought them up. I closed my eyes too. "I don't know. There's so much that hurts to think about that I can't seem to remember anything."

"I wish I was like that. I feel like I'm remembering everything at once. Dad and I were supposed to go surfing this weekend."

"I know."

"And Mom was going to chaperon the yearbook party, even though I didn't want her to."

I didn't say anything.

"It's not fair, Scott. They had no right to leave us like this. No money, no one to live with, nothing. What were they thinking?"

"They were thinking that they were only in their forties, and that they weren't going to die anytime soon. And I'm sure they didn't think they'd die together like that." They had been on their way home from a party. Neither of them had their seat belts on.

"Yeah, I know." Gregg sighed. "But after all the lectures about saving money and being prepared and doing things today instead of tomorrow, it's just a nasty surprise."

I knew Gregg was really upset about the money. We didn't have much now, which was going to be different after growing up in the upper-middle-class neighborhood of Hermosa Beach. The life insurance and sale of the house would cover the second mortgage, the funeral, and most of the credit card bills. The cars were both leased, so the one still in working order was going back to the company. The Lexus had been totaled beyond repair, but the insurance in the lease had covered it. There had apparently been some losses in their investments that had taken a big chunk out of the bank accounts.

Gregg had been accepted to UCLA, but he was nowhere close to getting any kind of scholarship. There was barely enough money left in the accounts to cover his first year in school. After that, he was either going to have to take out loans or get a scholarship somehow. He had been counting on Mom and Dad to put him through school. I had, too, but at least I had a few more years in high school, and if I could keep my 3.8 grade point average, I would stand a good chance of getting a scholarship.

We sat quietly for a long time like that, just thinking our own thoughts. I was confusing myself, because I knew I had come to their room on purpose, but now I just wanted to get my mind off my parents. Mentally, I was finishing the inventory in my room of what I was going to take with me. Clothing, books, a few tapes. Nancy had agreed to store some stuff for us. She would ship my computer and my models later. I was also trying to picture Colorado. I had always lived in California, and our family vacations had never taken us to Colorado. Gregg had a huge map of the U.S. on his bedroom wall, and before he took it down, we tried to find Buena Vista. We couldn't. That meant it wasn't a major town in Colorado.

And I didn't know what to think about Uncle Dave. He was apparently my father's brother. Why hadn't I even heard of him before? What kind of man loses touch with his only brother for over ten years? But then again, I didn't know if it was my uncle's fault or my father's. Knowing how much I loved my father and how close we had been as a family of four, I was pretty sure that if he couldn't get along with his brother, there was a good chance Gregg and I were going to have a hard time getting along with him too.

I heard a hushed whisper from the hallway. "Oh, look, they're finally asleep."

"Shh, Donna, you'll wake them."

I raised my head and looked toward Gregg, who was turning his head to look at me. We shook our heads at the same time, and I began to stretch.

"Well," Gregg yawned, "I guess we ought to get back to work."

"Are you sure about that?" I asked. "I think we could just lie here and let somebody else take care of everything."

"That's what we keep telling you," Donna said. "We can do all this for you. We can hire some packers and they'll do it all."

Gregg closed his eyes for a moment, and I could almost see him counting to ten. He never used to have such a short fuse, but in the last week he had been blowing up at everything and everyone. A couple of nights ago, he had blown up at me. I told him to quit being such a jerk and start counting before he answered people when he was mad. I was glad to see he was taking my advice.

"No, Donna," he said slowly, "that's not possible. We're not just moving. We have to get rid of most of the stuff, and we're the only ones who know what we want or need to keep. Therefore, we have to do this ourselves."

She opened her mouth to say something, but Gregg cut her off. "If you really want to be useful, why don't you go get us dinner? I'm really in the mood for Chinese food. In fact, I'd love some Szechuan beef from the Golden Star. Would you go get us some?" The Golden Star was about twenty minutes from our house.

"Yeah," I said, "I'd love some sweet and sour pork. And an egg roll."

"Mmmm," Nancy said. "That sounds great, but I'd like a spring roll instead. Tell you what," she said, turning to Donna. "Why don't you leave now, and I'll go call the order in. It should be ready by the time you get there." She began walking Donna toward the stairs.

"Nice work," I said in a low voice to Gregg.

"Thanks. I suppose now I'll have to eat some of it." He hadn't been eating much lately either.

"Small price to pay for getting rid of her, even for just forty minutes."

Gregg actually smiled. "She never had a chance, the way you and Nancy joined up with me so fast."

I nodded. "Hey," I said carefully, "why don't we let Nancy pack up this room? It'd be easier on both of us." I hurried on as I saw his face begin to shut on me. "And it would help her feel like she's doing something for us." He didn't say anything. "Come on, Gregg, neither of us is ready to go through all their personal stuff. At least let her help, so we don't have to do it all."

"Okay. Fine. Whatever." He got up and walked down the hall to his room. The door slammed behind him.

Nancy came back upstairs. "What was that all about?" She came into my parents' room and sat down on the bench in the bay window.

"I told him I wanted you to help us with packing up this room."

Nancy's eyes got a little bigger. "I didn't think either of you wanted me in here."

I shrugged.

"I'd be happy to help if you really want me to, but I don't want to bother Gregg by doing it."

"There's nothing that anyone could do right now that wouldn't bother Gregg," I said.

"I know he's upset."

"We all know he's upset. But deciding not to let you help us is stupid. You're basically part of our family."

"Thank you. I've always felt that way too, but it's nice to hear it."

I shook my head. "I still don't understand why we can't stay here with you."

"Life doesn't work that way. There's the matter of blood ties and the will, and the courts would be much more likely to award custody to an uncle than to a neighbor who merely watched you go to kindergarten the first day."

"And skateboard the first time."

She laughed. "And kiss a girl for the first time."

"You did not!"

"I most certainly did. You and that little girl Cindy, in, God, what was it? You were probably in fourth grade."

"Third," I said automatically. "I can't believe you were spying on me."

"I wasn't spying. I was in the backyard weeding. It wasn't my fault you chose the bushes by my house to try to kiss her."

"Hey, she tried to kiss me!"

"And I also saw Gregg drive for the first time, and get dressed in a tux for prom."

"And you went with us when he had to go to the hospital after he wiped out on his dirt bike."

"And I went with your parents to see you get inducted into the National Junior Honor Society."

"I remember drawing on your kitchen table when Mom and Dad would go out and you baby-sat us."

"I haven't had to baby-sit you for a long time," she said softly.

"Yeah, but you've always been there for us."

She smiled, even though there were tears in her eyes. "You know I'll always be here for you."

"'A phone call away' is what you've said a hundred times."

"It's true," she said quickly.

"I know, Nancy. But right now I'm afraid that even a phone call feels too far away."

"Yeah. I know what you mean. I wish it could be different, Scott."

"Me too."

"Well," she said briskly. "I suppose I ought to go place that order now."

"I thought you were going to do that as soon as she left."

Nancy winked at me. "I figured you and Gregg wouldn't mind if she had to wait an extra ten or fifteen minutes at the restaurant."

"Thanks, Nancy, you're pretty cool."

"I always have been, honey." She started down the stairs. "I'll help you with your parents' room," she said, loud enough for Gregg to hear, "but only if you're both in there with me. You should both have a say about what goes or stays."

Needless to say, a lot more went than stayed. We put their wedding album and our baby books into a box to be shipped to Colorado. Gregg kept Dad's pocketknife and compass. I took his wedding ring. He had hardly ever worn it, because he didn't like to wear jewelry. I also kept a ring he had given Mom for their twentieth anniversary. Gregg gave me a funny look when I put it in my pocket, but I still kept it. We each took a couple of his shirts. Then, whether it was sold in the estate auction, donated to Goodwill, or thrown away, everything else went.

Two days later, so did we.

Chapter Two

The two-hour flight from California to Colorado Springs wasn't too bad. Gregg and I both had our Walkmans and didn't talk to each other much. We hadn't really spoken since he, Nancy, and I had cleaned out Mom and Dad's room. Actually, he hadn't had a real conversation with anyone in days. He had yelled at Donna several times the last two days, but that was about it. He didn't really even say good-bye to Nancy. I was kind of pissed at him for that. She had done everything she could for us, and he was a total jerk to her.

When I hugged her good-bye, she had slipped something into my coat pocket. "It's my address, home number, and work number," she had said. "I want to make sure you take it with you."

"I'll stay in touch," I promised. "You're all the family I have left, other than Gregg."

"You have your uncle."

"But I don't even know him."

"Give him a chance," she said. "And take care of Gregg." She looked at him, standing away by himself. "I know you're the little brother, but I think he may need your help." And then she kissed me on the cheek and was gone.

When I got on the plane, I discovered that she hadn't just left me her address and number. The note read:

Scott—

You've been incredibly strong the last week, and I can't tell you how proud I am of you. I know your parents are watching and proud of you too, wherever they are. Gregg is going to need you to be there for him, no matter how much he tells you no. It will be hard, but try to stay with him, even when he pushes you away.

Give your uncle a chance. I know you're nervous about meeting him, but I'm sure he's nervous too. Don't worry about not having as much money as you used to. I know that you will succeed in whatever you choose to do. Keep up the fantastic job you've always done in school. Those awesome grades will come in handy when it comes time to find a college and scholarships.

Stay in touch whenever you have the time to remember me.

Nancy

She had included not only her number and address, but two hundred dollars cash as well.

When we got to Colorado Springs, my stomach was in knots. I couldn't believe I was going to meet my uncle for the first time.

We got off the plane and looked around expectantly. I searched the faces of all the people who were there waiting for friends or relatives, trying to find one that looked like my father. I thought I saw my uncle once, but then some lady flung her arms around him and they walked away.

"How are we supposed to recognize him?" Gregg muttered after we had been standing there for a few minutes, both of us feeling out of place.

"I don't know," I said. "Maybe we should just call out 'Uncle Dave' really loud."

I had been joking when I said it, but that's exactly what Gregg did. And he did it even louder than I thought he would. Everyone turned to stare at us, but no one stepped forward. *No wonder,* I thought. *Who would want to admit to being related to us now?*

"Maybe he's waiting for us at the baggage claim area," I said, hoping to get away from all those staring eyes. I started down the terminal wing toward the main concourse, only to discover that it was the only concourse. I was shocked.

"How small is this town?" I asked.

Gregg shrugged. "I have no idea how big Colorado Springs is," he said, "but I'm pretty sure it's bigger than Buena Vista."

"Oh God," I groaned.

We got down to the baggage carousels (there were only a few), and found our luggage pretty quickly. We didn't have much to pick up because most of it was being shipped to us. We each had a couple of suitcases, a backpack, and a box of extra stuff we had packed. A lot of people were still staring at us, so the next time Gregg started yelling "Uncle Dave?" I joined in. I figured I didn't have much to lose.

After getting no response, we went to make a phone call. It took Gregg about ten minutes to dig out the number before we could make the call. That's when we found out it was a long distance call to Buena Vista.

"How far away are we?" I asked Gregg.

"How am I supposed to know?" he snapped. This time he dialed collect.

"Yes, a collect call from Gregg and Scott," he told the operator. Then he waited a few seconds. His eyes got huge. He slammed the phone back down in the handset and cursed nonstop for two or three minutes. We got several more stares, and these were not the friendly type. I kept trying to get him to keep his voice down, but he wouldn't even listen to me.

Finally, he grabbed up his box and bags and said, "Come on." Instead of heading out of the terminal, he headed back down the concourse.

"Do we have to catch another flight?" I asked, hurrying to catch up.

He ignored me, and just fifty feet down the concourse he turned into a restaurant. He piled his stuff next to a table, went directly to the counter, and ordered himself two hamburgers, a large order of fries, and a chocolate milkshake. I stood by the table, feeling frustrated enough to hit him, except for the fact that he outweighed me by close to thirty pounds and was at least six inches taller. I had learned from experience how to defend myself, but I knew better than to attack.

When he came back with his food, he jerked his head toward the counter. "You better go get yourself some food," he said. "We're going to be here a while."

"Would you please tell me what the hell is going on?" I yelled. Again, heads turned to stare, but I really didn't care at this point.

"Someone will come get us in a while."

"Excuse me?"

"Someone will come get us in a while."

"What's that supposed to mean?"

"Exactly what I said."

"Well, what else did he say?"

"Nothing."

"What do you mean, nothing?" I felt like I was going in circles.

"The operator told Uncle Dave he had a collect call. Uncle Dave said 'someone will be there to pick you up soon,' and then he denied the charges."

"He denied the charges?"

"Would you please quit repeating everything I say?"

"Yeah, if you'll start telling me everything I need to know instead of just giving me bits and pieces!"

Gregg shrugged. "That's it. That's everything." And he bit into his burger. He just sat there, chewing, while I glared at him. Finally I went and got myself some food. I came back and we ate in silence. Gregg wouldn't even look at me. I couldn't stand it any longer.

"Gregg, tell me what's going on!"

"I did, Scott. That's the whole conversation."

"I don't get it."

He shook his head. "There's nothing to get. He's too cheap to pay for a collect call to tell us what's going on, and too lazy to come get us himself. That's all there is to it."

I stared at my half-empty plate and felt like throwing up or crying. I couldn't believe this was happening to us. We were going to live with this man? This man my father hadn't spoken to in years? This man who only talked to us for five minutes after learning of my father's death, and then wouldn't take a collect call when we finally arrived?

"This sucks," I muttered.

"Hey," Gregg said, "that's my line."

I looked up at him, and he smiled at me. It was the first real smile I had seen from him since my parents died. "We'll be okay, Scott."

I felt the tears even though I tried to hold them back. "How can you say that?"

"Because it can't get any worse."

I groaned.

"Hey," he said brightly, "how about a huge sundae? They've got hot fudge, caramel, and peanut butter."

"Okay," I said.

"Okay which one?"

"All three," I said.

He stared at me. "You didn't even finish your burger."

"I'll have it done by the time you get back with my sundae."

He grinned. "Okay. One peanut butter-caramel-hot fudge sundae coming up."

We were about halfway through our sundaes when the PA system announced: "Gregg and Scott Baxter, Gregg and Scott Baxter, please meet your party in the baggage claim area."

I dropped my spoon into my dish, and it splattered melted ice cream all over my shirt. Gregg looked at me, his eyes wide. I could see that his too-cool attitude was slipping just a little.

"Guess Buena Vista isn't quite as far away as we thought it was," I said slowly.

"Guess not." He scooped up another spoonful of ice cream and continued to eat. It hadn't taken long for his attitude to readjust.

"Come on, Gregg, let's go."

"Why?"

"Because he's here."

"So? He wasn't in any big hurry to get here. I paid for this ice cream. I'm going to eat all of it."

I sat there and waited for him to finish. It seemed like he took forever. I couldn't eat any more of my ice cream. It felt like everything I had just eaten was thinking about coming back up. My feet couldn't stop twitching on the floor.

"Come on, Gregg, hurry up!"

"I'm not done yet!" He was literally scraping every last drop of ice cream out of the bowl.

He took his time gathering his bags too. And when we walked down the concourse, I swear he was dragging his feet. Then he stopped and looked in the gift shop window.

"Come on, Gregg!" I pleaded.

"Gregg and Scott Baxter, Gregg and Scott Baxter, please meet your party in the baggage claim area," the anonymous PA voice droned again.

He stopped again, this time to check the monitor with the incoming flights. "Gregg, that's it! I'm going on." And I started walking faster, leaving him behind.

In three steps he caught up to me and grabbed the strap on my duffel bag. "What's the rush? You've never seen him before; what's a few more minutes going to do?"

"Gregg, I know you're pissed, but this is stupid. Let's get this over with. Let's go meet Uncle Dave and then go see what Buena Vista's all about."

He didn't increase his pace as much as I wanted, but at least he wasn't dragging his feet anymore.

We stepped on the escalator going down to baggage claim.

"What do you think he looks like?"

Gregg rolled his eyes. "I don't know and I really don't care," he said.

I turned back around to scan the baggage area as much as I could. We got off the escalator and turned toward the carousels. There was a lady holding a sign that said Gregg and Scott.

I glanced at Gregg. He looked bored. I went up to the lady.

"Um, excuse me," I began.

"Oh, hi!" she said brightly, looking at both of us. "You must be Scott." She took my hand and shook it. "And you must be Gregg." She reached out for Gregg's hand, but he ignored her.

"Do you have all your luggage?"

"Yeah, it's right here."

"Okay. Well, the van's waiting outside."

She turned to go.

"Um, who are you?" I blurted out.

"Oh, I'm sorry," she said, turning back around. "My name's Laura. I work with your uncle."

"Is he in the van?"

"Oh, no," she said with a laugh. "He had seven trips to send out today. He'll meet us at the office."

We followed her out to the van. It was painted a bright blue with Rugged Rapids written in purple across the side. There were already four other people in the van.

Laura quickly started loading our stuff into the luggage box on top of the van.

"Um, what's this for?"

She looked at me. "What do you mean?"

"This van, what's it for?"

"We provide a shuttle service for people who come in from out of state to take multiday trips with us."

"Trips?"

"Raft trips." She stopped. "Don't you know anything about your uncle's company?"

Gregg snorted. "No," I said quickly, "we've never even met him before."

"Oh," she said, raising her eyebrows. "Well, Rocky owns Rugged Rapids. And since I was coming down to pick up some clients, he asked me to get you as well."

"How convenient," Gregg muttered.

"Rocky?" I asked.

She looked at me funny. "Yes. Your uncle."

"Wait a minute," I said. "There must be some mistake. Our uncle's name is Dave. I'm sorry. You must be looking for someone else."

"You're Gregg and Scott Baxter, right?"

"Right."

"And you're moving out here from California to live with your uncle because your parents were killed in an accident?"

I winced. No one had said it that baldly before. "Yes."

"Then I'm pretty sure you're the ones I'm supposed to pick up. I'm really sorry," she said awkwardly. "Um...excuse me?" I still didn't move. "I guess you're going to have to get in the van so I can close the door and we can get out of here."

Gregg was already sitting in the van. All of the seats were taken except for the seat up next to the driver. I crawled in for a long ride.

The scenery to Buena Vista was breathtaking. The mountains amazed me, from the time we were outside of the airport when they looked like they were towering over the city, to the time we were surrounded by them as we drove through canyons and valleys. Once the highway turned sharply after we had finished climbing a hill. I hadn't realized how much of an incline it was until we reached the crest where the road spilled down into a huge sprawling valley.

Coming from California, I was also surprised to be driving these long stretches of highway, rarely seeing another car. The sky was a deep, velvety blue. The trees were dark green, but the grass was already beginning to lose its spring green and turn a little yellow. Along the way, I saw a hawk, some antelope, and even a few buffalo. I guess the buffalo really didn't count, since they were in a fenced-in field, but it was the first time I had ever seen them live and not on TV.

Gregg was still really angry. He put on his headphones before we got out of the airport parking lot and stared out his window the whole time. Even if I had wanted to sulk, I wouldn't have been able to do it that long, at least not without getting a crick in my neck.

The other four people in the van turned out to be a family in from Arizona for a week. They were taking a three-day trip with Rugged Rapids. The son, who looked to be about ten, was hooked into his Game Boy. The daughter looked about twelve, and she was trying to appear to be ignoring me while she stared at me. The mom and dad had a lot of questions for Laura.

Laura turned out to be pretty nice and she knew a lot about the area. She told us about the different wildlife we would see, what kind of weather we should have during the next week, and how the river was running. Even though I knew it was part of the package, it was still neat to listen to her. I liked the way she wore her dirty-blond hair, hanging perfectly straight down to the middle of her back. She didn't seem to be wearing any makeup either. Some of the girls I knew started wearing makeup when they were in elementary school.

She told us that she had just graduated from UCLA, but that she had grown up in Colorado. I looked quickly at Gregg when she said that, but he was into his music and hadn't heard her. She also glanced at Gregg in the rearview mirror when she said it, so I knew she knew some things about us. She had been a river guide for the last three summers and had been with Rugged Rapids for the last two.

"I'm Rocky's assistant manager this year, so I don't make quite as many river trips as I used to."

"How many river rafting companies are there in Buena Vista?" I asked.

"It varies a little from year to year, depending on who went out of business and who's starting, but right now there's around eight."

"How long has my uncle been doing this?"

"Rafting? You'd have to ask him that. But I know he's only had the company for three years."

"If you ask me, Rugged Rapids is a great outfit," the father jumped in.

"I've been rafting a lot, and I really enjoyed my experience with Rocky's company last summer. I was very impressed with the friendliness of his guides. That's why I decided to bring my whole family for this trip."

His wife rolled her eyes. "We were perfectly happy to let you have this as your personal escape every year," she said.

"I know," he said, "but I really think you'll enjoy this, and the kids will too, if you'll just give it a chance."

"That's why we're here with you, dear," she said, patting his hand.

"You've never been rafting?" Laura asked.

"No," she said, "just Jon. He's the only one who's been rafting."

"And now you're going on a three-day trip?" I asked.

"It might be a good idea," Laura advised, "if you were to take a one-day or even a half-day trip, just to be sure you're really going to be comfortable. Especially with young children."

The mother raised her eyebrows at her husband, just like my mother used to do, and I could almost hear her saying, "See? I told you."

Before she could say anything, though, Laura laughed. "Just don't tell my boss I suggested it. He'll kill me if you decide not to take the three-day trip after the shorter one."

The drive took about two hours. We dropped the family off at a motel, and after we unloaded their bags, Laura gave Jon a card with the Rugged Rapids number on it. "You might want to call and see if you can get on a short trip first," she said.

"Thanks," he said, "I'm starting to think that's a good idea."

The three of us continued. Gregg was still staring out the window. The sun had gone down behind the mountains, but there was still plenty of light. I guess we must have gone through the side streets, because there didn't seem to be very much to the town. Within minutes we were outside of the town and back on the two-lane highway.

"Um, I thought Uncle Dave lived in Buena Vista."

Laura shook her head slightly. "He lives south of Buena Vista, almost halfway to Salida."

"Oh."

She laughed. "You don't know much about Colorado, do you?"

"Never been here till now."

"I'm sorry about your parents," she said after a minute.

I shrugged, blinking back the tears. They kept trying to creep out at the most awkward moments.

We were quiet as we pulled into the gravel driveway. I surveyed the house and decided that Uncle Dave hadn't exaggerated at all. The house was tiny, and it looked really old too. It was one story, with two front windows looking out over a porch that ran across the front of the house. It had faded to a boring gray, and the trim may have once been white, but now it too was a dingy shade of gray. Huge trees surrounded and hung protectively over the house, and I could see where a couple of branches had been cut back when they had gotten too friendly with the roof.

The house sat all by itself almost a half mile off the road. Our neighbors' houses in California had only been twenty feet away. Dave's house looked lonely.

Laura got out of the van and began unloading our bags. I hopped out and started to help her. Gregg climbed out, stretched, and turned a slow 360, looking at everything. He still hadn't said anything.

Laura reached for a box. "Here, I'll take that," I said, taking it from her. It was mine, and I felt funny letting her carry my stuff. She grabbed a different one, and started for the front door. Gregg just watched, not moving to help with the pile of bags and boxes.

"Oof," she said, setting it down by the door while she fished in her pocket for a key. "It's heavy."

"It's Gregg's," I said, by way of apology.

She smiled at me. "I'm sure they're all heavy. When you move, you have to bring a lot of stuff with you."

She pushed the door open and stepped aside, waiting for me to go in. While I was shaking my head, gesturing for her to go ahead, Gregg swept by, carrying only his small backpack and his Walkman.

I followed Laura through the small living room to a tiny bedroom, where she set down the box. As she turned to go back for another load, I asked her which room was mine.

"Ahh." She fidgeted. "There are only two bedrooms in the house."

All I could do was look at her.

"This house has two bedrooms, one bath, a living room, and a kitchen."

"Oh." I dropped my two bags and box on the floor with a hollow thump and then followed her back through the living room. Gregg had sprawled on the sofa with his feet kicked up on the table in front of it. In addition to the sofa and table, there was a recliner and a stand with a small TV on it in the room. The kitchen had a table and two chairs jammed in the back. That appeared to be it for furniture.

When we got outside, I cleared my throat to get her attention, and then said in a low voice, "I'm sorry about Gregg—"

"Why should you apologize for your brother?" she asked before I could explain what he was doing. "You haven't done anything wrong. Neither has he, really."

"He's not being much help."

She shrugged. "When that becomes a crime, the courts aren't going to have time to deal with anything else."

We gathered the rest of the luggage, passed Gregg, who was still on the couch, and returned to the bedroom. This time I took a better look. Two twin beds stood along the longer two walls, with barely enough space to walk between them. At the foot of each bed was a small, banged-up dresser. I wasn't sure the drawers would open because the dressers were so close to the beds. But there wasn't much room for rearranging. None of the furniture or bed coverings matched. Laura put down the bags and left the room.

Since Gregg was being so obnoxious, I decided I would claim the bed that was under the window. I piled all my stuff on top of it and then went back out to the living room.

Laura was on the phone. I walked by Gregg and hit him on the head, knocking the headphones off.

"Hey! Watch it!"

"You watch it!" I hissed back.

"What?" He was still speaking too loud.

"Quit being such a jerk," I said, softly so Laura wouldn't hear.

"I'm not being a jerk. I'm sure Uncle Dave paid her plenty to help us move here." He put his headphones back on.

The front door swung open. A tall, muscular man entered and took off his sunglasses. He was very tan, and his long blond hair was slipping out from under a baseball cap. His hard blue eyes swept the room, taking in every detail quickly without resting on anyone very long. He looked to be about thirty. *He's too young and too big to be my uncle,* I thought. I glanced quickly at Laura, hoping for an introduction.

Out of the corner of my eye, I saw Gregg turn his Walkman off, even though he left the headphones on.

Laura turned around at the sound of the door, and said, "Never mind, he's here," before she hung up the phone. She smiled at him and said, "I wasn't sure you were back from the last run yet."

He nodded. "Yep. It was a pretty quick run. The new guides are fast learners. We should have everything down by next week."

He then turned his attention fully on me. I knew that I was being measured, and I was pretty sure I wasn't meeting all expectations. But I was doing my own measuring. This man couldn't possibly be my uncle. He was at least fifteen years younger than my father. And there was no family resemblance. My father had been a thin, dark-haired and dark-eyed man.

He always claimed to be five-foot-ten, but I was pretty sure he was really closer to five-foot-nine. I had inherited my father's build, short height, and coloring. Gregg had my mother's blue eyes and her lighter brown hair. He got his height from her side of the family, but he was skinny like my father. This man was easily six-foot-three, and was extremely broad through the shoulders and chest. He seemed to fill the entire living room.

It almost looked like he was going to grin, but he didn't. "Glad to finally meet you, Scott. Sorry about your parents," he said awkwardly.

"Hi, Uncle Dave," I mumbled.

He held up both hands as if warding something off. "No, no, please do not call me that! Just call me Rocky."

"Uncle Rocky?" I asked.

"No, Rocky. Just like everyone else does."

"Where'd you get that nickname?" Gregg asked, with more than a hint of scorn in his voice. "Were you a boxer? Yo, Rocky." He dropped his voice into an imitation of Sylvester Stallone and faked a few jabs at the air in front of him.

"Hello, Gregg," Rocky said smoothly. "I'd really appreciate it if you wouldn't use the coffee table as a footrest."

Gregg didn't move. "Not a boxer, huh? So are you called Rocky 'cause you're just so soft and lovable?"

Rocky bent down and yanked the table out from under Gregg's feet. "Thank you." He then looked Gregg over, and again I could tell that expectations were not being met. Gregg met his appraisal with an unblinking stare.

"Well, Rocky, we're here. Thanks ever so much for taking us in."

"You're welcome," Rocky said, ignoring Gregg's sarcasm.

"Um," Laura cleared her throat nervously. "I think I'll head on home now." She began walking toward the front door. "I'll see you tomorrow."

Rocky stood up and walked to the door with her. "Thanks for your help today."

"Sure," she said, smiling up at him as he opened the door for her.

They stepped out onto the porch, and although I could hear a low murmuring, I couldn't make out any words.

Gregg was shaking his head. "This really sucks."

I looked at him. "Yeah, well, all you're doing is making it worse."

"It can't get any worse than it already is," Gregg said. "Rocky. What a stupid name."

"That's your opinion," Rocky said as he came back in, "but I don't share it."

Gregg just stared at him, not even willing to be embarrassed for being heard. "So where'd you get such a stupid name?"

"If you think it's so stupid, then it certainly shouldn't be any concern of yours where I got it," Rocky said, sitting down on the couch next to Gregg.

"Whatever." Gregg turned his Walkman back on. I could hear it from halfway across the room.

"Gregg," Rocky said. "Gregg," he repeated loudly, when Gregg continued to bop his head in time to the music. He waited a minute, sighed, and then tapped him on the knee. Gregg still ignored him. He tapped him a little harder, maybe closer to hitting him. Gregg angrily slapped his hand away.

"Gregg," I said. "Come on."

Gregg made a great scene about turning the Walkman off. "I'm sorry, Scott. Did you say something?"

"Come on, Gregg."

"What?"

Rocky broke in. "Look, I really am sorry you guys are having to go through all this. I know this isn't easy for any of us, but we'll just have to make the best of a bad situation. First I need to talk to both of you about ground rules in my house," he said.

As soon as Rocky started talking, Gregg turned the Walkman back on.

Rocky looked at me and I shrugged. He sighed. "I only ask a few things. I ask that you keep the house fairly neat. What you do with your room and how clean you keep it is up to you. But I ask that the living room, bathroom, and kitchen be kept clean. When you finish with the dishes, wash them. Don't leave them for someone else. We all have to share the one bathroom, so try not to hog it too often."

I nodded. That was easy. I realized that I couldn't hear Gregg's music anymore, but I couldn't tell if he had turned it off or just turned it down. I didn't know if Rocky had noticed.

"Don't do anything illegal, here in the house or out at someone else's house. For both of you that includes drugs and drinking. That also includes smoking cigarettes."

"We don't smoke," I said.

"Good. Don't start. And if you're not going to be here at night, let me know where I can reach you."

I waited for a minute, but when he didn't say anything else, I asked, "Is that it?"

"It's all I can think of for right now. If something else comes up, we'll talk about it at that time."

"Beautiful," Gregg muttered.

Rocky turned to him and almost smiled. "Glad you caught all that so your brother won't have to repeat it for you." Gregg refused to look at him. Rocky just shook his head. "You'll both be working for me this summer," he began again.

Gregg sat up suddenly and looked at him. "What!"

Rocky continued as if he hadn't heard him. "You'll both spend days working in the shop, and while you're doing that you should have time to read rafting books and learn the river guides and terms. Scott, you're going to have to start as a swamper. We'll try to work you onto the rafts as much as we can, but you're too young and small to train for a guide. As a swamper, you'll not only do cashiering and transportation, but you'll also be assisting the cook, setting up tents, stuff like that on the river. The other guides will tell you it's all the crap work."

"You can't do this!" Gregg said.

"Gregg, we'll get you trained as a guide as quickly as possible. We'll start by just letting you ride along on as many trips as you can, so you can learn the river. If we work every day we should have you trained in a couple of weeks. Until you turn eighteen, you'll have to row the supply boat. After that, you'll be ready to start taking groups."

"You can't tell me where I'm going to work," Gregg said, shaking his head.

Rocky looked at him and sighed. "My business barely makes ends meet. To have the extra money to feed and clothe you, I had to let some of my help go. That means I need you to help pick up the slack."

Gregg stared at him. "You're not going to pay us, are you?" he asked in disbelief.

"I will pay you as much as I can. It won't be as much as the other staff members will get, but it will be more than an average allowance."

"You have no idea what an average allowance is."

"I've asked around, talked to some people about your age. Most of them have told me that at your age, allowances stop and work begins."

"Yeah, but that means you pick where you work!"

"In most situations," Rocky agreed. "But this isn't a typical situation."

"I hate being here already. I wish I had never seen you."

"So do I," Rocky said blandly.

Gregg and I both just stared at him. I'm sure my eyes were as big and shocked as Gregg's were.

"If you weren't here, that would mean your father—my brother—was still alive."

It took a minute for that to sink in.

"Laura said you've had the business for three years," I said, looking for a new topic.

Gregg rolled his eyes at me.

Rocky nodded. "Yeah. The first year, I lost over two thousand dollars, just because I didn't know how to manage a business. Last year, I think I actually made two hundred dollars. This year, I may be able to make enough to get me through till ski season...I mean get us through."

"What do you do then?" I asked.

"I'm a ski instructor," he said. "And if I can make enough money, then I might be able to take a little time off to fix some things up around here and get some new equipment—maybe even get by without having to work another part-time job between seasons."

"Oh," I said. And then without thinking, I added, "Am I going to have to get another job in the winter too?"

Rocky lowered his head. "I hope not, Scott. I'd like you to be able to focus on school. But right now I just don't know."

"Well, at least I won't have to worry about it," Gregg said. When Rocky looked at him, he added, "Don't even think about touching my college money."

"I won't," Rocky said simply. He hesitated, then added, "But my understanding is that you've barely got enough to cover next year. I believe you will find yourself needing a job to continue. Hopefully, I'll be able to get you enough to start a savings account this year. And if things work well, you can come back again next year."

"I can take care of myself. I don't need a guardian."

"No, I'm sure you don't," Rocky agreed. "But the judge says you do, at least until you're eighteen. I know your birthday is coming up real soon, so I'm not shoving a lot of rules on you right now."

"No, instead you're just forcing us to work for you. Gee, thanks, Uncle Rocky," Gregg said. His sarcasm was cutting.

I kept my mouth shut. Arguing with Gregg in front of Rocky wasn't going to help any of us get along.

"Do either of you have any other questions for me right now?" Rocky asked.

"Yeah," Gregg said, "I do. Why did you deny the charges?"

"Huh?" Rocky looked startled.

"The collect call this afternoon."

"Oh, that. It was an unnecessary expense."

"Excuse me?"

"Laura was already on her way. I knew she'd be there real soon. Collect calls are expensive. Since I knew I could get the information that you needed to you for free, I did."

Gregg shook his head in disgust. "Great, he's not only a jerk but he's a cheap jerk as well."

Rocky stood up, ignoring him. "I usually do the grocery shopping on Tuesdays, but it may take me a while to figure out how much food we'll need for the three of us. Just let me know if there's anything you want and I'll try to remember to pick it up."

"What's for dinner?" Gregg asked. At the mention of food, my stomach rumbled. I was hungry.

"Whatever you want. You can help yourself to anything you like in the kitchen." He went to the closet and pulled out a jeans jacket.

"Where are you going?" I asked.

"I've got some things to do," he said.

For a minute, we just watched him put the jacket on.

"What do you mean, you've got some things to do?" Gregg demanded.

"I mean I've got plans," Rocky said.

"You're just going to leave us here?"

He blinked and looked surprised. "You need to unpack. You'll eat dinner. And you're probably pretty tired, so you'll be going to sleep soon. You don't need me for any of those things." When Gregg didn't say anything, he added, "You don't need a guardian, remember?"

"Rocky?" I asked as he opened the door. "When are you going to be home?"

"There's an alarm clock in your room. We need to head to the office at 7:45 tomorrow morning." He looked at me, dropped me a wink, and pulled the door shut behind him.

Gregg waited until we heard an engine start, then he jumped up, threw his Walkman against the front door, and yelled "Damn him!"

I sat down on the edge of the recliner. Gregg stormed around the house, cussing and flinging his arms everywhere, and occasionally kicking the walls. I waited till he started to calm down and then I headed for the kitchen.

"What are you doing?" he demanded.

"I'm hungry. I'm going to see what there is to eat."

"I can't believe you're just going along with this!"

"With what?"

"With him and his attitude. Him and his you'll-work-for-me-and-I-might-pay-you attitude."

I shook my head.

"Doesn't it bother you, Scott?"

"Yeah, Gregg, it does. But there's not much I can do about it right now."

"So you're just going to accept it?"

"No, I'm going to wait till there's a time when I can talk to Rocky and figure something out."

"You can't talk to that guy."

"How do you know?" I countered.

"What's that supposed to mean?"

"It means you never gave him a chance. He came in here and you wouldn't even listen to him."

"I heard what he said!" Gregg shouted.

"Why are you yelling at me?"

"Because you're being stupid! You're just going along with him."

"I told you—" I began.

"Yeah, right, like you're going to talk to him later. You've always been such a goody-goody. You've always done whatever anybody tells you to do, Mr. Straight-A's. Mr. Computer Whiz and Bookworm. You're such a geek."

This was not the first time he had ever called me a geek, but it was the first time it ever sounded like he meant it. "I am not a geek!"

"You are too! All you do is study and read and obey all the rules. That makes you a geek!"

"Yeah, well, at least I'm not an egotistical, arrogant jackass who's so absorbed in himself that he can't even make an attempt to understand or cooperate with the rest of the world!" I shouted. "And if you give me two minutes, I'll find a dictionary so you can look up all the words you didn't understand!"

"I'm outta here." He turned and headed for the front door.

"Where are you going?" I demanded.

"I don't know," he said, "and I'm sure you don't care!" He slammed the door.

I went to the bedroom instead of to the kitchen. I had lost my appetite. I started to unpack, but I didn't know where to put anything, and I really didn't have the energy for it. After I opened the window, I stretched out on the bed and listened to the crickets. And then I began to cry.

Chapter Three

When I woke up the next morning, I was freezing. I had fallen asleep on the bed underneath the open window and had never crawled under the blanket. I was stiff and sore all over.

I got up and dug through my bags until I found a towel. I stumbled to the bathroom and took a hot shower. It helped my neck loosen up a little bit.

It wasn't until I was back in the room that I realized that Gregg wasn't in his bed. In fact, none of his stuff had been touched. I was sure he hadn't been home last night at all. I wondered where he had gone. Throwing on a pair of jeans and a T-shirt, I hurried into the living room.

He was asleep on the couch. I was torn between relief and anger. I was glad he was there; I really didn't know what I would have done if he hadn't been. But I was also more than a little angry with him. Throwing a tantrum like a six year old, and then sleeping out here on the sofa, complete with a warm comforter. He probably slept better than I did last night. Irritated, I went to the kitchen for some food. I had been hungry last night; I was positively starving now.

I rummaged through the kitchen cabinets, not all that worried about making too much noise. Gregg needed to get up anyway, and if I woke Rocky up, well, it was his fault for not showing us around the kitchen last night. In the very back of the refrigerator, I managed to find an egg carton. There were two eggs left. Then I located some oil and a skillet. Without bothering to look at the expiration date, I scrambled the eggs, but then I was disappointed not to find any ketchup for them. I was even more disappointed in the cereal selection. Granola? That was it? There wasn't even any milk for the cereal. No orange juice either.

As I sat there, munching on the dry and virtually tasteless granola, I spied a pad of paper and half a pencil. I started a serious grocery list. Milk, OJ, frosted flakes, bagels, cream cheese, Coke. After seeing the mostly empty shelves in the pantry, I added macaroni and cheese, spaghetti and sauce, wheat bread, and peanut butter to the list. Apples, oranges, and carrots. Lettuce. I stopped there. There wasn't much point in making a list. I might as well write "food." Rocky barely had anything to eat in the whole house.

"What time is it?" Gregg mumbled from the doorway.

"A little after seven."

"Ugh. I can't believe I'm up this early." He turned and slumped back down the hall to the bedroom.

I pulled a chair up to the table and looked out the window while I ate the rest of my eggs. I heard the refrigerator door open.

"There's not much in there," I said without turning around. "I'm surprised Uncle Rocky doesn't look more like an anorexic and less like the Hulk with the amount of food he keeps around here."

"I told you, it's just Rocky," Rocky said.

I jumped. "Oh. Sorry. Thought you were Gregg."

"So I gathered." He put some water in the kettle and came to join me at the table. "I'm sorry about the food. I told you I usually shop on Tuesdays."

"Yeah, but today's only Saturday."

"I know. I'll find time to get to the store today. Just write up a list."

"It's on the counter."

Rocky blinked. "Already?"

I shrugged. "Well, the first part. I'll have to really look and add to it later."

"What kind of grades do you get in school?"

I looked at him. "I've always done pretty well. Why?"

He just nodded. "Thought so."

"Hey, Scott, where'd you get this comforter?" Gregg called from the bedroom.

I looked at Rocky. "Just tell him to leave it on the couch," he said quietly.

"Leave it on the couch," I called to him.

"Can't do that, Scott. You know he wants us to 'keep the place clean,'" Gregg said in a deep voice as he came back into the kitchen. "We sure don't want to make him mad again—" He broke off when he saw Rocky.

"You haven't seen me angry yet," Rocky said mildly as he got up to take the kettle off the stove. "Anyone for tea?"

"I'll take coffee," Gregg said.

Rocky sighed and turned to me. "Where's that list?"

I nodded to the counter, and he turned and jotted coffee at the bottom.

"Thanks for the blanket last night, Scott," Gregg said. "I would have frozen without it."

I started to say that I didn't have anything to do with it, but Rocky started coughing and shaking his head pretty violently. I didn't say anything.

I stood up and stretched, wincing when my back cracked. Gregg looked at me. "You look awful. Didn't you sleep last night?"

I shook my head. "Not very well."

"No wonder. You must've slept with the window wide open all night long." He turned to the pantry and stared. "What are we supposed to eat?"

"Here," I said, pushing the box of granola to him.

He made a face. "You're kidding, right?"

"I'm afraid there's not much else," Rocky began.

Gregg turned to the refrigerator and yanked it open. "God, there's nothing in here!" He turned back to Rocky, furious. "What the hell were you thinking? You've known we were coming for the last five days! You don't even have enough to keep us on a bread and water diet!"

"Gregg, I'm sorry, but—" Rocky tried again.

"Why didn't you just tell the judge the truth, that you don't want us? Why didn't you just let us stay in California, where people are really human and we had friends we could have stayed with? You don't pick us up, you don't accept our calls, you don't have any food...We would have been better off on the streets!"

"Excuse me," a new voice said, and we all jumped.

Laura was standing in the door to the kitchen, holding a brown paper grocery bag and looking extremely uncomfortable. "I don't mean to intrude. I knocked, but I don't think anyone heard me."

"That's okay, Laura," Rocky said, rubbing a hand over his face. "What's up?"

"Um, I got to thinking last night about the way you tend to stock your fridge and I thought maybe the boys might need a little more than you have to offer right now."

He looked at her with a mixture of relief and embarrassment. "You couldn't be more right," he murmured.

She set the bag on the table, and Gregg dug right in. He pulled out an apple, two chocolate donuts, and a pint of orange juice. "Thanks," he said in Laura's general direction. Then he left, muttering under his breath.

We were all quiet for a few minutes. Laura was watching Rocky sympathetically. The sound of the bathroom door slamming broke the silence.

"Scott?" Laura turned to me. "Don't you want anything?"

I hesitated, then asked, "You have any fruit left?"

She nodded. "Apple or orange?"

"I'll take an orange. Thanks," I said as she tossed me one.

Rocky was leaning over his lap, elbows on his knees. He looked up at me. "I'm sorry, Scott," he said, shaking his head. "I was going to do some shopping yesterday, but a couple of checks bounced and I didn't have enough money to cover everything."

"Don't the grocery stores take credit cards?" I asked.

He grimaced. "Yes, but I don't have any credit cards. I don't believe in them."

Laura laughed and ruffled his hair. "You wouldn't believe in checks, either, if you had a choice."

He momentarily leaned his head into her hand. "Nope," he said. "How can you manage the store, your life, and my life all at the same time?"

She laughed again and just shook her head.

He straightened up and looked at me. "I didn't realize your window was open last night, or I would have closed it."

I shrugged. "It's all right."

"Well," he said quickly. "We'd better get going to the office." He looked at me. "You'll probably want to wear shorts. I know it's a little chilly now, but the forecast for later today says it's gonna hit the upper 80s."

When Rocky had said office, for some reason I pictured an office building with an elevator and lots of people working, wearing suits and ties. If I had thought at all, I would have realized that when you work for a rafting company, you don't wear a suit or tie. And you surely wouldn't have an office in a skyscraper.

The Rugged Rapids "office" was a small, one-story, two-room building only a mile from Rocky's house. The main room was the sales room. It had T-shirts, sunglasses, sunscreen, rain ponchos, and a bunch of other stuff. The small room in the back was Rocky's private office.

"Scott, I'm going to have you work with Bob today." He pointed in the direction of a wiry blond guy who had his left arm in a sling. "Bob, these are my nephews, Scott and Gregg."

"Hey," he said, nodding.

Before we could say anything, Rocky started up again. "Scott, you'll stay here and learn how to work the cash register and how to take reservations. You'll also learn the transportation run for Brown's Canyon." He paused. "When do you turn sixteen?"

"Um, November," I said, startled by the shift in conversation.

"November. Well, that's not going to do us any good this summer, but we should still get you your learner's permit." He turned to Bob. "When you book the rafts this morning, do the best you can to leave an empty spot on Roger's raft."

"Sure thing, Rocky. We gonna start a training run?"

"Yeah, I think so." He turned and headed toward a door in the back of the building. "Come on, guys."

I started to follow him out, but I stopped at the door. Gregg was still checking out the T-shirts. "Gregg!"

"In a minute, in a minute."

I waited, but I could tell that he wasn't going to hurry. I stepped out the door and almost walked into Rocky, who was coming back to get us. "Where's Gregg?"

"He's coming," I said, starting on my way toward the group of people pulling rafts out.

Rocky sighed and fell in step with me. "He sure has made up his mind."

"Can you blame him?" I retorted.

Rocky raised an eyebrow at me. "Not really. But then that doesn't explain you." He stopped walking and turned to me.

I shrugged as I stopped and faced him. "My brother and I have always been different," I said. "Most family members would know that by now."

"You two seem to be about as different as my brother and I were." He paused for a minute. "I just hope you respect each other's differences more than we did."

"How old are you?" I asked.

He laughed. "Older than I look and younger than I feel."

"No, really, how old are you? You can't be more than thirty."

Rocky smiled. "You're pretty close, Scott." He hesitated. "And I bet you're asking 'cause you're pretty surprised by the age difference between your father and me. And I bet you're thinking that our age difference might have been one of the reasons we were never very close." Rocky put a hand on my shoulder and started walking toward the rafts again. "And I bet that one of the reasons you get good grades is because you're pretty perceptive."

A wide gravel road led from the office to the river. Behind and to the right of the office stood a large dirty-brown barn. I watched as four guys carried out two rafts and lined them up behind six others on the bank of the river.

"Can I have everyone's attention for a minute?" Rocky called. They didn't stop what they were doing, but everyone kind of slowed down and drifted in our general direction.

"I'd like you to meet my nephews, Scott and Gregg," he said, tilting his head back and to the left. I looked over my left shoulder and was surprised to see Gregg about fifteen feet behind me. "They're going to be living with me now and helping us out around here. So when you get the chance, introduce yourselves, and if you see they need help with something, give 'em a hand."

There was a general murmuring and moving about before they all went back to work.

"Roger!" Rocky called.

A big burly blond guy left the side of the farthest raft and headed toward us. He appeared to be a younger version of Rocky. He looked a lot more like Rocky's brother than my father had.

"Yeah, Boss?"

"I'd like you to work with Gregg," Rocky said, drawing Gregg forward. "We're going to train him to be a guide. He doesn't have any rafting experience."

"How do you know?" Gregg demanded.

Rocky looked at him. "Okay, how much rafting experience do you have?"

"I went tubing down a river twice."

"Actually it was more of a creek," I chimed in. Gregg shot me a dirty look.

Rocky sighed and resumed his instructions. "He doesn't have any rafting experience, so the first few days he's just going to ride with you and balance out your crews. Make sure he pays attention to the rapids' names and their specific hazards. I'll take him for training on the oar boat when you think he knows the river well. He can be our supply man when he's ready to run the river, and by the time he turns eighteen, he'll be able to guide the paddle boats."

"Sounds good," Roger said. "Come on, Gregg, let's get you outfitted."

"Oh, Roger," Rocky said. "I've got their jackets hanging in the barn with the rest of the staff's."

Then Rocky led me to a tanned girl with short brown hair. "Carol? Would you teach Scott how to top off the rafts and show him how to fit a life jacket?"

"Sure thing," she said brightly.

"I've got to get back up to the office," Rocky said. "Pay attention, and you'll learn a lot. Ask any questions you need to. In this business, you can't know too much." Then he left, leaving me with her.

"Okay, Scott," she said, "Rocky didn't really do an official introduction, so I'm Carol." She shook my hand with a firm grasp. "I've been a guide for the last four years, but this is my first year down here on the Arkansas."

"Where were you before?"

"Up in Fort Collins, working the Poudre. But I graduated this spring, and I wanted to try something new."

"Cool," I said, because it felt like I should say something.

We walked over to a gray raft. The bright purple Rugged Rapids logo on the sides stood out in contrast.

"This," she said, slapping the raft, "is your typical sixteen-foot paddle raft. It has four separate air bladders. The ones on the outside of the raft are just called tubes. The two center ones are the thwarts." She tapped a round valve. "Each bladder needs to be topped off every time we take the rafts out. They should be tight, like a drum."

She handed me a pump. "I'll let you try this by yourself, and I'll be back in a few minutes to see how you've done."

"Um, Carol," I said as she turned to go. "I have absolutely no idea how to do this."

She grinned and came back. "Good."

"What do you mean, good?"

"Promise not to tell?"

"Sure."

"You passed my test. Most guys who think they're macho would have just tried it without asking for help. Now I know that I can give you instructions and if you don't understand, you'll ask."

We spent the next ten minutes topping off the raft. She also explained that it was important to check them again after they were set in the water. "The cold water makes the hot air contract, and the tubes deflate a little," she said when I asked why we had to do it twice.

In the barn, there was a storeroom full of life jackets. We made several trips carrying them outside, until we had created a pile behind the rafts. "You'll have to help us get the patrons fitted for jackets before they leave." She picked up a jacket and had me put it on, then showed me how to tighten it. "How's that feel?"

"Fine, I guess."

"Okay, now here's an important test for each jacket. After they're on and fastened, you need to lift it up at the shoulders." She grabbed the shoulders and jerked up hard. I was lifted an inch or two off the ground. "Now that's a good fit." She loosened the straps a little and did it again. I stayed on the ground, and the jacket started to come off over the top of my head. "That's a bad fit."

I nodded. "Why does it have to fit so tight?"

"If anyone falls off the raft, the best way to get them back in the raft is to lean over, grab them by the jacket, and lift them in. If the jacket's too loose, it might slip off, and the patron could very easily drown."

"Oh. But that doesn't happen often, right?"

"What?"

"Drowning."

Carol shrugged. "People die every year on rivers. Last year we had a lot of high water, and ten people drowned in Colorado."

"Any on this river?" I tried to sound casual.

"Two, I think."

I started to say something, but nothing would come out. I think Carol finally realized that I was nervous. "Scott, this is a sport that people enjoy because it is a little dangerous, even for very experienced rafters. It only gets very dangerous for people who are inexperienced or who do stupid things. More than half of last year's drownings happened because the person wasn't wearing a life jacket. You have to respect the power of the river."

I nodded and tried to relax, but all I could do was look around restlessly. Gregg was talking to Roger at his raft, testing the fit of a life jacket.

Carol laughed and gave me a playful shove. "Hey, relax, we're pros here."

When I didn't give her a wholehearted grin in return, she continued, "Scott, listen. Roger may act like a jerk sometimes, but he's really a pro. He grew up on this river, and he's been a guide for the last four years. He's never flipped a raft, which is amazing for anybody. He won't let anything happen to your brother. Jeez, I didn't know you were gonna get so serious on me," she said.

"I'm sorry," I mumbled. I never used to worry about Gregg. He was always the daredevil and I was the bookworm, and that's just the way things were. Now his fascination with stupid stunts scared me. I didn't want to lose him too.

I helped her carry out another raft and we topped it off. She explained the safety line, a rope that hung around the outside of the raft all the way around. It was a place to grab on if you ever went for an unplanned swim while rafting.

This raft was an oar boat, and it had a metal frame on it. She explained how the guide would handle the oars, while the patrons just got to sit back and relax on the ride. She also told me that oar boats were a little more stable, a little easier to turn quickly on the river. I looked at the other boats. Three of them were missing the oar frame.

"Why do you use the other boats, if the oar boats are better?"

Carol grinned. "Well, that's all a matter of opinion. One reason people really enjoy paddle boats is because then they're directly involved with the rafting. They help control where the raft goes. The success of the trip depends on each paddler doing his or her best. It's more of a personal challenge."

She showed me where to stow the extra life jacket and paddle or oar, depending on the type of raft. State law requires that each raft carry a spare. What the spare would be for, I couldn't see. From what she had said about somebody slipping out of a jacket, it seemed more likely to me that we'd be left with an extra jacket and no body, not the other way around.

A few of the guys began loading rafts onto a trailer behind an old school bus. Other people were wandering down to the rafts in groups and pairs. Some of the guides began helping them search through the huge mound of life jackets for one that fit. I walked over and helped a couple of ladies. I tried to hide my nervousness, because they just assumed that I knew what I was doing. I made sure their jackets were tight, and gave them each a tug. They took it all as something they expected.

I noticed Rocky standing on the trailer by the rafts. He waited a few minutes, and then whistled really loud. "Okay," he boomed, "it looks like everyone has a jacket, and I know you all signed the release form up at the store. Thanks for reading all the material we gave you and paying close attention to the instructions. I just want to remind you that it is extremely important for you to listen to the guide on your raft. I'd like to say just your life may depend on it, but I can't do that. The fact is, *everyone's* life in your raft may depend on it!

"Your guides are all experienced professionals who have been through rigorous training to be able to work for me. They are also trained in CPR and first aid.

"Today's weather looks pretty cloudless, so make sure you've got plenty of sunscreen with you and use it. Wear a hat and good sunglasses. You're going to need them. Your guides will go over additional rules and responsibilities with you when you board their rafts."

"Those of you who signed up for the Royal Gorge trip, please go ahead and board the bus at this time. And just in case you forgot which trip you've signed up for, here's who should be on the bus."

Rocky stopped and drank some water while Laura called out the names for the Royal Gorge trip. "By the way, make sure you pick up a helmet before you get on the bus. Rafters are required to have helmets in the Royal Gorge."

"Okay. Now for our Brown's Canyon trips. First, we have Lou's boat." A man with fiery red hair lifted a Rockies baseball cap in the air. Laura called the five people on his boat. Then she moved on to Joe, Barb, Rocky, and finally Roger. She had only four people on Roger's boat; Gregg was going to learn and balance out the crew at the same time.

I wandered over to Gregg. He wasn't wearing one of the ugly orange jackets that all the patrons had on. He had a sharp blue one on, with his name written on it. "Where'd you get the jacket?"

He jerked his thumb back toward the barn. "There's one with your name too," he said.

"Don't you need a helmet?" I asked him.

Gregg was watching Roger. Roger was talking to the girls I had helped with the jackets. They looked to be a couple of years younger than Roger, and the blond was batting her eyelashes for all she was worth. The brunette kept sliding glances at Gregg. He grinned back at her.

"Gregg?"

He tore his eyes away from his admirer with an effort. "What?"

"Where's your helmet?" I repeated.

"Oh." He shrugged. "Roger said they're not required in Brown's Canyon." He gazed back over to the girls.

"Hey, Gregg," I said. "Be careful, huh?"

He looked at me funny. "Why? This is going to be a rush!"

Then Roger said, "Come on, Baxter Boys, let's get this baby in the water!" He grabbed his side of the raft and Gregg grabbed the other, which left me with the back end to grab. I felt pretty stupid, pretending to carry it with them, but I didn't want to look like I wasn't carrying any of the weight either.

"Okay, Mark and John? Is that right, John?" Roger continued, almost ignoring the nods he got. "Mark and John, you both take the front positions. Then we'll have Debbie in the middle in front of Gregg." He pointed the brunette over to my brother. "Stacey will be in front of me," he added as he directed her over to his side.

Lou and Barb's boats were already beginning to drift downriver, and their lighthearted chatter floated toward the shore.

"You're riding sweep, Roger!" Rocky hollered as his raft left the shore.

"Okay, go ahead and hop in," Roger said to his crew. Then he motioned me over to him. He was holding the line that was keeping the raft from drifting. "This is the bowline," he said, rolling it in loops. "It's very important to keep it free of tangles and to keep it coiled up when not tying the boat off." He finished the loops and wrapped them into one bundle. Everyone else was in the boat, waiting for him. "Tomorrow, you're in charge of my bowline." He gave the boat another push and hopped in.

Gregg turned and waved his paddle at me as they drifted down the river.

I spent the day with Bob in the shop.

"Do you read a lot?" was one of his first questions.

"Well, yeah," I said, shrugging and wondering if Gregg had been spreading the word about my geeky bookworm habits.

"You might want to pick out a few good books to read and keep here. The days that you're stuck here seem to go on forever. We'll finish the cleaning in about forty-five minutes, and then we just sit here for the rest of the day."

I looked at him. He was tall and had an athletic build and a good tan. "You don't look like this is what you usually do."

"Oh, no," he said with a huge crooked grin. "I'm a river runner. But last week I took a group on an oar raft down the Gorge, and one of the oar locks popped." He pointed to his sling. "Sprained my wrist. But Rocky's cool. He's trying to get me as much office time as he can. It's only minimum wage, but every bit helps. He also gives me a cut of the tips."

"Sounds fair."

"Yeah, but it's not something all rafting companies would do. You take care of Rocky and work hard, and when he gets the chance to take care of you, he will."

I raised my eyebrows. "And how much is he paying you to say that?"

"Say what?"

"Never mind."

"So, we start by sweeping the floor and doing the windows. Which one do you want?"

"Which one is easier for you to do?"

He grinned. "I'm a little better at the windows."

"Sounds good."

He got out the window cleaner and the "manual vacuum," a little push-brush contraption that was used on the stiff carpet, and we started to work.

"How long have you been a river guide?" I asked.

"Oh, about three years."

"All of them with Rocky?"

"No, just the last two. I knew Rocky before, though. When I was in high school, I helped out at a rafting company upriver where Rocky was a guide."

"How long has he been a guide?"

"Rocky? I don't know, since the river started flowing maybe?"

We laughed and worked in silence for a few minutes. Then the phone rang, and Bob took a reservation. He motioned me over and showed me the paperwork as he filled it out. When he hung up, we went over it again in detail, and he showed me where the trip schedule and price list were, as well as how to ring a sale on the cash register.

As we resumed cleaning, Bob asked me, "So when was the last time your family got to visit Rocky?"

"I met him for the first time last night."

"Seriously?"

"Seriously."

"Wow, that's got to be hard. I mean, losing your parents like that, and then having to come out here. It would be bad enough having to leave home and come out to live with your uncle, but man, if you don't even know him!" He was shaking his head.

"It hasn't started off as the best summer in my memory," I said.

"No, I guess not." He hesitated. "What happened to your parents? If you don't mind me asking, that is."

I shrugged. "They were driving home from a party. Dad misjudged a turn and ran head-on into a bus. They weren't wearing seat belts."

"Oh, God, that sucks!"

"Yeah, that's pretty much what Gregg and I have been saying." I went back to sweeping the floor, putting my back to him and hiding the sudden tears.

"How old are you guys?"

I cleared my throat and covered it with a cough. "I'm fifteen, he's seventeen. You?"

"I'm twenty-one, same as Roger, Jim, and Carol. The rest of the staff is between eighteen and twenty-six."

"So far they seem like a pretty friendly group."

Bob nodded. "Rocky's gonna make Gregg a guide?"

"That's his plan right now. Gregg wasn't too excited about it last night, but he seemed okay with it this morning."

"He'll like Roger. Roger knows how to have a good time." Bob laughed. "Roger really knows how to have a good time. He just turned twenty-one a few months ago and he's really gotten into his drinking. Our whole staff likes to party, but Roger, he's our chief partier."

"Then he and Gregg will get along," I agreed. "Gregg's always been into parties and pranks."

Bob laughed again. "Then Rocky either has a perfect partnership in the making, or a huge rebellion on his hands."

"What do you mean?"

"Rocky used to be quite the party animal too, from what I've heard, but he's not anymore. In fact, several staff members from last year quit. Rocky was always on their case for partying too much. According to them, he's become really lame."

"Which means either Gregg and Roger are going to have a lot of fun by themselves—" I began.

"Or they're going to have too much fun and get in a lot of trouble with Rocky," Bob finished.

Chapter Four

"Oh, man, what a day!" Gregg said as he flopped onto my bed.

I grunted and went back to sorting through my clothes, trying to decide which ones could actually fit in the tiny dresser and which ones would have to be stored in boxes under my bed. We still had several more boxes being shipped to us. I had no idea where we were going to put our stuff. Even though we had sold or donated more than half of our personal belongings, we still had at least twice as much stuff as could fit in the room.

"River rafting is a blast! I can't believe how awesome today was."

I still didn't say anything. Bob had been fun to hang out with, but being stuck inside the store for the whole day and only seeing people before and after their trips did not make for an awesome day. Gregg, on the other hand, had done the Brown's Canyon run twice with Roger. He had been excited about it after the first run and he was convinced that the second run was even better.

"Hey, what are you doing?"

"What do you mean?"

"Don't be putting your stuff in my dresser," he said.

"This is my dresser, not yours," I said, putting another T-shirt in and shutting the drawer firmly.

"No way, little buddy, this bed and this dresser are mine."

"I don't think so," I said, shaking my head.

"I think so," he retorted. "I'm taking the bed under the window, and that's all there is to it."

"Bull! You weren't even in here last night, remember? I already claimed this side of the room while you were out throwing your fit."

"I did not throw a fit!"

"You did too, and I've got a news flash for you: you're doing it again!"

"You mouthy, snotty, little..." Gregg lunged for me.

It wasn't until my head hit the corner of the bed frame that I cried out, in spite of the fact that he was using his height and weight as an advantage against me, as always. I had gotten pretty good over the years at wrestling with him and holding my own simply by twisting and turning away from him and breaking out of his grasp. We were both used to fighting and wrestling with minimal noise; neither of us had wanted our parents to come settle personal matters for us. When my head hit, though, it hit hard, and I couldn't help yelling out.

Gregg stopped, but he was still on top of me. "Are you okay?" He may have wanted to kill me a minute before, but we were still brothers. That meant even more to us now than it used to.

Rocky was at our bedroom door in an instant. "What's going on in here?" he growled.

Gregg hopped off me quickly. "Nothing," he said, shaking his head.

"Nothing," I echoed instinctively.

"Doesn't look like nothing. What's the problem?"

"It's none of your business," Gregg said stubbornly.

"It most certainly is," Rocky insisted.

"No, it's not. You have nothing to do with this discussion."

"It's taking place in my house."

"So?"

"So it's got something to do with me."

Gregg laughed. "Actually, it doesn't. We're not discussing how much of a jackass you are. We'll call you back when we get to that part if you want us to."

"Watch your mouth, kid. You're not too old to be punished."

"You try it and I'll nail you with a child abuse suit so fast it will make your head spin."

Rocky took a step into the room. "You've seen what I've got. All I'd lose at this point is custody of you. And right now that doesn't really seem like much of a penalty."

"I told you he didn't want us, Scott."

"You leave him out of this. You're the one who's being a jerk, not him."

"Oh, look, Scotty, you've done it again! You've followed all the rules and you've got everybody loving you and thinking you're the perfect child." Gregg gave me a mock bow. "I'm impressed. It took less than twenty-four hours this time to prove how perfect you are."

I didn't say anything.

"So are you going to tell me what this is all about?" Rocky asked.

"Go ahead, I'm sure you're just dying to tell Rocky how perfect you are and that I'm being a bad boy," Gregg said to me.

I looked at Gregg, then I said, "We were just discussing which bed we were going to take. I decided after freezing last night that I wanted the one by the door. Gregg didn't want to take the one under the window, but I think I've talked him into it."

"Good," Rocky said, turning around to leave. "If you check the kitchen, you should find some better choices tonight." He said over his shoulder, "I haven't made it to the store yet, but Laura made a run for us this afternoon. Don't sleep in too late tomorrow. And Gregg, you might want to get up early tomorrow and stretch. You'll probably find yourself tight and sore from paddling when you wake up."

"Going out again?" Gregg asked.

"Yep. If you two decide to go out, leave me a note where you'll be."

"Where will you be?" I asked, but the front door was shutting on my question.

"Nice working for you," Gregg called as the door clicked shut.

We sat there, me on the floor, him on the bed by the window, for a couple of minutes. He finally looked at me. "You can have this bed."

"That's okay. You take it. But you have to put all my clothes I just put in that dresser into the other one."

Gregg looked at the dresser for a minute, then he looked at the bed. "This is the bed you slept in last night, right?"

"Yeah."

"Then I'm not sleeping on your dirty sheets. You take it."

"You sure?" I asked, neglecting to tell him I had slept on top of the covers.

"Positive."

"Okay."

We spent most of the evening putting things away. We wanted to reorganize the room, but after trying to shove the beds and dressers in several different positions, we discovered that the only way they all fit in the tiny room was the way Rocky had set them up.

In the kitchen, we found hamburger meat, a box of macaroni and cheese, and lettuce. I fixed the hamburgers and salad while Gregg cooked the macaroni. We tried to watch TV while we ate. Rocky's old TV didn't have a remote. It only got five channels, and all of them were fuzzy. After a while Gregg got up and turned it off and we finished our meal in silence.

When we climbed into bed, we talked a little before we went to sleep. It almost felt like a sleep over, since we had never shared a bedroom before.

We talked about Rocky; Gregg was sure he was a jerk, but I wasn't convinced. I didn't think he was great, but I told Gregg he was being unfair.

"Life is unfair," Gregg mumbled. "Look at where we are now."

"I know," I said tentatively. "I still can't believe they're gone." It was hard to get Gregg to talk about the accident, and he was the only one I wanted to talk to about it.

Gregg was quiet for so long, I almost thought he had fallen asleep. "It's weird," he finally said. "I go between feeling like they just died yesterday to feeling like they've been gone for a really long time."

"Me too!" I exclaimed eagerly. I knew exactly what he was talking about.

"I don't know which is worse. In a way it's easier when it feels like it's been a long time—" he started.

"But then you feel guilty for not thinking about it," I finished for him.

"Yeah," he said soberly.

"Hey, do you remember when—" I began.

"Scott," Gregg cut in. "I'm too tired to play the do-you-remember game, okay?"

I shut up. For a long time, we both were silent.

Then, as Gregg started to drift off, he tried to tell me about the river, but I didn't get much of what he said, other than it was a rush and just totally awesome.

The next morning I was the first one up again. I took my shower, pulled a pair of sweatpants on over my shorts, and went into the kitchen. I had noticed the night before that there were some bagels in the pantry now, along with OJ and a dozen eggs in the fridge. I scrambled three of the eggs and had two of the bagels toasted when Rocky came into the kitchen.

"Morning," he said as he started to fix some tea.

"Morning. I've got eggs here," I said, indicating the pan.

He gave me a funny smile. "Fixing breakfast for everyone, huh?"

"Fixing it for me," I said, "but I ended up with some extra for anyone who wants it."

"Hey, Scotty, what's for breakfast?" Gregg asked, coming into the kitchen in his boxers.

"I don't know," I said. "What are you making?"

He made a face at me as he grabbed a glass of milk, one of the bagels, dumped the remaining eggs onto a plate, and then retreated to our room.

Rocky stirred honey into his tea and shook his head. A small smile tugged at the corners of his mouth. "You and Gregg have taken the opposite roles your father and I did. I always thought the younger brother was the irresponsible one."

"Gregg's not irresponsible."

Rocky raised his eyebrows. "I bet he gets into more trouble than you do."

I decided to change the subject.

"So where were you last night?" I asked.

"I was out."

"Are you trying to keep it a mystery?"

"Are you trying to be nosy?"

I shrugged. "You said we had to let you know where we're going to be when we go out, so I thought we should know where we can reach you."

"I'm an adult."

"So? I consider myself an adult too."

He regarded me carefully for a minute.

"I'm not trying to be smart," I began.

"You don't need to try," he said, "it comes naturally for you. And you're right. You should know where you can reach me. From now on, I'll leave you a number, but it's for emergency use only, clear?"

"Sure."

I sat down to my breakfast. He just looked at me for a few minutes, which started to kill my appetite.

Finally, he said, "I noticed you got stuck back under the window last night."

"I decided I wanted it back."

He watched me again without saying anything.

"What?"

He shrugged. "It's neat to see brothers sticking up for each other."

"What do you mean?"

"I'm not completely stupid, Scott."

"I never said you were."

"You and Gregg look out for each other, and that's a good thing. Just make sure that while you're looking out for him you don't forget to look out for yourself."

He stood up and stretched. "Time to get going."

When we got to the parking lot, I went directly down to the raft barn to help set up and top off the rafts. It was a lot more fun than being inside the store. I was going to be in there enough today as it was.

Gregg hooked up with Roger right away, and they started talking and working together as if they had known each other for years. I kind of floated around, giving a hand wherever it was needed and exchanging just a few words with some of the other guides.

The patrons started to arrive, and I helped several people find life jackets that fit correctly. I was surprised to see the family we had driven up with standing near the barn. I offered to help them all get outfitted. The dad, Jon, turned just a little red when he explained that they were taking a half-day run down Brown's, just to make sure everyone was up for the three-day trip.

"Sounds like a good idea," I said, checking the straps on his son's jacket.

His daughter turned crimson when I tugged on her straps, and then she squealed when I lifted her off the ground by the shoulders.

Rocky came down to the barn with Laura again. He ran through his speech, and she called off the names for each raft. Roger's raft had five paid passengers, and Gregg was there to round out the crew.

I was watching Gregg and Roger clown around in front of a couple of girls who were going to be on Lou's boat, and was startled to hear my name called on a passenger list.

"Huh?" I said, looking up.

Laura was trying not to laugh at me. "You're on Rocky's boat for this run."

"Oh," I said, and reached for a life jacket out of the pile.

"No, no," she said. "Go get yours out of the barn. It's with the rest of the staff gear."

I jogged up to the barn and turned into the small room that had lockers for the guides' personal belongings. There were pegs along one wall, with names above each one. My name was next to Gregg's at the end, written on a newer, cleaner piece of duct tape than the rest of them. A blue life jacket, matching Gregg's, hung on the peg.

When I lifted it off the peg, I saw my name on the front right of the jacket. It only needed a little adjusting to fit nice and tight. It had a small, open-weave pocket on the front and a whistle attached to the zipper.

When I got back down to the rafts, Lou's boat was shoving off, and Barb's was getting ready to go next. The family from Arizona was milling around Rocky's raft. Rocky was checking the safety line and the extra paddle and jacket.

The mom's name was Barbara, the daughter was Sarah, and the son was Chris. Rocky had Jon and Barbara up front, with Sarah and Chris in the middle. We all climbed awkwardly into the raft.

"Sit sideways," Rocky instructed, "and wedge your feet between either the tube or the thwart and the bottom of the raft."

The position felt a little unnatural, so I experimented with a couple strokes of the paddle.

Rocky shoved us off, and we drifted down the calm water.

He spent some time giving us instructions and drilling us. "Make sure that you're not only pulling on the paddle with your bottom hand, but that you're also pushing with your top hand."

I focused on trying that and was surprised at the power I got from the full stroke.

"Now, as close together as we are, we need to pull together. The lead paddler is our right front position, Jon." Jon smiled and nodded to his wife across from him. "So Barbara will match her strokes to Jon's, and then those of us in the back will just follow the person in front of us."

We practiced getting our timing right. I had Sarah right in front of me, and it took her a few strokes to figure out her mom's rhythm.

"When I call 'power right,' it means that everyone on the right side has to paddle forward as hard as you can, and everyone on the left has to back-paddle. 'Power left,' and everyone on the left paddles forward hard and the right side back-paddles. 'Power forward,' and we all just paddle forward as hard as we can. Got that?"

He drilled us a little longer, having us power forward to get to a tree leaning out from the bank or to an outcrop of rocks, practicing our left and right turns.

"Good, good. You all work together pretty well. Just make sure that you keep that power when we're in the rapids. You've got to dig in hard with the paddle so we'll all make it. You'll also find that digging in hard with your paddle braces you and helps you keep your balance.

"On the off chance you do get thrown out of the raft, there are some things you need to know. First, don't panic. We'll get you back in the boat as soon as possible. If you can, we'd like you to try to hang on to your paddle. They float downstream faster than you do, and they're expensive. If you don't have your paddle, you can't do us much good back on the raft, and we just might decide not to pick you up."

Jon, Barbara, and I laughed at this joke, but Chris and Sarah didn't seem too sure.

"Just kidding. We always keep a spare paddle on board. Second, you need to get clear of the raft in the rapids. I know you'll want to be close to us, but we won't be able to pull you up during a rapid, and there's a good chance you'll get hit with a paddle or even get run over if you try to stay too close to the boat. The best thing to do is to stay on your back and get your feet up in front of you. Let your legs and feet act like shock absorbers in case you hit any rocks.

"When we can get you, we will come pick you up. Get your paddle in the raft first, and then someone will help you climb back into the raft. The best way to get you in is for one of us to grab the top of the life jacket and pull you on board. Sometimes we have to dunk you first to get the momentum going to lift you up. You also have to kick as hard as you can to help."

As we drifted into the mouth of the canyon, Rocky talked about the proposed dam that the locals in Buena Vista were trying to keep from being built. "It will destroy all the rafting along this section of the Arkansas. It will also flood out a beautiful part of the canyon. We're encouraging everyone who enjoys this trip to write to your representatives in Congress and ask them to vote against the dam."

We drifted along the river quietly for a few minutes, everyone just looking. When I took a deep breath and closed my eyes for a second, I felt completely relaxed. The raft bobbed gently up and down, and I could hear the light slapping of the water against it. The sun was up and warm, but it wasn't blistering hot yet. A swallow trilled a song from the shore, safe in its mud nest.

"Let's just do some light paddle forward right now," Rocky said.

We all paddled forward, and Jon asked Rocky some questions about the water level. He was showing Rocky that he wasn't just your average tourist; he knew something.

"Yeah, the water level's pretty high right now, but this early in the season, that's what we expect because of all the spring runoff. It's not as high as it was last year when the Bureau of Land Management supervisors had to close the Royal Gorge to all rafting for a week."

"What happens when the water's high?" I asked.

"Different things in different sections," Rocky said. "If you've got a section with rocks exposed during low levels, then they can either get washed almost all the way out or they will create standing waves. Other places, the water can come up enough to cover a large boulder and create a hole behind it."

"What's a hole?"

"A hole is a place where the water comes rushing back in to fill up the area behind the rock. If you get stuck in one, you feel like you're in a washing machine. The water's churning around, not really seeming to go anywhere. It's got a lot of crosscurrents, and it can suck a person or the pontoon of a raft down before it will let it go."

Sarah and Chris were looking at Rocky with terror all over their faces.

"There aren't any holes on this section, are there?" Chris asked.

"There are a couple. We'll do everything we can to avoid them. But that means that everyone needs to listen to the captain and paddle hard."

They both nodded. "How often do people get thrown out of the rafts?" I asked, mostly because I was curious, but also partly because I could tell Sarah was really nervous. I wanted to see how spooked she'd get.

Rocky shrugged. "It depends on several things. Water level, guide ability, patron ability, whether the people are focused on the river, lots of things. I can't tell you how often we have people get thrown out of rafts."

"Yeah, but on average," I pressed.

He gave me a funny look for a second, then leaned over and gave me a shove. It came so unexpectedly, I didn't even have time to get a breath of air before I went under water. I came up sputtering and cold.

"Jeez," I hollered.

"Water's cold, huh?" Sarah was laughing at me. I splashed her and she shrieked, but she didn't stop laughing.

Rocky had a huge grin on his face. "I forgot to tell you that 99 percent of the people who pester guides get thrown out, especially when they're relatives." He nodded to me. "You kept your paddle. Nice job. Kick on over here."

I kicked to the side of the raft and handed my paddle up to him; he handed it to Sarah to hold. Standing next to the rafts or sitting on them, I hadn't realized how high above the water the tops of the tubes are. I knew there was no way I could get back in by myself.

Rocky leaned over and grabbed the shoulders of my jacket. "On the count of three, I'm going to dunk you, then lift you in. You need to kick as hard as you can."

"Okay."

"One...two..." He bobbed me up and down. "Three!" He shoved me under water and then yanked me out real hard. I kicked the whole way. In fact, I was still kicking when I landed in the raft.

Now they were all laughing at me. Sarah said I looked like a fish flopping around. I thought briefly about shoving her in too, but Rocky caught my eye and shook his head. I knew that if I hadn't been his nephew, he never would have shoved me in. I didn't know how to feel about that.

I was glad the breeze was warm. I didn't want to have to spend the rest of the day in cold, wet clothes.

We hit a somewhat bumpy section in the river, and Sarah screamed for all she was worth.

Rocky made a great show of rubbing his ears. "Ye gads, Sarah, if you scream like that for a simple riffle, you're going to blow out our eardrums when we hit a rapid."

"Wasn't that a rapid?" she asked, concern showing plainly on her face.

"Oh, no," Rocky said with a grin. "Rapids are muuuch bigger."

"Oh," she said in such a small voice I almost felt sorry for her.

The farther along we drifted, the closer the canyon walls came in. When we left the raft barn, we couldn't even see the canyon. Now, steep walls were closing in; red and brown rock dotted with sparse green plants loomed over the raft. Places to pull up along the riverbank and load a raft became fewer and farther apart. We hit several more riffles, and the water splashed us a little. Even though I was still wet from my unplanned swim, the water felt cold.

As we were rounding a bend in the canyon, I could hear a kind of static.

At least, that's what it sounded like to me, the white noise that you get on the radio when you get out of range. The farther we went, the louder the static became. I looked at Rocky and he nodded to me.

"We're approaching our first rapid," he said loudly for everyone's benefit. "It's called Canyon Doors. We want to follow the tongue to the left of the first rock, but we need to be careful once we pass it, because the water gets really squirrelly. Then we need to skirt the hole on the right. After that, we'll have to work to the right to set up for Pinball, the next rapid. There's not much room between the two. In Pinball, we need to stay to the left of the big rock that's on the river right. It's a rock that's notorious for wrapping rafts."

We could see the churning water in front of us. I stared. The river was a murky brown where it was calm, but all I saw in front of me was a furious mass of white water. I felt my mouth go dry, and my stomach tightened up. I could hear Carol's voice casually telling me that ten people had died on rivers last year, and now I could see why.

"All right," Rocky called above the din of the rapid. "Paddle forward, everyone!"

We all dug in. It was amazing. The raft became a roller-coaster car, but instead of gliding up and down all the hills, it crashed through some of them. The waves were four or five feet tall in some places. Gallons of water rained down on Barbara and Jon. We topped the crest of a wave, and I could see a boulder looming directly in front of us.

"Power left!" Rocky yelled. The raft turned to the right, and we scooted by the rock with a couple of feet to spare. Two more small waves, and the rapid was over.

"Not bad, crew, not bad at all. You keep up this work and you won't need me back here," Rocky said easily.

Rocky looked at me. "You're a natural, Scott. A couple of years, a few more runs, and a good growth spurt, and you'll make a great guide."

I was grinning from ear to ear from the ride, and even Rocky's comment about my small size couldn't make me stop.

We went through Zoom Flume, Squeeze Play, and Big Drop just fine. We had our timing down, so we weren't smacking each other's paddles anymore. Chris loosened up a little and hollered like a banshee on the last wave of Big Drop.

Rocky showed me some things to watch out for. He told me what "sleepers" look like; they are rocks just under the surface with the water "pillowing" over them. And he talked about the dangers of hitting a "strainer," a tangle of dead trees and branches caught between rocks. I listened and enjoyed it. He knew a lot, and he was talking to me like I was another adult, not some kid he had to entertain.

"Okay," he said, "now we've got Staircase coming up. It's got seven stairs, or drops. With the water as high as it is, it's just going to seem like a bunch of standing waves. We'll need to dig hard and keep the nose of the raft facing downriver."

The waves were huge, definitely the biggest we had seen. But we were confident. We knew what we were doing. All we had to do was paddle and listen to Rocky.

I dug in, a grin on my face. This was awesome. The challenge was thrilling, the weather was beautiful, and I was a natural. This was easy.

I reached out with my paddle and sank it down into thin air. The wave that had just been there dropped out from under the raft, and there was nothing to stop my paddle, nothing to stop my lean. My feet came untucked from the raft, and I went over.

Even though I was already wet from the dunking and all the splashing, being submerged in the cold water was still a shock. I came up, sputtering again, and got another mouthful of water instead of air as a wave crashed down on top of me. I tried to kick, but my feet were sluggish and it felt like the water moved them, not the other way around. The raft was easily ten feet in front of me now, and gaining distance.

The paddle was still in my hand, and it was a huge pain. It interfered with my swimming. I wanted to drop it, but I didn't. With a struggle, I was able to get my feet up in front of me, the way Rocky had told us.

Staircase had to be the longest rapid on the trip. It took forever to get through. Wave after wave slammed down on me. I couldn't see, and only every once in a while was I able to get a breath of air. I was exhausted. The water was numbingly cold.

I had just realized that I was actually swallowing more air than water when I heard my name being called. I looked around, blinking and trying to clear my eyes. The raft was off to my right, about thirty feet downstream.

"Come on, Scott! Start kicking," Rocky called.

"I can't," I said, even as I turned over on my stomach and tried to get my feet going.

"You've got to do better than that if you're going to make it," he yelled.

I was still kicking, just not very fast or strong. The raft was now about twenty feet away.

"Why don't we go get him?" Sarah asked.

"Yeah, come get me," I said, liking Sarah for perhaps the first time.

Rocky grinned, but he shook his head. "This is good training for you."

"Why?" I asked. Ten feet. I might actually make it.

"It will help you respect the river. The most dangerous thing you can do on a river is get cocky."

I reached up and grabbed the safety line with a sigh.

"Okay, hand me your paddle."

I shook my head. "Too...tired."

"Come on, Scott, we've got two more rapids. Let's get going."

"Go...on...I'll just...walk...meet you...there."

"Let's go." He reached down.

I handed him the paddle. He grabbed my jacket and dunked me without counting to three. I think I kicked, but I sure wasn't kicking this time when I got into the raft.

I looked around the raft. Jon was nodding encouragement to me, and Barbara was giving me a reassuring smile. Sarah looked scared. Chris was looking at me with curiosity. Suddenly I felt very stupid.

I sat up and got back in my seat, clapping my hands. "Okay, that was great! What's next?"

Rocky grinned and gave me my paddle. "Next one's Widow Maker."

"Oh, boy, I can't wait!" I said sarcastically.

We made it through the last two rapids with no problem. We got out at the pullout, and I helped the rest of the guides load the rafts onto the trailer while the patrons enjoyed soda and beer. We shoved all the life jackets into the bottom two rafts, stacked the rafts, and then tied the five of them together. Afterwards, we all piled on the bus and headed back to the store.

I sat in front of Gregg and Roger, but they were involved in their own discussion about the two girls from yesterday's trip and they made it clear I wasn't part of their conversation. I watched the scenery out the bus window and listened to the chatter around me. I could hear Rocky's voice from the front of the bus but could only make out an occasional word.

After we unloaded the rafts and equipment at the barn and set them up for the next group, the staff members broke up for a quick lunch. We had about an hour before the next groups would start arriving. I started thinking about dry clothes. I didn't want to spend the rest of the day in these clothes. They were still damp, and the river left them feeling stiff and gritty.

Rocky overheard me telling Joe I was going back for some dry clothes. "I wouldn't worry about them, Scott."

"Why not? These are dirty, and I want to change before working in the store this afternoon."

"You're coming with me again."

I blinked. "I am?"

"Yeah. We've got the time and the room. I'd like you to start learning about the river."

"How about I wait a couple days?"

He shook his head. "Need to get back on the horse that throws you."

"Huh?"

"You need to get back on the river today. I know you got a little spooked when you got thrown out. I don't want that fear to build."

"I did not get spooked! And I got right back on."

"I want you on this trip anyway, Scott." He paused a minute. "I talked to Jon and his family. They're lined up for our three-day trip day after tomorrow. You're coming with us. We need a swamper."

"Wonderful," I said.

"Come on, Scott. You were enjoying it before."

"I'm tired," I said, and even I could hear the whine in my voice.

"So, you'll sleep well tonight." Rocky paused. "I know it's scary the first time you swim a rapid. That's one of the reasons I pushed you in the calm water. It was a slow spot where a lot of people swim on hot days, and it's good to have some experience swimming in the river."

I turned and started back toward the rafts.

"Scott?"

"What? I'm going, aren't I?" I didn't look back or stop. I heard him sigh and then turn to head back to the office.

I sat around with the other guides at the barn, eating lunch with them and listening to their conversations. They were friendly toward me, but I could tell they weren't interested in being my friend. I was too young.

Rocky and I had another family for the afternoon trip. In spite of my decision not to enjoy the river, I did. I had a great time. It's hard to feel sorry for yourself for long when you are concentrating on the water.

On the bus ride back, I sat up front and listened to Rocky tell rafting war stories.

At the raft barn, we got everything stored away quickly. Almost all the guides were gone before I realized it. I was hanging my life jacket in the barn when Gregg came bounding up to me.

"Hey, Scotty!"

"Hey," I said, trying not to sound depressed.

He hung his jacket next to mine and pounded me on the shoulder. "Isn't rafting just awesome?"

"Yeah, it's pretty cool."

"Roger and me are taking a three-day trip in a couple of days. Man, I can't wait! Camping and rafting! And," he said with a big grin, "Debbie and Stacey are going too."

"Who are Debbie and Stacey?"

"The girls who were on our raft yesterday. Roger convinced them to ditch their boyfriends and come with us."

"I'm going too," I said.

"You sure about that, Scott?"

I shrugged. "That's what Rocky said this afternoon."

"Rocky's going?"

When I nodded, he groaned. "Oh, man, that sucks!"

"Why?"

"He'll ruin everything!"

"What were you planning on doing?"

"Nothing."

"Then how is he going to ruin it?" I asked.

"Just by being there. He's such a jerk."

I didn't say anything. I knew Gregg couldn't stand him, but I wasn't sure why. He had been okay to me so far, except for making me go rafting again.

"Oh, well. If he notices I'm not home tonight, just tell him I'm at Roger's."

"Can I come?" I asked without thinking.

Gregg looked at me funny. "No, you can't. We're going out with Stacey and Debbie. I don't need no tagalong little brother."

I didn't say anything. I had never been a tagalong before; Gregg and I had always had separate friends and interests. But I didn't want to stay home alone.

"Why don't you ask Bob or Joe to go do something?" Gregg suggested in a rare display of compassion.

"Yeah, sure," I said, nodding. I knew they had already gone, but I wasn't going to tell Gregg that. I didn't need his pity.

Of course, by the time I had been in the empty house for a couple of hours, I probably would have enjoyed pity of any kind, as long as it meant company. Being this lonely was a new feeling for me. It was a feeling I hoped would go away soon.

I felt really strange wandering around the house. I had only been here for two days, and I just didn't feel comfortable poking into a stranger's belongings. Rocky may have been my uncle, but I still didn't know much about him.

The house didn't give many clues either. It was old and run-down, but clean. The furniture was all mismatched. The only things that looked like a set were the kitchen table and chairs. There were some pictures around the house, but they were all of mountains, rivers, bighorn sheep, bears, and wolves. There weren't any pictures of people. Twice I walked toward his bedroom door, and twice I chickened out. I wanted to know more about him, but not from snooping.

Finally I got an inspiration. I went into my room and pulled out Nancy's phone number. I don't know why I hadn't called her before. I knew she'd be worried about us.

I tried three times to call her. Each time, I got the annoying tone in my ear, followed by a taped message saying, "We're sorry, that call cannot be completed as dialed." After the third time, I was frustrated enough to call the operator for assistance.

"How may I help you?"

"I'm trying to make a long-distance call," I said, "but it won't go through."

"What number, please?"

I gave her the number, and she said, "Just a moment."

Thirty seconds later, she was back. "The number you're calling from does not list a long-distance carrier."

"What?"

"You don't have a long-distance carrier."

"What does that mean?"

"It means you can't place long-distance calls from that phone."

"Oh. Thank you."

I hung up, completely confused. No long-distance calls? How did Rocky live like this? How could I live like this?

Trying not to get even more depressed, I decided I had to do something. I dug through some of the cabinets in the kitchen and finally found some paper that I could write on. I wrote to Nancy, telling her as much as I could about our situation. I didn't want her to worry about us, and if I told her about the rafting company and the apparent lack of money, she might feel bad. As I finished the letter, I looked around the room, still amazed that I couldn't make a simple long-distance call. Gradually, as I stared at the old mismatched furniture, I began to understand. You could live without long distance, if you couldn't afford it.

Glumly I wondered what else we couldn't afford.

Chapter Five

"Hey, Scott?"

"Yeah?"

"Can I have some more corn?"

"Sure," I said tiredly, and dumped another spoonful onto Sarah's plate.

"Thanks," she said with a giggle. She returned to the campfire with her parents.

This was our last night on the river, thank God. The trip would have been great, except for Sarah...and Gregg.

There were three boats on this trip. Rocky, Laura, and Roger were the guides. Bob came along as the cook. His wrist was still wrapped in an Ace bandage, but I could tell he was glad to be back on the river. Laura had the oar boat with all our food and gear on it. Bob rode with her. There were eight patrons, four on each raft. Rocky and I were with the Arizona family, of course. Roger and Gregg were with Stacey and Debbie and their boy-friends. Apparently Debbie had neglected to tell Gregg that their boyfriends would be with them again. I could see the tension building on that raft. At camp it wasn't a whole lot better. Roger and Gregg were obviously trying to look important to Stacey and Debbie. It was embarrassing to watch.

As long as I ignored them, I could really enjoy the river. The rafting seemed to get better every hour, and so did the scenery. We were having hot days and mild nights, so things couldn't have been better weather-wise.

Rocky had told me that I'd be a swamper on this trip, so I was prepared for that, but I wasn't prepared to be the only one. I wasn't supposed to be either, but Gregg had a fit when Rocky told him he had to help. Gregg conveniently waited till we got to the first camp to tell Rocky he wasn't planning to be a swamper.

"No way, man. I'm training to be a guide, not some stupid chef."

"Gregg, Scott can't set up the tents, help cook, and set up the latrine all by himself. You're enjoying the rafting, but you're not a guide yet. The reason you're on this trip is to be a swamper and help us out."

"Sorry, you got the wrong guy." Gregg stalked off. I could tell that Rocky was angry, but he wasn't going to make a scene in front of everyone. Gregg just avoided Rocky for the rest of the trip. He always made sure there was at least ten feet between them and a patron close by.

Laura and Rocky tried to help me a little with the tents and setting up the latrine, but I ended up doing almost all of it by myself. Part of the trip package included evening activities such as hiking, swimming, and volleyball, so they spent a lot of time helping with those things too.

Not only did I have to help with the cooking, but I also had to do the dishes. In the river, no less. I had to boil water, put it in separate buckets, wash and rinse the dishes, and then I had to strain the water before I put it back in the river. With so many people using the river, you couldn't just let stuff wash downstream, because if everyone did that, the river would be trashed in just a couple of days.

I was mad at Gregg anyway, but then he and Roger had to make matters even worse. They started giving me a hard time about Sarah. She had been following me around everywhere, always asking me questions. She had also offered to help me cook, but I didn't want her around me that much. I guess she was kind of cute, but she was only twelve, and besides, she was leaving in a couple of days.

Roger picked up on her crush before Gregg did, but it wasn't long before both of them were ragging me about it. I couldn't help it if she liked me! Every time she was near me they made kissing noises, and they kept calling her my girlfriend. I tried to ignore them, but they were both really good at being irritating and stupid.

"Oh, Scotty, will you please give me some more corn," Gregg giggled in a high-pitched, mocking voice. They had come up from behind me, as if just thinking about them was enough to get their attention.

"Oh, Scotty, you're just so cute!" Roger squealed, pinching my cheek.

I smacked his hand with the corn spoon and splattered kernels all over him and Gregg.

"Now, Scott," Gregg said, wagging his finger at me, "that's not being a very nice boyfriend. You're supposed to give her a kiss with the corn."

"Shut up."

"Oh, Roger, I think it bugs him to get instructions about how to treat a girlfriend."

"We're just trying to help you out, Snotty Scotty, since you don't know what you're doing yet."

"You guys are such jackasses."

"Hey." Roger yanked the spoon out of my hand. "There's no reason to call us names, little boyfriend, unless you want to get the tar beat out of you. Now why don't you be nice and go give your girlfriend a kiss?"

"She's not my girlfriend!"

"Uh-oh, denial. Yep, that's the first stage of love," Gregg said.

"Well, at least I could get her if I wanted to," I muttered.

"Excuse me?"

"Nothing."

"No, you said something." Roger shoved the spoon under my chin and jerked my head up. "What did you say?"

"I said I could get her if I wanted to."

"And that's supposed to mean what?"

"I just know you guys are frustrated 'cause you can't get your girls," I said with a shrug.

I turned around and lifted the hot water off the stove, confident that I had scored the last point. I had just noticed the sandaled feet a few feet in front of me when someone shoved me in the back. I flew forward and instinctively threw the water out away from me. Just as my face landed in the sand, I heard Chris scream.

He had been waiting for us to finish talking so he could get some hot chocolate. The water went down his right leg, from the shin all the way to his toes. By the time I looked up, his skin was already turning red. Chris was sobbing uncontrollably. His parents came running, and so did Rocky.

Rocky scooped him up and took him to the river, quickly submerging his leg in the cold water. Over his shoulder, he said, "There's an instant cold pack in the first aid kit. Get it."

Feeling sick to my stomach, I turned and ran to back to the camp. Laura was already pulling the kit out. "What happened?" she asked.

"Chris got a pan of hot water spilled on him," I said.

"Is it bad?"

"Yeah, I think so."

When we got back to the river, Chris was still whimpering, but he had calmed down quite a bit. We put the ice packs on his leg and helped him back to the campfire.

"How'd this happen?" Rocky asked. His voice was mild, but I wasn't fooled.

I didn't say anything right away.

Chris looked up at me. "It looked like you tripped," he said.

I opened my mouth, and a hand came down on my shoulder, squeezing. "Yeah, Scott, it looked like you tripped." I looked back at Roger, and he squeezed a little more.

I still didn't say anything.

"I thought you tripped," Gregg said from the other side.

I turned and looked at him. His face was blank, unreadable.

"It's understandable," Roger said. "It's getting dark, and you were in a hurry, trying to get all cleaned up. There's a big rock sticking out of the ground over there. I'm surprised you didn't stub your toe." He actually looked down at my foot as if he wanted to make sure it was all right.

"Scott?" Rocky said softly.

"I guess I tripped." I turned around. "I'm really sorry, Chris."

He shrugged. "It was an accident. I'll be okay."

"Guess I'll go get the rest cleaned up," I said.

"I'll help," Gregg said quickly. He looked over at Roger, but Roger was sitting down by the fire next to Stacey, telling her that he made the best s'mores on the Arkansas.

Gregg and I did the dishes in silence. Rocky put on some more hot water for coffee and hot chocolate, but he didn't say anything either. When everything had been cleared away, I headed for my tent. I was beat.

"Hey, Scott," Gregg said.

I stopped but didn't turn around.

"Thanks." I waited for something more, but he turned and went to the campfire. In a few minutes, I heard his voice joining Roger's in a bad rendition of "Jeremiah Was a Bullfrog." I went into my tent and curled up, but it was a long time before I was able to sleep.

We managed to finish the rest of the trip without any other major incidents. I apologized a few more times to Chris, especially when I saw the blisters that were forming on his leg. He tried to smile and be tough, but I could tell that it hurt. His last day on the river wasn't as much fun as it should have been.

We got back to the office and unloaded and cleaned all the gear. I was in the middle of hosing out the coolers when I looked around and realized that Roger and Gregg were gone.

"Figures," I muttered to myself. We were the last trip to come in that day, so everyone else was already long gone. It looked like I would be stuck cleaning and storing the rest of the kitchen gear all by myself.

I grabbed the handle of the huge cooler and began dragging it up to the raft barn.

"I really don't care!" I heard Gregg shout. I was so startled I dropped the cooler. Apparently they were in the raft barn. I picked up the handle and started forward again.

"I don't care if you don't care," Rocky said. "Either you can cooperate and work for me, or you can start paying rent and work wherever you can find a place that will deal with your attitude."

"I don't have an attitude, you do!"

I stopped just outside of the barn. I could see them through the open door.

"You came here with an attitude."

"You never wanted us in the first place!"

"You don't know that. You won't even talk to me."

"That's because every time I see you, you're giving me orders and making me your slave."

"Wait a minute. I knew this would be hard for all of us. I have tried to set simple guidelines to make things easier. I don't ask much out of you at home. I do ask that you help me pay the bills by working for me, but you won't even do that. Instead you flirt and fart around and make your little brother pick up your slack."

"Yeah, well, Scott's always been perfect, so—"

"This is not about Scott, this is about you trying to get out of doing your share! Now either there will be more cooperation from you or you can find yourself another job and pay me a hundred dollars a month in rent and buy your own food."

"Ha! That shack's not worth a hundred dollars a month."

"You'd be surprised. And you," Rocky turned to Roger. "I expect a whole lot more out of you. You've been in this business long enough to know you don't screw around when you're on the job. Screwing around is for staff trips and parties only."

Roger nodded in cool acceptance.

"I should just pull him off your raft."

"No, don't do that, Rocky. We'll settle down. He's doing real well on the river. After another couple of weeks and CPR certification, he'll be ready to guide."

Rocky gave Roger a considering look. "I've known you for years, Roger. I'm trusting your judgment and your word that the horseplay stops here. Don't let me down. I know your father taught you better."

As he got up to go, Roger sighed and said, "I know."

"Both of you need to help Scott put the kitchen gear away. No one is to leave without checking with me first."

Roger came out of the barn. He looked at me but didn't say anything.

Rocky stopped Gregg when he moved to follow him. I couldn't hear what was said, just Rocky's deep voice rumbling. I'm not sure if Gregg said anything at all. After a few minutes he came out, too, and followed Roger to help with the rest of the gear. Rocky just shook his head, then he headed up to the office.

The night we got back from our three-day trip, I went home alone again. Roger and Gregg went off to who knows where after we finished with the kitchen gear. All I wanted to do was sleep for a few days. I couldn't believe how tired I was. Then the phone rang.

It was Sarah. They had given her Rocky's phone number and told her that I asked them to do it. They may have found it hilarious, but I found it embarrassing and awkward. I knew Roger or Gregg would have just blown her off, but somehow I couldn't do that. I tried to let her down easy.

The next few days passed without any major problems cropping up. I went on a raft trip about every other day, sometimes a full day, sometimes just a half. I was getting pretty confident with Brown's Canyon, but I still wasn't too sure about the Royal Gorge. I was very comfortable with the register and working the store. Helping people find the right size wet suit to rent or letting people know what personal items to take with them on the multiday trips was easy and even a little fun.

Bob and I tried to liven up the hours spent working the store, but it still got boring in the afternoons. We played card games like crazy. I also started getting to know Tom and Joe a little bit more. They were both nineteen and getting ready to go back to college in the fall. Since this was their first year as guides, they were low on the list and didn't get to take as many trips out as the other guides did. Trips were assigned based on seniority, because the guides got paid per trip, not per hour or day.

Roger and Gregg continued to get along real well. They pretty much ignored the rest of the staff, except to give people a hard time for bad sunburns, for letting patrons get thrown out of the raft, or for lack of girlfriends. They thought they were funny, but I'm not sure the rest of the staff agreed. I know I didn't.

I rolled out of bed one morning and did my standard bathroom routine. Then I started breakfast. Rocky came in as usual, but he didn't want anything to eat. We sat quietly for a few minutes.

"Hey, Rocky," I said suddenly.

"Yeah?"

"Is there anyway we can get a long-distance carrier?" I asked.

He looked at me blankly.

Quickly I explained what had happened when I tried to call Nancy. "It'd just be nice to let her know we're okay," I said. "And I've got some friends I'd like to call too."

He nodded. "I think we can arrange that. But you'll have to be real careful with the amount of time you spend on the phone."

"I know," I said easily. "You can take it out of my paycheck."

He looked like that hurt him. "I don't want to do that." He hesitated and added, "But if the bill gets too big, I will."

"Sure," I said. "Is that why you lost touch with Dad? Because you couldn't afford it?"

Rocky shook his head slowly. "I shut down the long distance because I had a roommate for a while. She never paid the long-distance bills, and she ran up over four hundred dollars worth of phone calls."

"Wow," I said. I waited for a minute, then asked, "So why did you lose touch?"

He made a cross between a snort and a chuckle. "I'll tell ya when you're older."

"Come on," I said.

"No, Scott, not today. It's a long story." He stretched his arms up over his head. "Hey, where's Gregg?"

I blinked. He had usually come in, grabbed food, and left by now. "I don't know," I said, getting up. "I'll go find out."

I took my bagel with me down the hall.

"Hey, Gregg, come on, you're going to be late."

"Mghff..."

"What?"

"Go away."

"Come on," I said, pulling the blanket off him.

"Quit it, Scott!" He yanked the cover back up. "It's my day off."

"Your what?"

"My day off. Now go away."

I turned and ran into Rocky who was standing in the doorway. For a big guy, he could move awfully quickly and quietly. I didn't know how long he'd been there, but from the look on his face, I guessed correctly that he had heard what Gregg had just said.

He flipped on the light switch. "Get up, Gregg."

"Today's my day off," he said again, louder. "Now, if you don't mind, I'm sleeping in."

"Who said it was your day off?"

Gregg rolled over so his back was to us.

"Gregg? When did I tell you that you had today off?"

"Go to hell!"

I sat down on my bed, just watching.

"I thought we agreed there would be more cooperation from you."

"From me?" Gregg sat up in bed. "There's been nothing but cooperation from me these last few days! What about some cooperation from you? When does that start?"

"What do you want from me?"

"I want my day off!"

"We can discuss your schedule and days off, but not right now. I've already got you lined up on a raft. If you had wanted today off, you should have asked me earlier."

"You *told* me I had to come out to live with you. You *told* me I was working for you. Then you *told* me I was going to be working with Roger. Roger has Mondays and every other Tuesday off, so I get today off, too!"

"Gregg," Rocky said, and I could tell he was trying not to yell. "Roger's schedule is set. You're training right now. I need you on the river, learning as much as you can. Once you're ready to go, we'll discuss your schedule. Now let's go. I don't want to be late."

"This is such a crock!" Gregg shouted, jumping to his feet. "You are such a pushy, demanding, unbending, stubborn jackass!"

"And what are you?" Rocky demanded. "Are you trying to tell me you really think you're being reasonable and cooperative?"

"Yes, I am! I've worked for you, I've listened to your stupid rules, I've done what you've told me to do. I'm seventeen! You can't make me work this many hours a week without a break! Not without some sort of extra pay. There are child labor laws or something. We've worked every day since we've been here. Even God took a day off." Gregg sat back down.

Rocky shook his head. "I've got to get to the office. You want today off, fine, take it. But I'm not going to start paying you until you start running the supply boat or guiding the trips, and you're not going to start guiding till I say you're ready. You need every trip on the river you can get to prepare for my test."

"What do you mean, you're not paying me?" Gregg yelled.

"You haven't been working. Hell, everyone else *pays* to do what you've been doing the last week! The guides do the work. So do the cooks, cashiers, and swampers. I was going to pay you for being a swamper on the last long trip, but you decided that was beneath you." He turned to go.

Gregg glared at his back. "You can't do this. This is slave labor."

"Wrong." Rocky turned back around and stopped in front of him, leaning down till his face was just inches from Gregg's. "You're in training on the river right now. You ask any other guide, and they'll tell you they paid anywhere from one to three hundred dollars for their training course. I'm giving you a gift, and you're too bullheaded and selfish to see it. I'm sorry I don't have a Beverly Hills mansion for you to recline in this summer, but I'm giving you everything I can." He stopped for a minute and then stood up. "And I ask the same of you."

He thought for a minute, then said, "Tell you what. I'll give just a little bit more. I'll give you...both of you," he said, nodding toward me, "Mondays *and* Tuesdays off for the rest of the summer."

Neither of us said anything at first. I was trying to figure out how I kept getting dragged into these fights.

"That's okay," Gregg said. "I'll just take Mondays and every other Tuesday off, like Roger."

Rocky shook his head slowly. "Nope. Every Monday and Tuesday. I don't want to push you too hard. And besides, I've got guides who are fighting to take trips. They need all the trips they can get, because they're saving for college. But of course you're not worried about that," he said to Gregg, "because this year's already taken care of for you."

"I hate you," Gregg said, glaring at Rocky.

"I can tell," Rocky said simply. Then he turned around and left.

I was torn. I was tired and I really wanted the day off, but I didn't want Rocky thinking I couldn't handle it. I thought about getting up to go after Rocky, but the look on Gregg's face stopped me.

He looked like someone had just knocked the wind out of him. He started shaking. Then he started to cry.

I got up and awkwardly tried to put my arms around him, and he pushed them away. He turned his anger on me. "Go on, get out of here! I know you think Rocky's all cool, so why don't you just go and lick his boots some more!"

I didn't move at first. He got up and shoved me out of the room, then slammed the door.

I wanted so many things. I wanted to go back and make Gregg talk to me. I wanted to talk to Nancy. I wanted to talk to Rocky and find out why he was doing this to all of us. I wanted my parents and my old life back.

But at that moment, I just wanted to get out of the house, to go to the office and hang out with Bob, or go down to the raft barn and help Laura and Carol rig the rafts. But I knew I couldn't betray Gregg that way.

I guess I was more worn out than I thought I was. I fell asleep on the couch, which wasn't too surprising, considering the junk that was on TV. I thought I had only dozed off, but when I looked at the clock, I was surprised to see that it was nearly noon.

I sat up slowly and listened. The house was absolutely still, except for the talk show rattling on TV. I got up and turned it off, then padded quietly to our room, expecting to see Gregg crashed out on his bed.

He was gone.

I sighed and sat down. This was just great. He drags me into his argument, forces me to take the day off too, and then bails on me, leaving me with nothing to do for an entire day.

I wandered to the kitchen and ate an orange for lunch. I decided to go exploring, since there wasn't much else for me to do.

The front of the house I was already familiar with, so I went around to the back. There wasn't much there. An old tire hung from one of the huge cottonwood trees. The ground was covered with some strawberry plants growing around in a random pattern, so I assumed they were wild. An old wooden storage shed stood a few feet from the house.

The hinges squealed a little when I opened the door. The air was musty, and there were thick cobwebs everywhere. In the dim light I could see an odd assortment of old tools, skis, a black bike, and even a lawn mower, although there wasn't really a lawn around the house.

My eyes went back to the bike. It was covered with dust but it seemed to be in good condition. I pulled it out, and I was surprised to find both tires with good tread. The back one was just a little low. I went back in the shed, rummaged around and found an air pump, and fixed that problem.

It was an older model ten-speed, but the brakes seemed to work, and the chain moved over the gears pretty smoothly. I would have preferred a sharp mountain bike, but this would certainly work for now. This was my way out. I wasn't going to be stuck in the house anymore.

I went to the house and got a damp towel. When I wiped down the bike, I could see it was navy blue. There was an old bike lock around the bar, but no key. I dropped the seat. It had been set at its highest point, and I knew I wouldn't be able to sit on it that way. It was a tall bike as it was. Obviously it was Rocky's, and he was almost a full foot taller than me.

I ran back into the house and grabbed the yellow pages, turning to the city maps. I looked carefully at the streets in both towns, and decided that it looked like Salida might be a little bit bigger. However, it also looked like I was a little closer to Buena Vista. I hopped on the bike, eager to see what I could find.

After thirty minutes in the sweltering sun, some of my eagerness had faded. I hadn't realized how far from Rocky's house Buena Vista was. And I was also pretty sure I had been riding uphill the whole time. Plus, noon was not the coolest hour for a bike ride along a two-lane blacktop.

When I finally hit town, I stopped at the first bike rack I saw. My butt was sore and I was ready to walk around a little bit. I didn't have any way to lock up the bike, because I hadn't been able to find the key to the old lock in the shed.

I stood there for a few minutes, not quite sure what to do. But when I took a good look at all the high-class mountain bikes in the rack, I decided no one would want to steal a beat-up old ten-speed. I parked it and walked on into town.

I didn't think it would take me long to explore the town, at least from what I could see. The main part of town was only two main streets about three city blocks long. There were all sorts of little sports shops, a couple of gas stations, a few restaurants, and a couple of knickknack stores.

There was also a movie theater, which made me feel better, but it only had two screens. At first I was really disappointed, but then I saw an announcement for a drive-in that showed movies on the weekends. This helped, but not much. All of the movies in town were at least a couple of months old, and I had already seen them.

I wandered in and out of a few stores, but I hadn't brought my wallet with me. I dug in my pockets and found almost three dollars, but that wasn't going to go far.

While I was in one of the T-shirt stores, I asked if there was a library nearby. The guy at the counter was watching a portable TV. He looked like he was about seventeen and my guess was the last book he had read was probably by Dr. Seuss.

I repeated my question.

"Um, yeah, we got a library. It's in the high school."

"There's not a public library?"

"Well, yeah, dude, that's it."

"Oh. Okay," I said. "Where's the high school?"

"Like, turn down the next street, and it's, like, about a block down there."

"Which way do I turn?"

"Oh, right, turn right," he said with a laugh.

"Thanks," I said.

"Sure, dude," he said, turning back to the MTV Beach Bash.

I managed to find the high school pretty easily, not because of the descriptive directions he had given me, but because just down the street there was a sign pointing the way. Apparently the school was a pretty important part of the town.

Buena Vista High was an old red brick building with wide steps leading up to the front door. Two large columns stood impressively to either side of the entrance, and the trees along the walk had to be close to a hundred years old. I couldn't really get a feel for how big the building was as I walked up to it. It was just a standard block building, but it gave off vibes of being ancient.

I was pleasantly surprised when I walked into the relatively cool air of the hallway. The school colors appeared to be red and black, and their mascot was the Demons. The lockers lining the hall were incredibly tall and narrow. The whole building had a still, almost dead quality to it, and my footsteps echoed down the hallway. It felt like it could have been empty for years.

All the classrooms were shut, of course, and the couple of doors that I tried were also locked. I peered in the window on one of the doors to see what the room looked like. The desks were all wooden; they could have been part of a movie set for the old one-room school house.

The library was on the left off the main hall. A sign on the door read, The Buena Vista City Library Welcomes You! I opened the door and the feeling of dead air evaporated.

My old school's library had several rooms and sections, but this was just one large room divided up by bookshelves set at angles.

The library was doing a pretty fair amount of business. There was a group of little kids gathered around a silver-haired gentleman who was reading *The 500 Hats of Bartholomew Cubbins,* which used to be one of my favorites. The kids were all entranced, and several of them had forgotten to close their mouths.

Three people were sitting in chairs in the center of the library, just reading, and there were two middle-aged ladies in the romance section. They were passing books to each other, giggling like little girls. A guy who looked like a college student was working at a computer.

I wandered through a couple of rows of books, looking for either the sci-fi or horror section. I found the sci-fi first. In the middle of a row, I stopped and glanced up at the checkout desk.

The girl behind the counter appeared to be about my age. She had wheat-gold hair and a generous amount of freckles across her nose. She was helping another older man check out a book, and every time she said something, he said "What?" really loud. Her voice got louder through the whole conversation, but she still kept smiling and sounding nice.

"No, Mr. Kinney, it's due back in two weeks."

"What?"

"It's due in two weeks!"

"What?"

"Two weeks," she almost shouted, tapping the date on the book.

"Oh, of course," he said, nodding.

"Have a good day," she said as he shuffled out.

"What?" He turned around.

She just smiled and waved. He smiled and waved back.

"Can I help you?" she said suddenly.

With a start, I realized I had been standing in the middle of the row, just staring like an idiot, even though she had turned and was facing me. "Um, yeah," I said, blindly grabbing a book off the left shelf.

I took it up to the counter and set it down. We were about the same height, which was nice. The ceiling fan blew the sweet smell of her perfume over to me. "Can you tell me if this is any good?"

"I've never read it myself, but it looks educational," she said. She raised her eyebrows and tried not to smile, but her brown eyes were laughing at me.

When I looked down at the book, I could have kicked myself. In the middle of the science fiction section, I had to grab a thick textbook entitled *Red Stars: Their Lives, Components, and Distances*. I couldn't believe it, and I couldn't think of anything witty to say.

"I guess it was misplaced," she said sympathetically.

"Yeah, well, sometimes truth is just as interesting as fiction," I said, trying to come up with a reason why I'd pick up such a dull, boring book to read during summer vacation.

"I prefer to study the stars outside," she said.

"Yeah, me too. But I don't really know a lot about them, and..." I trailed off, convinced I was sounding like a moron.

"I don't either. I just like to look at them. Kind of like rainbows. I'd rather not know how or why they're there, 'cause that just takes all the mystery out of them."

I must have looked at her funny because she kind of gave herself a shake and said, "Well, do you want to check it out?"

"Sure, why not?"

"Do you have a library card?"

"Um, no," I said, suddenly realizing that this might get complicated.

"Okay. Would you like to get one today?"

"No, that's okay, maybe I'll come back tomorrow."

"Are you sure? You could check the book out today, but we just need to have you in the computer. It doesn't take long, if you're in a hurry."

"Um, no, that's not it." I could tell by the look on her face that I was confusing her. I decided that the only option open to me was the embarrassing truth. "I don't know my address or phone number. I just moved here."

"Oh," she said slowly. "That could be a problem."

"Oh, hey," I said quickly. "Do you have a phone book?"

"Yeah, but if you just moved here, you won't be listed," she said doubtfully.

"Oh, no, I know that. But I moved in with my uncle and he's been here for a few years."

"Okay," she said, moving down the counter. She got the book and brought it back to me. "Where're you from?"

"Southern California," I said, thumbing through the white pages.

"Cool. I've always wanted to go to California."

"It's a great place."

"So I've heard."

"How long have you lived here?" I asked.

"All my life." She sighed. "I've never even been outside this state. I've been to a few other towns, but I've never been outside of Colorado."

"Wow," I said. I couldn't even imagine that. I had always lived in California, but at least we had taken a few vacations to Mexico, Oregon, and Canada.

"Yeah, well, my parents are late hippies. They believe in living with the earth. They've never worried about jobs or money, they just live month to month. Right now they're into organic gardening. They don't believe in modern society, which is fine, except they won't even work within it. They don't realize that they can't just write everyone else off like this. Their life-style would be fine if it was just them, but they never stop to consider..." she broke off suddenly, flushing. "I'm sorry. I didn't mean to go off on you like that."

"No problem," I said with a grin. "What's your name?"

She grimaced. "Summer."

"Free-spirited parents, huh?"

"Yeah. Who are you?"

"Scott," I said. "Conservative parents, traditional name."

She laughed. "I guess so."

"Well, I found it," I said.

She looked at me blankly.

"My uncle's address," I reminded her. She still looked confused. "I can still get the library card, right?"

"Oh, yeah, sure," she said, blushing again and looking miserable.

I was beginning to feel almost confident. If she was this nervous and uncomfortable, maybe I had a chance.

She pulled out a sheet of paper and passed it to me. "Let me find you a pen," she said.

"Got one," I said, picking it up off the counter.

She got a little bit redder.

"So how old are you?" I asked.

"Fourteen."

"Going into ninth grade?"

"No, tenth."

"Really? Are you going to be fifteen soon?"

"No," she said, shaking her head. "I got put ahead a year in grade school. My antisociety parents about had a fit. But then in seventh grade, when the school recommended I be moved up again, they said no. They wanted to homeschool me, but I liked being with other kids."

"Wow," I said, "you must be pretty smart."

She shrugged. "I can hold my own."

A woman with a child walked up and put several books on the counter. Summer checked the books out and handed them to the little boy.

"What's this high school like?" I asked when she finished.

"It's school."

"But what's it like?"

"What do you mean?"

"Well, I'm going to be coming here next year," I said, hoping it was true, "and I was just wondering what it's like."

"Seven class periods in a day, one for lunch and one for study hall. All the basic core classes are offered. And there are some electives. You want to get here early on registration day, because the good electives all go fast."

I nodded. "How many students are here?"

She shrugged. "I don't know. Around five hundred maybe."

"It's a small school."

"Not really." She sounded defensive.

I laughed. "My high school last year had over two thousand."

"Oh," she said. "Well, yeah, we're smaller than that. And I bet your high school was just grades nine to twelve, right?"

"Yeah," I said. "Isn't this one?"

"No," she said, smiling. "This is grades seven to twelve."

"Wow," I said. "It is really small."

"That's what tends to happen in a small town."

"Yeah, I guess so," I said, handing her the pen and paper back. "So what's there to do around here, anyway?"

"Oh, lots of stuff. Biking and rafting, rollerblading and hiking. And of course in the winter there's skiing and snow boarding..." she trailed off.

"You don't sound real enthusiastic about it."

"After growing up here, I'm just a little tired of it all. I'd like to try some new things."

"I noticed the movie theaters in town. How often do they get new movies in?"

"Oh, they try to swap one out every week, so the movies are only here for a total of two weeks. The big theater is in Salida. It has three movies at a time. The ones that are there now are pretty good, if you haven't seen them."

"What are they showing?" I asked.

She got a newspaper out and we looked it up together.

"I've seen them all," I said without thinking. *Great,* I thought. *I just blew that chance.*

"Well," she said, handing me the book and my new card. "Here you go. It's due back in two weeks."

"Yeah, thanks," I said. "By the way, how often do you work here?"

She shrugged. "It depends. I'm just part-time, and they call me when they need me. Last week I was only in here two days, but the week before I was in here all five. The schedule's not very set."

"I see." We stood there for a minute, just staring. I could tell I was starting to flush this time.

"Well," she said suddenly, "I've got to get back to work. Mike's almost done reading, and I haven't gotten out the cookies for the kids yet."

"Yeah," I said, "I've got to get going anyway."

She turned to leave, and then looked back. "Hopefully I'll be here when you bring the book back. That way you can teach me about red stars." She smiled shyly at me and walked away. It wasn't a date, but at least it was a little bit of encouragement.

To my relief, the bike was still there when I got to the rack. It was a pain trying to hold the book with one hand and steer with the other, but it was a heck of a lot better than walking all that way.

Gregg was still gone, and it looked like Rocky was out for the night again. I made a batch of macaroni and cheese and settled down on the couch for a night of sitcom reruns and red stars. I tried to stay up until Gregg got home but I fell asleep on the couch.

Chapter Six

"Hey, Scotty, wake up!"

I almost jumped out of my skin. I had been sound asleep, and Gregg jumped on top of me on the couch, thinking it was a fun way to wake me up.

"Get off me!" I shouted when I could breathe again. I tried to shove him but my arms were trapped under the comforter that had somehow appeared while I was asleep. It was the same one Rocky had put over Gregg our first night here.

"God, I forgot how cranky you are in the mornings," he said, getting off me. "Get up, lazy butt."

"Why? What time is it?"

"About nine o'clock."

"So? We have today off, remember?"

"Yeah, but I'm bored. Let's go find something to do."

I sat up on the couch and stretched.

"Come on, man, let's go!"

"Would you relax?" I said irritably. "I'm not in any hurry. If you've got somewhere to go, go. I want to shower and eat breakfast before I go anywhere."

I walked to the bathroom and climbed into the shower, muttering to myself. I was mad that he was pushing me like this, especially since I knew if Roger had been off today, Gregg wouldn't even have stopped to give me the time of day. But at the same time, I also knew I didn't want to spend the day alone again. I hurried through my shower and got dressed.

It had been a few years since Gregg and I had done anything just the two of us, but we used to have a lot of fun together. I figured that even though he had been acting like a spoiled brat and blowing up at stupid stuff, he was still my brother, and basically all the family I had left. I should at least give him another chance.

When I got to the kitchen, I was surprised to find Gregg cooking. I don't think I had ever seen him cook before. But there he was, scrambling eggs.

"Hey," he said. "Breakfast is almost ready."

"What brings this on?" I asked suspiciously as I sat down.

He shrugged. "I don't know. Just thought it was time I made you breakfast, in return for all the stuff you cooked for me last week."

"Well, thanks," I said. I still wasn't convinced.

"So what'd you do yesterday?" he asked, straddling a chair and watching me begin to eat.

"Not much," I said. "There's not a lot to do here." I knew he wouldn't be interested in the library.

"Boy, you said it. This is one dull little town."

"What did you and Roger do?"

"We hung out at his house," he said casually. "You know, watched a few movies and had a few beers."

I didn't say anything. My parents had had pretty strict rules about drinking, and Rocky had specifically forbidden us from doing anything illegal, but if I brought that up, he'd just call me a goody-goody and go storming off again. I was lonely and I had missed talking to him these last few days. I didn't want him mad at me again.

"Where does Roger live?" I asked instead.

"Oh, he and his friend Josh have a house about fifteen minutes from here. Josh guides for another company, further up the river, I forget which one." Gregg shook his head. "Roger used to work for them too, and if Rocky doesn't lighten up soon, he'll probably go back to them."

"What do you mean, lighten up?"

"Well, he's been on his case so much lately. It's really been uncool. I mean, you saw him on the trip this weekend. He was a complete jerk to Roger. Not to mention what he's been pulling with you and me here at the house." He laughed a little. "Roger thinks we ought to call the ACLU or the social workers or something and report him for violating child labor laws with you."

I looked at him. "Oh, hey, don't go do that. I'm sure he'll come around soon."

"Anyway," Gregg said, "at this other rafting company, the whole staff parties like once or twice a week. It's a much better outfit than Rocky's."

"So why did Roger come work for Rocky?"

"Well, he pays five dollars more per half-day trip, and twenty dollars more per two-day trip," Gregg admitted. "And I guess Roger's cousin and Rocky used to work together or something." Gregg shrugged. "He says that during Rocky's first year as owner, he was a lot more fun."

"Yeah, but he lost all that money," I said. "Maybe he had to change a little."

"A little, but not this much. Besides, it's more important to have fun in life. Money's not all that matters."

I looked at him. This from the guy who wanted to be a stockbroker and rake in the money. This from the guy who was mad because he only had enough money for the first year of college. "So why are you pissed that Rocky's not paying you for last week?" I asked. "Isn't it enough that you've been having fun?"

He rolled his eyes at me. "It's the principle of the thing. Besides, you have to have some money to be able to have fun. Stuff costs money." He looked at me. "Are you done eating yet?"

"Yeah," I said, standing up and putting the dishes in the sink. I knew I should do them now, but Gregg was waiting impatiently at the door. I made a mental note to make sure I did them as soon as we got home.

"So where are we going, anyway?" I asked as we stepped outside.

"First to the office. Then wherever we want."

"And how are we going to get wherever we want?"

Gregg held up a set of keys. "Roger said we could have his truck for the day, as long as we're back to pick him up at six."

"Cool," I said, relieved that it wasn't going to be a matter of either walking everywhere or riding double on the beat-up old bike.

As we walked along the road, he talked about the movies he and Roger had watched and their plans to go meet Debbie and Stacey later that night.

I shook my head. "I don't know, Gregg."

"What do you mean?"

"Well, it just doesn't seem real cool, you know, to be stealing someone else's girl."

"Ah." Gregg waved it away. "If their boyfriends were serious, or if they were really interested, Debbie and Stacey wouldn't have agreed to meet us in the first place."

I had to admit, from that point of view, it made sense.

"How long are they here?"

"They're spending the summer with Debbie's grandmother or something," Gregg said with a shrug.

"Hey," he said, changing the subject. "Next Monday night, when Roger has Tuesday off too, he and Josh are throwing a party. Everyone from both rafting staffs are invited. It should be a huge blowout, and they've already got two kegs reserved."

"Cool," I said, because he expected it.

"Come on, Scott!"

"Come on what?"

"You've got to come. Everyone will be there. It'll be great!"

"I don't know."

"Scott, don't be a geek. It's a party in the middle of summer, for Pete's sake! Besides, we've got Tuesday off, so it's not like we'd have to get up early or anything."

"Could I bring someone?" I asked, thinking that maybe it'd be a good way to get together with Summer.

"Sure," he said quickly. Then he stopped and looked at me. "Who?"

"No one you know."

"A girl?" He started grinning, and I could feel the blush creep up my face.

"Well, yeah, maybe," I hedged.

"Little miss kiss-kiss? Sarah?"

"Knock it off," I said, giving him a halfhearted shove. "I was never interested in her and you know it. Anyway, I said it's no one you know."

"Come on, who is it?"

"No way. I'm not telling you. Besides, I don't even know if she'll come or not."

"What if I say you can't come if you don't tell me who she is?"

"Fine," I said.

He rolled his eyes. "You're such a loser, Scott. I bet you don't even have anyone in mind to ask. You're just trying to get out of coming to the party."

"Whatever, Gregg."

It took us a few minutes to get to the store. I thought we'd go straight to the truck and take off, but Gregg headed right inside, so I followed him.

"Hey, guys, what's up?" Bob asked as we stepped in.

"Not much," I said easily. "Just enjoying a day off."

Gregg didn't say anything. He headed directly to the counter and pulled out the slush jar. All of the guides kicked in a percent of every tip they got, to divide among the staff who were stuck working the office. The money from the soda machine went in there too.

"What's going on?" Bob asked.

"Nothing," Gregg said. "Just getting Scott's tips for last week. Rocky said we could get them today so we can get some stuff in town."

Bob just stared at him. Clearly he didn't believe Gregg, but wasn't sure if he should call him on it either. I couldn't believe Gregg was lying like that. I looked at the wad of money he had pulled out, and looked at Bob. He had already taken a cut in pay because of his arm. If I didn't say anything, his share from the slush jar would be even smaller. On the other hand, I didn't want to snitch on Gregg.

"Gregg," I said quickly, "we really only need fifteen for today."

He looked at me in surprise. "Not if we're going to go to lunch and then go shopping."

I glared at him. After a moment he said, "Well, maybe we can get by with a little less." He put a couple of bills back in the jar, but I was sure they were just singles.

"We'll be sure to bring change back," I said to Bob.

"Sure," he said. "I mean, it is Rocky's business. If this is what he told you to do, then do it." He went to the back of the store and picked up the broom. I felt awful.

In the truck, I waited for Gregg to say something. He didn't. Instead, as we pulled out of the parking lot, he punched in the cigarette lighter, reached under the driver's seat, and pulled out a pack of Marlboros. I felt like I was watching a stranger as he stuck a cigarette in his mouth and lit it. He had never smoked in front of me before, and from the way he coughed a little when he first inhaled, I figured he hadn't been smoking long. I remembered how Mom would change out of her clothes as soon as she got home after being around someone who smoked.

"What are you doing?" I finally demanded.

He should have been an actor. He was very good at looking innocent. "What do you mean?"

"Taking that money. Rocky never said we could have it. And smoking? Since when have you smoked?"

He sighed. "You worked in the shop last week, right?"

"Yeah? So what?"

"And that money gets split up between the people who work the shop, right?"

"So what?"

"So we just got your money a little early, that's all."

"Then give it to me."

"No way."

"I'm the one who worked in the shop last week, not you. That's my money."

"Yeah, well, we're going out to lunch today, right?"

"It's still my money."

"Yeah, but I'm driving, so you're buying."

"No deal," I said.

"And we have to fill Roger's tank."

"What?"

He looked at me. "If you borrow someone's car, you fill the tank."

I looked at the gauge. It was already on the *E*. "No way, man. We put a gallon or two in there. We're not going to use more than that."

"It's common courtesy to fill the tank, Scott."

I glared at him. "Give me my money."

"No. You wouldn't even have this money if it weren't for me."

"So what? Give me my money."

"Why? All you'd do is go put it in some stupid savings account or something. You don't know how to have any fun."

"Just because I don't go around stealing doesn't mean I don't know how to have fun."

"We're going to go have a good time, Scott. Just relax about the money. You'll get what you need."

"Give me my money, Gregg."

He yanked the steering wheel and pulled over on the shoulder. "You want your money? Fine, here's your stupid money." He threw his cigarette out the window and then shoved the cash into my hand. "Now get out!"

"What?" I exclaimed.

"You heard me. I thought it'd be cool to go spend the day and have lunch together, but if all you're going to do is be selfish and whine, then you can just get out of the truck and go home."

"No," I said, folding my arms across my chest.

"What did you say?"

"I said no. I'm not getting out of the truck."

"Get out!" He shouted so loud it made me jump, even though I knew it was coming.

I just sat there and ignored his cussing and shoving. I did lock the truck door so he wouldn't be able to reach over and open the door with one hand and push me out with the other.

After a few minutes, he shut up. He lit another cigarette. We sat in complete silence for at least five minutes.

Finally he let out a big gusty sigh and leaned his head back. "I'm sorry, Scott," he said, tossing the butt out the window.

I didn't say anything.

He shook his head. "I don't know what I'm doing. I know I've been kind of a jerk lately. But Rocky just... he just really pisses me off."

"Give him a chance, Gregg. This hasn't been real easy on him either. He's trying to do the best he can."

"I know he says that, but it just feels like he's holding back."

"Maybe he's waiting for you to try too."

"I don't know." He shook his head again and looked at me. "I still love ya like a brother, man."

"I know. Me too."

"And the cigarettes, they're just..." he trailed off.

"Just what?" I asked.

"They're just to help me calm down. They help me relax."

"They stink and they help you kill yourself, Gregg. That's all they do."

"Hey, I'm just doing what I can to deal with this situation, okay?"

I didn't say anything.

"Are you still up to going for lunch?" he asked after a few seconds.

I hesitated.

"I've got some money," he said, reading my thoughts. "I'll put the slush money back."

"Okay," I said. "I've got some money too."

As we pulled back onto the road, he said he was sorry one more time.

"Me too," I said. And even though we both meant it, I also knew that we still had a lot of things to work out.

We spent a lot of time in town looking at mountain bikes. Gregg was hoping his bike would be arriving in the next few days, along with the rest of our stuff. I had never been much into biking, but after my ride yesterday, I could appreciate why Gregg looked longingly at the bikes with extra gears, full suspension, and aluminum frames.

"Man," he said, looking at a new model, "I wish I could get one of these."

"What's wrong with your bike?"

"In the first place, it's still in California. Besides, it's almost two years old."

"So?"

"So, it's heavier than the new ones. And the seat doesn't have that new style cushion. And this one's got better gear ratios."

"Oh," I said, trying to sound as if I understood how two years could make a bike old.

"Man, we're going to be in for a rough summer if Rocky's really not going to pay us."

"Gregg," I said tiredly. "Let's not get into this again."

"No, no, I'm not going to sit and complain. I think we need to do some planning. I mean, seriously, how much money did you bring with you?"

"Today?"

"No, how much did you have to bring from home?"

I shrugged. "A couple hundred," I said, even though it was closer to three hundred fifty, and that wasn't including the money Nancy had given me.

He shook his head. "I wish I had saved like you did. I've got less than a hundred to my name. And if Rocky's not paying me...how am I supposed to get through the summer?"

"I don't know. I mean, I'm sure Rocky will help us with clothes and stuff, but I don't know how much he can."

"Well, yeah, even just for little stuff like movies." Gregg shook his head. "I don't know what I'm going to do after next year," he said.

"What do you mean?"

"I mean for college. I may not be able to finish."

"Sure you will. You'll just have to make sure you keep good grades so you can get a loan or a grant or something."

"Loans follow you around too much. I'd probably spend the next fifteen years just trying to pay them off. I'd be better off just getting a job. Besides, I'm not sure college is what I want to do. I've never gotten good grades."

"You can get through college, Gregg. And you have to if you want to be a stockbroker."

He looked at me for a minute and then sighed.

"Keep being a geek, Scott. That way you can get a scholarship. I mean, we both know Rocky's not going to be any help. God, I can't wait for school to start! I just want to get out of his stupid house and out of this lame town."

I bit my tongue. He was in a down mood, and there wasn't anything I could say to help him right now.

We ate lunch at El Duran, a little Mexican café that actually had really good food. The whole time, Gregg kept talking about what a cool guy Roger was and how much fun they had together. I didn't have much to add to the conversation.

We went to a hardware store and looked at some plastic storage units. We both agreed we were going to have to find a way to store the rest of our stuff when it arrived.

Gregg picked up a four-inch pocketknife to wear on his life jacket. He said all the guides needed them in case anyone gets tangled in a line because it's faster and safer just to cut it. I priced some padlocks and chains. I knew I couldn't afford a new bike, but if Rocky let me keep riding his, then I was going to need a way to lock it up.

When we got back to the office, I returned the money to the slush jar. Gregg made sure that Bob saw me do it. "We decided to wait a while on the shopping," he said, "so we didn't need it after all."

We went back to the house and measured our room, arguing about which storage chests would work better for it. Then we watched one of the cheesy talk shows for an hour and had some hot dogs for dinner.

Around a quarter of six, Gregg left to go to the office to meet Roger. "In case we miss Rocky, tell him I'm staying at Roger's tonight," he said as he left.

"Sure," I said, but I was talking to the door.

When Rocky came in two hours later, I was sprawled on the couch, once again watching fuzzy TV.

"Hello," he said with a smile. "You and Gregg seem to like that couch better than your own beds to sleep on. How were your days off?"

I shrugged. "Fine, I guess. Nothing really special."

He went back into his room for a few minutes. When he came out, he said, "Is your brother around?"

I shook my head. "He's staying at Roger's tonight."

He hesitated. "They certainly became good friends fast."

"Yep."

He looked at me for a minute like he was going to say something, but then he just said, "Never mind," and went into the kitchen.

A mountain bike commercial came on, and I called, "Hey, Rocky?"

"Yeah?"

"Do you have the key to your bike lock?"

"My what?" He came back into the living room.

"Your bike lock."

"I have a bike?"

I started to laugh. "Well, I thought you did. I found one in the shed."

"Really? Well, I'll be damned. That's where it went. Did you find anything else in there?"

"There's a lot of junk in there."

"Maybe I ought to go back and check it out sometime," he said, mostly to himself.

"The key?"

"Hmm?"

"Do you have the key?" I asked, even though by this time I knew what the answer would be.

"Oh, God, I probably do, but I have no idea where it would be." He looked at me. "Does the bike still work?"

"Yeah," I said. "I rode it into town yesterday. I hope you don't mind if I use it. That way I'm not stuck in the house all day."

"Oh, no, not at all," he said. "Glad it's still useful. Just be careful on the highway. We probably ought to get you a helmet."

"That's all right," I said. I knew they were almost in style since everyone was wearing them, but I couldn't stand them.

He went to the front door.

"Going out again?"

"Yeah," he said slowly, grabbing his jeans jacket. "You going to be okay?"

"What do you mean?"

He looked kind of uncomfortable. "I didn't realize Gregg was going to be gone so much. It leaves you alone an awful lot," he said finally.

I just looked at him.

"Well, if you need anything, the phone number's on the refrigerator," he said.

"Yeah, I know."

"Good night, Scott."

"See ya."

Chapter Seven

If it hadn't been for Friday, it would have been a good week. I was slowly beginning to feel accepted by the other staff members, except for Roger. I couldn't say if he wasn't accepting me or if he was just ignoring me as much as possible, but either way the results were the same.

On Wednesday, Joe, Barb, and I went to lunch, and we made plans to go bowling on Friday night. They were a fun crew to work with, and even more fun to go out with. Joe, Barb, and Tom were nineteen, Lou was eighteen, and Gary was twenty, so it was a little easier getting to know them. They were at least a little bit closer to my age than Roger.

Bob and I continued to have a good time when we worked together in the store. We had an ongoing poker game, and each day we invented a few new rules for it. It was getting a little crazy, and expensive. By the time we closed Thursday night, I "owed" Bob nearly four million dollars. In spite of the fun, though, I have to admit I started getting upset on the days I had to stay with him instead of rafting with the others. Bob was counting down the days till he could get back to being a guide. We were both pretty happy on Tuesday when a group called in for a two-day trip on Saturday and Sunday, and Rocky signed us up as the cook and swamper.

Wednesday night, I was in the kitchen when Rocky came home. He went to his room first, then came and sat at the kitchen table.

"Where's Gregg?"

I snorted. "Where do you think he is?"

He sighed. "Roger's." When I just nodded, he said, "What's for dinner?"

I looked at him. "Huh?"

"What smells so good?"

"It's a tuna melt casserole."

"Enough there for two?"

"Um, yeah, sure." I laughed. "There's enough here for three or four."

He got up and started getting plates and silverware out.

"You're staying in tonight?" I asked after a minute.

"Yep."

"Can I ask why?"

He shrugged. "Just kind of feel like it."

"Oh," I said. I couldn't think of anything else.

Dinner was a little uncomfortable at first. It was, after all, the first time he had sat down with me without the intent of leaving within five minutes. But after a while, we started talking about the river and some of the other staff members. He told me a few funny stories about some of the crazy things the guides had done as rookies, and even told me about some of his own embarrassing moments.

When we finished eating, he helped me do the dishes and then we wandered out to the living room. I turned on the TV.

About ten minutes into the sitcom, he looked at me and frowned. "You like watching this stuff?"

"Not really," I said. "But there's not much else to do."

"Do you play chess?"

"Yeah." I looked around. "Do you have a set?"

"Hang on." He disappeared into his room and returned with a box. When he blew on it, dust flew everywhere. "Haven't played for a while," he said sheepishly.

"I'd never have guessed," I said with a grin.

We spent the evening playing. Even though he said he hadn't played in years, he was still pretty good. When he made the comment that I was better than he had thought I would be, I laughed.

"My dad taught me when I was eight or nine. I was on the chess team last year."

"You hustled me!"

"I did not!"

"You did too! Me, your uncle! And you hustled me." He shook his head and we both laughed.

Then he got kind of serious. "Your dad's the one who taught me how to play too."

"Really?"

"Really."

"How old were you?"

"I think I was seven or eight. Does Gregg play?"

I shook my head. "Dad tried to teach him a few times, but he could never get Gregg to sit still long enough."

Rocky chuckled. "Your dad had to wait till I was laid up with chicken pox to get me to sit still long enough." He sighed. "Your poor dad had a hard time putting up with me."

It got quiet. I wanted to ask him again what had happened between him and my dad, but I didn't know how. His next move put me in checkmate, and we ended our evening tied, two games apiece.

I went to the movies with Lou and Tom on Thursday night. By that time it didn't matter that I had already seen the show; I just wanted to get out of the house. Every time I went into town, I hoped I might see Summer. Rocky hung around for dinner with me again that night. I told him that if he wasn't careful, I was going to get used to having him around. When I told Rocky that I was going out, he looked almost disappointed.

"Well, I guess I'll see you tomorrow then," he said as I was heading out the door.

"Yeah," I said.

"I suppose it's my turn to cook dinner tomorrow night."

"Actually, we're going bowling in Salida tomorrow after work, so I won't be around."

"Well, next time then," he said.

Friday morning was a little cloudy. The mornings in Colorado's mountains were cold, even though they warmed up quickly in the summer sun. The breeze that whispered through the aspen leaves made the air feel even crisper. I decided to wear my sweats to the office that morning; I just hoped I'd remember to bring them home that night. They needed to be washed before the weekend trip.

I helped Carol and Jim rig up the rafts. We got three rafts set up in the same amount of time it took Roger and Gregg to get one done. They joked and horsed around so much that they rarely did the same amount of work done by the rest of the staff. I had noticed that while I was getting closer to the others on the staff, they seemed to be pulling away from Roger and Gregg. I very rarely saw Gregg or Roger speaking to anyone else.

After the rafts were set, we kicked around and waited for Rocky to come down to assign trips. Fitting patrons for life jackets was a little more interesting this time. I had never watched Roger help patrons pick jackets before.

There was a group of college girls who wandered down to the river. Roger grabbed Gregg and the two of them went over and spent a great deal of time making sure they had jackets that fit exactly right. After the girls were fitted, however, neither Roger nor Gregg seemed to feel any responsibility for getting anyone else a jacket.

I had to help a family of three, and the mom was very heavyset. Finding a life jacket to fit her was uncomfortable, both for her and for me. We finally found one with a fifty-six–inch chest, and by loosening the straps on it practically all the way, we were able to get it on her. Her husband and son were both fairly skinny; in fact, the little boy looked to be about nine and couldn't have weighed more than sixty-five pounds. They were an odd-looking group.

Roger and Gregg made some very unflattering comments about the family, and they made them loud enough for me to hear while I was helping the woman get into the life jacket. Rocky walked past me while they were talking, and from the way he stopped and looked at them, I was pretty sure he'd heard what they said. He shook his head and made a note on his clipboard before climbing to the platform to give his standard speech.

I was a little surprised to see Rocky assign the family of three to Roger's raft. I kind of suspected that he did it to correct Roger's behavior, but from the way the lady looked at Roger when she learned she was assigned to his raft, it seemed almost like he was punishing her more than Roger.

But the real surprise for me was when Rocky assigned me to Roger's raft as well. I had never been on his raft, and I had assumed that it was because Rocky only wanted one trainee per raft. I didn't have time to ask Rocky about his decision before he left to drive the shuttle for the Royal Gorge run.

"Grab the bowline, Snotty," Roger said.

He asked for introductions quickly, and we learned that the lady's name was Mindy, her husband was Mike, and their son's name was Max.

"Okay, here's where I want you." He started to rub his hands together, but then he stopped and turned to Gregg.

"You should take this one. Where do you want them?"

I stared at him. Rocky had specifically said Gregg was not to guide a boat until he had tested him.

Gregg didn't seem surprised at all. "I'd like to have Mike on the front left. Scott, you take the left middle, Mindy, you'll go on the right front, and Max, you're in front of me on the right here."

They all got to their positions. Gregg came up to me to take the bowline. "Go ahead and get in, Scott."

"Gregg," I began.

"Hey, I know what you're going to say," he said in a low voice. "It's no big deal. I've done this a few other times. Besides, Roger's right here to help if I need it. I'll do my test with Rocky pretty soon. This is just practice, okay?"

I couldn't argue, not with his smooth logic and not with patrons right there. I went to my place on the raft and watched him pick up the guide's paddle. The guide's paddle has a larger blade that can be used as a rudder to steer the raft.

We shoved off. After the usual introductory remarks, Gregg started to give the instructions. "Okay, now you're all going to need to listen to what I tell you to do, and do it right away when we're in the rapids. If we don't work together in the rapids, we'll have someone get washed out, or we may flip the boat." He showed them how to use the paddles. "Now, when I call power forward, everyone paddles forward. Ready? Power forward!" he called.

We all started paddling forward. I focused on following Mike's strokes and not hitting his paddle. I heard Mindy and Max apologize to each other several times when their paddles hit. The raft began turning to the right. We weren't evenly balanced for power.

"Okay, that's enough."

I stopped and looked back at him, waiting. I knew he needed to tell both Max and Mike to follow Mindy's strokes, and he needed to change some positions.

"Now the next term you need to know is power right. Power right means everyone on the right paddles forward, and everyone on the left paddles backwards. Ready? Power right!"

It took us quite a while to get the left turn done. Not only were Mindy and Max very weak paddlers, but Roger put his paddle up and lay back on the raft tube. When I looked back and asked him what he was doing, he smiled.

"Just catching some rays, Snotty. The raft's unbalanced, so if I don't paddle, it evens up."

I opened my mouth to tell him that maybe he should suggest to Gregg that he balance the raft, but he cut me off. "Just turn around and paddle. I'll do my work in the rapids. I don't need any practice."

I turned back around to face the river with a sinking feeling in the pit of my stomach. I was more frightened by the thought of the upcoming rapids than I had ever been.

We practiced power left one time, and then we just drifted down the rest of the flat water toward the canyon. Every time I had been on Rocky's raft, he had the crew practice power right, left, and forward three or four times each, mixing them up. With the inexperienced family we had, we should have practiced at least five times, maybe a little more. But after we had done each turn once, Gregg turned to Roger and they began talking about the upcoming party. I was extremely uncomfortable. It was their job to be instructing and entertaining the patrons, and all they were doing was gossiping. The other guides talked to the patrons about the proposed Two-Forks Dam, about home states, the weather, other sports, other rafting experiences, anything. But they never ignored the patrons.

The tension on the raft grew as we drifted down the river. I could tell Mike and Mindy were getting angry, and Max was bored. We were the last raft to shove off and the other rafts were already so far in front they were out of sight. There was no one behind us.

"Hey, Mike and Max," I said cheerfully. "It will be easier on all of us in the rapids if we follow Mindy's strokes. Max, you especially need to follow your mom's strokes with the paddle so you guys don't keep hitting each other. And Mike, if you try to time your stroke with Mindy's and I follow you, then the whole raft will be on the same rhythm."

They all nodded in agreement.

"Also," I continued, "when we do get into the rough water, you'll need to dig even harder with your paddle."

I went on talking about river strategy, and they began to relax a little. Mike asked a few questions, and Max practiced following Mindy's stroke. Gregg and Roger continued to ignore us.

When I could hear the river static coming up the canyon, I looked back at Gregg again. He was lying back on the raft, too, talking to Roger.

"Hey, Gregg, the first one's Canyon Doors, right?" I asked. I knew perfectly well that it was, but I didn't want to take away what little authority he had left.

"Why, yes, Scott, it sure is." He sat up. "You all ready for your first rapid?" he asked with a really fake smile.

Mike nodded. "I think we are. It's what we paid for."

"Yes, you did. We're going to get you as much excitement for your money as we can. And just a friendly reminder, we guides only get twenty dollars per trip, so tips are greatly appreciated."

I stared at him. He was practically begging for extra money. I knew the guides weren't supposed to mention tips. And he hadn't told them anything about how the rapid was laid out or how there was barely any space before the second rapid.

"Okay, everyone, power forward!" he called.

We entered the rapid just to the right of the tongue. That appeared to be a good place to enter this rapid, because it would let you avoid the rock on the left, but if you entered there you would be heading right for the hole at the bottom on the right. It was a particularly bad choice for this trip, because we had already shown a tendency to push to the right since the right side was weaker. Just by blind luck, we made it through Canyon Doors, but we had no chance once we were in Pinball.

The first big wave in Pinball broke right over Mindy. She screeched and quit paddling, leaning into the raft trying to get away from it. When she stopped, Max stopped too, because I had told him to follow what she did. With two more strokes from Mike and me, the raft turned to the right and started through the waves sideways. Our side of the raft dropped suddenly.

Gregg called out "Power right!" and I could hear a note of panic entering his voice.

I dug in backwards as hard as I could, and so did Mike, but Mindy and Max were both hunched over trying to duck from the waves.

"Paddle!" Gregg screamed at them. "You've got to paddle forward!"

From the corner of my eye I saw Gregg dig in. *What's he doing paddling?* I thought frantically. *He's supposed to be steering and helping us turn.*

Mindy sat up just as a wave came thundering across the bow of the boat. She went with it. Max began to scream. Mike stopped paddling to stare at the spot where his wife had just been.

"Paddle!" I shouted at him over the noise. "We've got to get turned back forward!" He dug his paddle in again.

Behind us, Gregg kept paddling and hollering at Max to shut up and paddle. When he finally did, the raft slowly turned so the bow was once again facing downstream, but it was too late to miss the hole.

The raft dropped down into the hole, and the first wave that came down on us was the biggest I had ever seen. We weren't going anywhere. The churning water of the hole held us above it and began turning us sideways once again.

"Power forward!" Gregg hollered. We dug in, fear giving us even more strength than we knew we had to give. A wave grabbed us and spit us out of the hole.

We made it through the last few tail waves, and I turned around to see if I could spot Mindy. It was a shock to see that Roger was gone as well. That explained why Gregg had started to panic.

Gregg stood up, wobbling just a little. I couldn't tell if he was shaking because the raft was unsteady or because he was upset.

"Found him!" he shouted. "Power left!"

"Where's Mindy?" I asked.

"Let's get Roger, he's closer," he said.

"Gregg!"

"Dammit, Scott, power left!"

We paddled forward to get Roger. He tossed his paddle into the raft and then Gregg pulled him in.

"Whew!" Roger said, shaking the water out of his hair. "What a ride!" He started to laugh. "I guess I'll have to pay more attention on the next one."

They both sat back on the raft.

"Gregg!"

"What, Scott?" he snapped.

"We need to find—"

"There she is!" Mike hollered, pointing farther downriver. I could just barely make out the orange of the life jacket bobbing along.

"Let's go," Gregg said. "Paddle forward easy."

"What?" I turned and stared at him in disbelief.

"Paddle forward."

"Let's power forward. We need to hurry."

"Scott, we're all a little tired here."

"So what? She's in the water, freezing and probably terrified."

"Look, we're already gaining on her."

"Yeah, and it's not like she doesn't have any natural insulation," Roger muttered.

Mike turned around. "I don't know who you think you are, but I am sick of your cracks. Just shut up and get this raft over to my wife!"

He turned back around and began power forward strokes. Max and I followed his lead. We began turning to the right again. Roger and Gregg were paddling halfheartedly, but that still meant we had three strong paddlers on the left, and only Gregg and little Max on the right.

I hopped over to the front right, and we straightened out a little bit. We were gaining on her, but it was a slow gain. I could already hear the dull roar from the next rapid drifting up the canyon.

So far she hadn't given any indication that she knew we were behind her.

"Mindy!" I yelled, hoping she could hear me. I didn't see any response. We kept paddling. Soon we were within twenty feet of her. "Mindy!" I yelled again. This time she turned her head around in the water, looking. "Mindy!" Mike and I yelled together. She lifted her hand a little bit out of the water.

We kept our slow gain, but we were getting close to Zoom Flume faster than we were closing in on Mindy.

"Come on, honey, kick over this way," Mike called.

"Kick, Mommy!" Max echoed.

As we turned the last bend in the canyon before the next rapid, we finally reached her.

"Pull her in, Scott," Gregg said.

I set my paddle down and leaned over the side, even though I knew there was no way I was going to be able to get her in. She was easily three times as heavy as I was. As we continued to drift closer to Zoom Flume, I tried unsuccessfully to pull her in four times. Mike came over to help. Gregg and Roger sat in the back and watched.

The rapid was less than thirty feet away. Mindy was struggling in the water, choking, shivering, and crying. She was terrified. "Get me in! Oh please, get me out of the water," she kept crying. I could barely hear her over the roar of the rapid.

"Can we get a little help up here?" Mike yelled.

Roger sighed and stood up, coming to the front of the raft. He pushed Mike and me aside, leaned over, and grabbed her jacket.

Looking straight into her eyes, he said very clearly, "Mindy, I'm going to dunk and then lift you. You need to kick as hard as you can. If we can't get you in here on this try, you'll have to push away from the raft and we'll pick you up on the other side of the rapid."

"What?" Mike exclaimed.

"One...two...three!" Roger dunked her and then lifted and leaned back as far as he could. She didn't make it in. She was still sobbing.

"Mindy," Roger said. "You've got to get away from the raft. Keep your feet up and in front of you. We'll see you on the other side." And he pushed her away from the raft.

"You bastard!" Mike yelled. He stood up and shoved Roger out of the raft.

While I could understand Mike's reasons for doing that, I also knew we were now even shorter for paddle power.

"What the hell were you thinking?" Gregg hollered.

"I'm thinking you two are the biggest jackasses I've seen in a long time!"

"Okay," I broke in. We were on the tongue of the rapid. "Everyone power forward!"

Somehow we managed to make it through Zoom Flume in one piece. It was a blur for me, and I still don't know how we did it. I tried to keep an eye on where Mindy was through the rapid.

She and Roger both got caught in the big eddy at the end of the rapid, and got out. We powered over to the eddy, and just caught the end of it. When we reached the bank, I grabbed the bowline and hopped out, pulling the raft up on the shore.

Mike leaped out, and when I saw the way his jaw and fists were clenched, there was no doubt in my mind that he was going to beat the tar out of Roger. I was sort of looking forward to seeing it. But Mindy stumbled toward him and wrapped her arms around him, sobbing. He couldn't leave her, so he just hugged her tightly, staring daggers at Roger. Max ran up and joined the family hug. He was terrified too.

Roger went over and sat next to Gregg on the raft. No one said anything for a long time.

After a few minutes, when it became clear that neither Roger nor Gregg was going to say anything, I walked over to the family.

"Mindy, I know you're scared, but other than that, are you okay? Did you hit any rocks?"

Sniffling, she shook her head.

"Are you starting to warm up? Because we do need to get going again, as soon as we can."

Her eyes got huge. "I can't get back in there!"

"Look, Mindy, the only way to get out of the canyon is by raft. You and I can switch spots. The middle is a little bit more secure, and if we keep the strength balanced, we'll be okay."

"Why didn't we balance the strength before?" Mike demanded, staring at Roger and Gregg. They were having a quiet but intense discussion by the raft.

I shrugged, unable to give an answer.

"What the hell kind of operation is this, when you shove your clients away from the raft when you enter the most dangerous section?"

I sighed. "That should have been explained earlier, before we got into the rapids. It's actually for the person's safety. If you go through the rapid next to the raft, you run the risk of being run over by the raft, or even pinned between the raft and the rocks."

Mike considered that for a minute. "So it's standard policy?"

"Yeah," I said. "Also, if we've got people trying to pull someone in during the rapid, then we've got even fewer people paddling, and the raft is likely to run into more problems."

Finally he nodded. "I guess that makes sense. But I wish we had known that earlier."

"I know. You should have been told all that stuff at the beginning."

Mindy had stopped sniffling.

"Are you ready?"

"I guess so," she said doubtfully.

"Oh, and another thing. Don't duck to avoid the water. That's when you need to dig in with the paddle. It actually works as a brace for you and helps keep you in the raft."

They all nodded and we began walking back toward the raft.

"Let's get going," I said.

Gregg nodded. "We really do need to make up the lost time," he began tentatively.

I noticed that Roger now had the guide's paddle in his hand. "Let's change a couple of positions," Roger said enthusiastically. "Scott, I think we'll do a little better if you and Mindy change places."

I didn't answer him although I felt vindicated that he arranged the raft the same way I had started to. Mindy climbed in behind Mike. "You okay?" I asked.

She tried to smile. "I'll be okay."

"You sure, Mindy?" Roger asked with a great show of concern. She nodded without looking at him.

"Good. Now let's have some fun!" No one seemed very happy as we pulled out.

We made it through the rest of the rapids all right. Everyone was tense, and Mike was still very angry, so it wasn't much fun. Roger made a few comments about the river, but when icy silence was all he got for his effort, he stopped. I tried to lighten things up once with a joke, but Max was the only one who laughed. Then I tried to tell them some of the things I knew about the canyon, but Mindy started asking more questions than I knew the answers to. All in all, it was a miserable trip.

By the time we got to the take-out, the other half-day trips were already there and waiting, as I knew they would be. The rafts were stacked on the trailer, and the clients were waiting on the bus.

"Hey, guys, where've you been?" Lou called as we pulled in. "How in the world did you get so far behind?"

"We had a small delay," Roger said, shrugging it off.

"You're nearly half an hour late," Carol said. "You know we're supposed to be on a schedule here."

"Hey," Roger snapped. "So we're a little late. Let's just get the raft loaded on the trailer and not make us even later by turning this into some kind of an issue!"

Lou shook his head, and Carol rolled her eyes at him.

As I took the life jackets from Mindy and Max, I heard Mike ask Lou who was in charge.

"Um, Rocky is the owner…"

"And where is Rocky?"

Lou looked at Carol. "He took the Royal Gorge trip today," I offered.

"When can I talk to him?" Mike asked.

"He'll be back at the office around four o'clock."

"Fine," Mike said, his anger evident in his voice. "I'll be back then."

"Is there something we can help you with?" Carol asked.

"Not unless you have the power to give me a refund and fire those two jerks," Mike said, pointing at Roger and Gregg as he climbed on to the bus.

Jim and Joe helped Gregg get the raft on the trailer. Roger grabbed a can of Coke from the cooler and stood fanning himself in the shade. Lou came up to me.

"What happened?"

I shook my head. "Tell you later," I muttered.

I got the last of the life jackets tucked into the rafts and went to get on the bus. Roger and Gregg were sitting at the back as usual. Mike and his family were in the front of the bus. I went to sit with Joe about halfway back.

"Hey, Scott, come sit back here with us," Gregg called, smiling a huge fake smile.

I smiled back at him, just as big and just as fake, and said, "No, thanks!" as I sat down. I knew they would ask me to cover for them.

Joe turned to me. "Exciting trip today?"

"More than I wanted," I said with a sigh.

"Come on, Scott." Roger's hand fell on my shoulder. "Come sit in the back with us."

"No, thanks," I said, shaking off his hand, "I'm just fine where I am."

"I don't think you are."

"Look, Roger, blow off, okay?"

I looked up at him and wanted to laugh at the angry and frustrated expression on his face. Clearly he wanted to try to bully me, but since I was in the middle of the bus with not only a bunch of patrons but also several staff members around me, he couldn't do anything.

Joe looked up at him too. "If you want to talk to him, why don't you just sit up here with the rest of us?"

"No, thanks," Roger said, mimicking my tone of voice. I watched him as he went back to sit with Gregg. They put their heads together in a very intense conversation. When I turned around I could feel their eyes boring holes into the back of my head.

I just sat and listened to all the chatter around me on the ride home. I didn't really hear any of it, though. I knew that Gregg and Roger were plotting something back there, and that they were going to try to get me to back up whatever story they came up with.

When we got back to the office, I managed to avoid Roger and Gregg by helping to set up the gear for the afternoon trips. Joe seemed to understand that I was trying to avoid them and stayed pretty close to me while we worked. And then I invited myself to go out to lunch with him and Ray and Jim. Roger and Gregg were climbing into the truck as we pulled out of the parking lot. After we got back from lunch, I hung out in the office with Bob. For the first time, I was glad I wouldn't be on the river in the afternoon.

Gregg came in after I had been there for about a half hour. "Hey, Scott, can you come down and help us with the rafts for a few minutes?"

"Umm..." I said, trying to think of an excuse.

"Go ahead, Scott, I've got things covered here," Bob said from the register.

Gregg smiled and I knew I was sunk.

We walked out of the office toward the raft barn, and Roger joined us along the way. They put me in the middle. No one said anything. When we got close to the river, I asked what we needed to work on.

"Actually, we need to do some repairs to the storeroom in the barn," Roger said.

I sighed. "Whatever."

Inside the storeroom Roger shut the door behind us. I sat down on a cooler and waited for one of them to say something.

"Now, Snotty," Roger began, "we appear to have a small problem."

"We need your help, Scott," Gregg broke in nervously. Roger scowled at him.

I just looked at both of them.

"That family seems to have something up their butt about the way we ran the trip today, and I have the feeling they're going to give old Rocky an earful when he gets back," Roger continued. "And I'm afraid that after Mindy got thrown out, their perception of what happened and our explanation of what really happened will be different. I think her fear and Mike's concern for her might lead them to exaggerate the danger of the situation." He paused. "We need to make sure that Rocky hears the truth from us."

"Oh," I said, nodding. "Well, no problem there." I stood up.

Roger shook his head. "We need to make sure that we all have the same truth," he said.

"Why? If we're telling the truth, then of course it will all be the same."

"Sit down, Scott," Gregg said. He sounded very tired.

I had just sat back down when Joe came into the room. "Oh, here you are. Bob needs you back at the office, Scott."

"We're still working down here," Roger said. "He'll be up in a minute."

Joe looked around. "Just tell me what you're doing and I'll take Scott's place," he said.

I grinned at him. "See ya," I said as I left the room. It took all my self-control not to run.

Joe caught up with me before I got out of the barn. "How're you doing, Scott?"

"Fine." I looked back over my shoulder. Gregg and Roger were still in the storeroom. "You guys already finished?" I asked Joe.

He laughed. "It was the strangest thing. As soon as you were out of the room, they said they were finished with whatever work you guys were doing."

"Strange," I agreed.

"Seriously, Scott, don't let them push you around."

"Thanks," I said gratefully. "I take it they really don't have anything for me to do in the office?"

"Nah, I made that up."

"So you just came down to get me out of there?"

"Well, when Bob said Gregg had come up to get you..."

"Thanks, man."

"No problem."

"We have a problem," Lou said as Rocky came in the door. Mike was standing right behind Lou.

Rocky ran his hand through his hair. His face was a little redder; I could tell he hadn't worn his hat today. He looked tired. "Can it wait till tomorrow?"

"I don't think so," Mike said, pushing past Lou. He had been waiting in the store for the last fifteen minutes. He had arrived just before the afternoon trips returned. I had tried to keep him occupied, showing him some maps and books on the area, in hopes that things wouldn't get worse. Roger and Gregg had been sitting at the back of the room, watching him warily. When Rocky walked in, I looked back and just caught the back door as it swung shut. *Cowards,* I thought.

"Okay, then. How may I help you?"

"I'd like a full refund for today's trip, a formal apology made to my wife, and I'd like to strongly suggest that you fire your incompetent, asinine guides."

Rocky blinked. "Would you mind explaining exactly what happened?"

"That's why I'm here."

"You were on a half-day trip this morning, right? Roger's boat?"

Mike nodded. "Roger and Gregg's." He looked to the back of the room. "They were here. They must have just left."

Rocky looked at me. "You were on their boat too," he said.

"Yeah," I nodded.

"He was the only courteous and helpful member of the team," Mike said.

Rocky turned and motioned for us to follow him. "Let's go talk in the back office. Hey, Lou, see if you can round up Roger and Gregg for me, will you?"

"Sure thing," Lou said.

"I'll go. I think I know where they went," Joe said, dropping me a wink.

We got to Rocky's office, and Rocky sat at his desk, while Mike took the chair directly in front of it. I just leaned against the wall to the left of the door.

"Now, what seems to be the problem?"

"There are several problems. The first is the attitude of your guides. They don't seem to realize that we've paid for their services. They're abusive."

"Abusive? In what way?"

"Verbally abusive. My wife may not have the figure of a model, but that doesn't make her any less of a person."

"No, it certainly doesn't. I apologize for anything my guides may have said that was out of line."

"I appreciate that, but it doesn't mean anything coming from you."

"I understand. What else?"

"I don't feel that the guide was competent."

Rocky raised his eyebrows in surprise. "Really?"

"Gregg forgot to fill us in on several key factors before we got into the main canyon. In fact, most of the useful information we did get came from Scott."

I shifted uncomfortably when Rocky looked at me and said, *"Gregg forgot to tell you things?"*

Mike nodded. "He never told us what to expect if someone got flipped out of the raft. Nor did he tell us about digging in with the paddle to keep your balance. The raft was apparently unbalanced in terms of paddling strength, but it wasn't until we had to stop to pick up both Roger and my wife that it was corrected, and it was Scott who made the changes!"

"Is that so?" Rocky hadn't taken his eyes off me. "Roger got thrown out of the raft?"

"Excuse me, but not only was my wife thrown out, she also had to swim through two rapids simply because we didn't get to her in time!"

"Oh, I didn't mean to imply that your wife getting thrown out wasn't important," Rocky said quickly. "That's not what I meant at all. I'm just surprised that Roger was thrown out at this water level."

Mike was sitting up straight, tension radiating from him. "Look, because of the incompetence and rudeness of your guides, my son and wife had a terrifying and unpleasant weekend, and my wife's life was unnecessarily put in danger!"

"Now Mike, I know you signed the waivers before you got on the raft. You understood before you got on that rafting is inherently dangerous and potentially life threatening. That's why it's popular...it's a challenge."

"Yes, but I also understood that I would be with professional, trained guides. At this point in time, I would challenge applying either of those terms to Gregg."

Rocky steepled his hands under his chin and sighed. "Mike, I understand all of your concerns, and I'm relieved that you chose to come back and give me all the details in person. I don't want to let you leave without an apology from Roger and Gregg for their behavior toward your wife. As far as firing them goes, that will have to be between them and me. Meanwhile, I don't want to just refund you your money and have you leave Colorado with a bad rafting experience. I would rather give you three certificates for a full-day trip, and I'll take you myself."

Mike looked at him. "I'll have to discuss that option with Mindy, but I have the feeling she'd rather just get the money and never see this place again."

Rocky grimaced. "It was that bad?"

"It was that bad."

There was a knock at the door. "Come in," Rocky called.

For a minute there, I didn't think anyone was going to come in. Then the door opened, and Roger casually strolled in and sat down on the one empty chair remaining in the cramped office. Gregg followed him in, looked around, and then chose to stand against the wall next to me.

"What's up?" Roger asked, as if there was absolutely no problem and he had just come in to chat with Rocky.

"Mike has some complaints about the way Gregg guided this morning's trip," Rocky said. His tone was calm, but his eyes were blazing.

Gregg shifted against the wall, but before he could say anything, Roger started talking again. "Yes, we're glad he came back. We wanted to apologize for any misunderstanding there might have been about the procedures to follow when a patron gets washed overboard in a rapid."

Mike looked at him for a moment. "If that was all I had a complaint about, that might be enough."

"And we're sorry for all the statements you might have overheard and thought were about your wife," Gregg mumbled.

"*Thought* were about my wife? I *know* they were about my wife!"

Roger sighed. "Actually they weren't. They were references to a woman we saw last night."

"Son, I'm not a fool," Mike snapped. "Don't try to play me for one."

"He's not your son," Gregg snapped back. He turned to Rocky. "This was part of the problem we had today. Mike and Mindy had a hard time accepting authority from me. I guess they thought I was too young to know what I was doing. They weren't willing to listen to all of the instructions I had for them."

"What?" Mike stared at him in disbelief. "It had nothing to do with your age. It had to do with your lousy attitude toward my wife and your inability to explain the procedures while on the river."

"See?" Roger chimed in. "He admits that he had a problem listening to what Gregg was telling them."

Rocky looked from one to the other, and then looked at me. I knew he was trying to decide who to believe. "Scott?"

I struggled. Things were bad enough between Rocky and Gregg. My life would just become more miserable if things got worse between them. I just wished I could protect Gregg without helping Roger. "Maybe Gregg would have told them a little more if they had seemed more interested in what he was telling them," I hedged.

Mike shook his head. "I don't believe this. I already explained that Scott, who is much younger, gave us the most useful information. Now, however, he seems too concerned with protecting his buddies." He stood up. "I want my money back right now," he said, his voice shaking with anger. "I think I'll have to report this to the Better Business Bureau."

Rocky held up his hands. "Wait a minute, Mike. Can we finish this?"

"There's nothing to finish. Obviously they're going to lie and cover for each other. You won't know who to believe. I want my money back, right now!"

"Okay," Rocky said with a big sigh. "Okay." He stood up and walked him to the office door. "You three wait here," he said, and they walked out.

We stayed there in absolute silence, just staring at each other, until Rocky came back to the office. I kept waiting for them to start in on me, but somehow the silence was worse.

"Now then," he said, shutting the door firmly. "I have told you how important our patrons are. We must keep them safe on the river, and we must also keep them happy. The gentleman who just left us said his family was neither safe nor happy. So what happened today? I want the truth."

No one said anything.

"Gregg, were you guiding the raft today?"

He nodded.

"And who told you to do so?"

No answer.

"Roger?" Rocky looked at him. "Weren't you the guide in charge of your boat?"

"No."

"Why not?"

"Because Gregg was ready."

"What did I tell you to do when Gregg was ready to guide?"

No answer.

"It's state law that all commercial guides be at least eighteen years old. How much liability insurance do you pay every month, Roger?"

He glared at Rocky. "It's not a big deal, man. So we might have pissed off a couple of patrons—who cares? It's not like we hurt them or anything."

"We were lucky this time. I want to make sure there won't be a next time." Roger shrugged. "You've become an old worry wart, Rocky."

"Without patrons, you don't have a job, Roger," Rocky said, visibly trying to control his anger. "And if you don't worry about safety, then people get hurt. I put Gregg on your raft so you could teach him how to respect the river. I'm beginning to think you've lost that ability."

"I had everything under control."

"Who owns this rafting company, Roger?"

He didn't answer.

"Gregg, who is your boss and supervisor? How much have you paid in training classes? How much have you paid for liability?"

Gregg stared at the floor.

"Now hear me, gentlemen, both of you. You work for me. I own this company, I pay for all the insurance, and I call all the shots. When I give orders, I expect them to be obeyed. You were told, Roger, to let me know when you thought Gregg was ready to be tested. Gregg, you were told to be an assistant and learn what you could."

He paused to take a breath. "Roger, you are my best guide. I thought you would be the best teacher for Gregg. I now see I was wrong.

"Mike thinks you should both be terminated. It's not going to do any of us any good for me to fire you. I've decided to keep both of you on a trial basis. Understand that you are now in sudden death. One more mistake, however minor, and you will be out so fast you won't know it until you've bounced on the asphalt a few times. You will not be paid for today's trips, Roger. In addition, you will no longer be teamed together. Roger, you're back on your own. Gregg, you'll be with me for the next few days, until I decide that you're ready for your own raft. End of discussion."

They simply looked at him for a few seconds, and then Roger stood up and left without saying anything. As Gregg watched after him, he reminded me of a puppy seeing his master leave. Then he looked at Rocky.

"I'm sorry," he said. That was it, but it was the nicest thing he had said to Rocky so far.

Rocky gave him a weary look. *Come on,* I thought, *be nice back. Open up the door a little.*

"So am I," he said flatly. And I could almost hear the door shut.

Gregg shook his head and left.

I didn't want to move. I was kind of hoping that Rocky had forgotten I was even there. I should have known better.

"Do you want to tell me what really happened?"

I shrugged. Once again, I was stuck between doing what I knew was right and protecting my brother. "It was pretty much like what they said."

"Who? Mike? Or your brother and Roger?"

"A little of each," I said reluctantly.

Rocky didn't say anything for a few moments. He just sat there, massaging his forehead. When he did speak again, what he said took me by surprise. "Sounds like you're getting ready to guide," he said mildly.

"Oh, no. I've just listened to what you and the other guides have been saying on the trips."

"Which appears to be more than Gregg has done." He shook his head again and rubbed his forehead. "Has he always been like this?"

"What do you mean?"

"Has he always been this difficult to talk to?"

I shrugged. "I don't know. My mom always said he was difficult. I didn't think he was."

"And your dad?" he asked softly.

"He and my dad got along great," I said, "until he turned sixteen. Then they started having some problems. Gregg wanted more freedom and no curfew, but Dad didn't think he was ready. His grades dropped, and he wrecked the car twice in one month. They had a lot of fights and Gregg was grounded almost every other week. But they were doing okay this last year. He started to settle down, and Mom and Dad started to lighten up on him."

"Sixteen, huh?" Rocky closed his eyes. "I guess history is doomed to repeat itself."

"What do you mean?"

"I'll tell you when you're older."

"I think I'm old enough now. I should at least know why you and my father didn't talk, why he never even mentioned your name."

"You're right, Scott, you should know." He yawned and rubbed his eyes. "But right now, I'm too tired. Both emotionally and physically. I just can't talk about it right now."

"But we will talk about it?" I pushed.

"Yes, Scott." Rocky smiled. It was a tired smile. "We will talk about it."

Chapter Eight

hardly saw Gregg or Roger at all until Monday. I guess Gregg stayed at Roger's house on Friday night. Then on Saturday I only saw them briefly in the morning, because Bob and I went on the weekend trip. We had a great time. Joe, Carol, and Barb were the guides. Not only did all of the staff members get along really well, but our patrons were a really fun group as well. Everyone was relaxed and worked together.

It was the best weekend I had had since my parents died. I thought of how much Mom would have loved the wildflowers at the campsite, and I could almost hear Dad whooping it up through the rapids. I missed Gregg too. I wished he was there to talk to.

Sunday night when I got back from the trip, I was amazed to walk into the house and find Rocky cooking. So far I had been the only one, other than Gregg when he had the cooking spree on our day off, to do anything more complicated than boil water or turn on the oven and insert a frozen pizza.

"Wow! Something smells fantastic!"

Rocky grinned and I almost thought he blushed, but I wasn't sure because of his sunburn.

"What is it?"

"My specialty."

"Which is?"

"Chicken Cordon Bleu."

"That's your specialty?"

"Yep."

"Man, you should have been cooking the whole time!"

He laughed. "How'd the trip go?"

"Excellent. There were absolutely no problems. I had a blast." I laughed. "This river is so awesome. It's never the same. I mean, I've done the short section of Brown's Canyon how many times this week? And every time it's different, even though it's the same rapids and the same rafts."

"So what do you think changes?"

I thought about it for a minute. "The people. You know, the different levels of experience of the groups, and the way they treat each other. And the way we run the rapids. Every time it's just a little different, and that makes the whole thing different."

"You like it though."

"No! I love it."

"Glad to hear it."

"How were things at the base?"

"Oh," he said, "they were okay." There was a definite lack of enthusiasm in his voice.

"Any major problems?"

"No. But I had to reassign Gregg. He's been doing pretty well as a guide working with me, but he's awful in terms of attitude, both toward me and toward the patrons."

"Who'd you assign him to?"

"I teamed him up with Ray. I'm hoping Ray can settle him down and undo the damage that Roger did."

"Such as?"

"Such as the belief that the guide is the most important person on the raft." He sighed and shook his head. "I thought if I gave Roger the responsibility of training Gregg, it would be good for both of them. I don't know what happened to Roger during the off season, but I don't like it. He keeps this up, he won't be here much longer."

"I think you've said that before."

Rocky looked up at me.

"You've said it twice since I've been here, and according to some of the other staff members, you threatened to fire him several times before that."

"I'm afraid you've got me there. That's why my business didn't do well the first year. I hate firing and disciplining people. Especially someone like Roger. I've known him since before he became a guide. I met him through a good friend of mine, who happens to be his cousin. We used to guide together, and then when Roger started guiding, my friend asked me to help him out. Roger didn't really need my help, because he took to the river so naturally. Now, though, it seems like he's been regressing. Ever since his father died."

"Roger's dad died?" I asked, intrigued.

Rocky nodded. "He had been fighting cancer for a long time, so we knew it was coming. He was practically all the family Roger had. As long as his dad was around, he tried to do well. He had plans and set goals for himself. Once his dad died, though, it's almost like he's becoming younger mentally. Now all he wants to do is party. And he's lost his respect for the river. That's what scares me the most."

"Yeah, but—"

There was a knock at the front door.

"Come in!" Rocky hollered. Then he turned to me quickly. "I forgot to tell you I invited Laura to join us for dinner. Hope you don't mind."

"No, not at all," I said, smiling. I had been trying to figure out their relationship for a while now. They hardly ever touched each other or said anything, but somehow I got the feeling that they were more than just friends.

Dinner was excellent. We had a great time sitting around, talking about all sorts of things. And when dinner was over, Laura suggested we go into town and get ice cream.

"Oh, wow, you have no idea how great that sounds right now," I said with a huge grin. "After two days on the river, I'm more than ready for a hot fudge sundae."

"I think you've got a winner of an idea," Rocky said, nodding and grinning himself.

Laura was starting to back out of her parking space when I suddenly realized I was about to pass up a fantastic opportunity. "Stop. Hang on a second. I forgot something." And I bolted out of her car.

When I got back, she had pulled the car around so they were waiting in front of the house for me.

"What was that all about?"

"I forgot something."

"A book?" Rocky asked, arching his eyebrows.

"Yeah. I have to return it."

"What book is it?"

"Um..." I held it up and Rocky read the title.

He made a face. "You actually checked that out?"

"Yeah."

"Did you read it?" Laura asked.

"Um, not exactly."

"Then why did you get it?"

"Well, because..." I fidgeted.

Rocky turned around and looked at me. "You're blushing!"

"I am not!" My cheeks were on fire.

"Laura, look at him!"

Rocky hounded me until I finally told them about meeting Summer and wanting to see her again.

"In that case," Laura said, "we can't take you to the library tonight."

"Why not?" I demanded at the same time Rocky asked, "Are you going to stand in the way of a possible true love story?"

She laughed. "Oh, no, I'd never do that. In fact, I'm trying to help this one."

"By not letting me go to the library?" I asked.

"Well, Scott," she said, "the library's not open on Sunday. If I took you now, all you'd be able to do is drop the book in the overnight return box."

"Oh," I said. "Thanks."

"I think you'll be better off going tomorrow."

"Yeah," Rocky said. "On my bike."

Laura looked at him. "You have a bike?"

I started laughing. "That's exactly what he said."

"I don't know why the two of you are so amused just because I can't remember what's in my own storage shed," Rocky said, trying to pout.

We pulled into the Dairy Delight at Buena Vista. As I got out of Laura's car, I glanced across the street and saw Roger's truck parked in front of the gas station. The door opened and Gregg and Roger walked out, each carrying two six-packs of beer.

"Come on, Rocky, let's go!" I said, grabbing his arm and dragging him toward the ice cream shop. I desperately hoped he hadn't seen Gregg carrying the beer.

I managed to drag Rocky all the way to the door before he decided to stop. Before I could get the door open, he turned back.

I couldn't help looking over quickly toward Roger's truck. Roger was getting in on the driver's side. Gregg was nowhere in sight. I could only assume that he had spotted us and was lying down either in the truck bed or in the front seat.

Rocky turned to Laura. "Be a sweetheart and order me a root beer float, would you? I need to pick up something."

"Okay," Laura said with a smile, "but I am not responsible for the condition of your float when you return."

She and I walked into the shop. The place was packed...for Buena Vista, that is. There were about five people in line. We got behind them.

"So," she said, turning to me. "What do you think now?"

"About what?"

"About Rocky and the rafting. Neither you nor Gregg seemed very happy when you got out here."

"Do you blame us?"

"Well, no, but is it getting any better?"

"Yeah." I sighed. "I like it now. And I'm starting to get to know Rocky."

"Not an easy thing to do," she said with a smile.

It was the perfect chance for me to ask about her and Rocky, but I just couldn't. Instead I said, "So what's with Roger?"

Laura shook her head. "I honestly don't know."

"It seems like everyone else thinks he should be fired, but Rocky won't do it."

"I think he will if he has to, but he's just giving him a second chance."

"A second chance is one thing, but it sounds like Roger's on his fifth at least."

"Well, Rocky and Roger have worked together for a long time."

"Yeah, I know that. But that should mean that Roger knows more and understands what to do better than the others on the staff. And it doesn't give him an excuse to blow everything off."

"You are observant, aren't you?" Laura sighed. "Roger *was* a lot better last year."

"That's what Rocky keeps saying. Is that when his dad died?"

Laura blinked. "Yeah. But we all knew he was dying. And he had made plans for Roger."

I looked down at my sneakers. "I'm not sure that knowing something is going to happen would make it any easier."

"What do you mean?"

I shrugged. I had this vague feeling that maybe Roger thought his dad could have lived longer, but quit trying. Maybe because of that, Roger thought he might as well quit trying too. But I didn't know how to say all that.

"Scott?" Laura asked gently. "How are you doing?"

I shook my head. "I don't know. Okay, I guess, most of the time. I miss them a lot, though. And it's especially hard, 'cause I can't really talk to anybody."

"Not even Rocky and Gregg?"

"I still don't know Rocky well enough. And Gregg is...I don't know what Gregg is doing right now."

By that time we were at the front of the line. Laura ordered two large root beer floats, and I got a hot fudge banana split. We spotted some people leaving a table and we hurried over. Just as we were sitting down, Rocky came in the door. He set a brown bag on the table and pushed it across to me.

"What's this?"

"Happy late Christmas," he said.

I opened the bag and laughed.

"What is it?" Laura asked.

I pulled out a shiny new padlock and chain.

"I didn't want you saying you couldn't go return that book because you didn't have a lock."

"Good idea," Laura said, "because otherwise he might get an overdue fine."

"Thanks, Rocky," I said.

He waved his hand. "No problem. Just make sure you're a gentleman."

"Oh, I'll try. But if she shoots me down, I may not be able to."

"Who could shoot down anyone as cute as you?" Laura said, reaching across to muss up my hair.

"Yeah, right. Whatever."

"There he goes, blushing again," Rocky said, chuckling.

I shook my head. "You've heard about people who bruise easy, right? It's a physical condition, not anything to laugh about. Well, so is the condition that makes people blush easy."

"It's a condition, huh?" Rocky asked.

"It sure is. And right now there's no known cure. All we victims can do is ask for mercy and support from everyone else."

"Nice try," Rocky said, "but I gave at the office. I can't do any more."

"Aww, man," I groaned. "I tried."

We continued to joke around and have fun for the rest of the evening. We went home and played a few games of chess. Laura only played once, because she said she wasn't any good. Rocky did beat her, but I think she was trying to back out so he and I could play.

She left around ten, and Rocky and I played one more game. Then he went to bed. I went to bed too, but couldn't sleep. Finally, I got up and wrote a long letter to Nancy, telling her everything that had happened in the last two weeks. Then I went back to bed. I blinked back a few tears, thinking about Mom and Dad, and Rocky and Gregg, but this time I didn't really cry.

I had been planning to sleep in Monday morning. The phone rang and woke me up at eight-thirty. At first I was just going to let it ring, but I've never been good at ignoring a ringing phone. On the third ring I got out of bed and stumbled out to the living room. By the time I got to the phone, the caller had hung up.

"Shoot," I muttered. I sat down on the couch for a few minutes, just in case they called right back. They didn't. I headed back to the bedroom, but by then I was awake and there wasn't any point in going back to bed.

After I ate and showered, I called the library.

"Buena Vista library, this is Summer, how may I help you?"

I froze. She was working today.

"Hello?"

"Um, yeah," I said quickly. "What are your hours today?"

"We're open from nine to five."

"Okay, thank you."

"Sure," she said. "Thank you for calling." And she hung up.

I rode into town and locked up the bike by the high school. When I walked into the library, I went up to the front desk and dropped the book into the return bin. Summer wasn't at the desk. I looked around and didn't see her.

With a sigh, I wandered back over to the sci-fi section. If nothing else, at least this time I could get a real book to read on the days I had to watch the store. When I started down the row, I realized that this was actually the fantasy and sci-fi section combined. I kept moving down the row, checking to see if they had the new Robert Jordan book. From time to time, I pulled out a book that had an interesting title and then put it back. When I got to the J section, I started looking more closely. I was so into the books that I bumped into someone right next to me.

"Excuse me," I said, moving over to reach for a book I had just spied.

"No more stars?"

"Huh?" I looked up, and there was Summer, grinning at me.

"Oh, hey there! How are you doing?"

"I'm fine. Did you finish the book? The one on stars?"

"Well, I finished some of it. Turned out to be a little drier than I thought it was going to be."

"I think I tried to tell you that," she said, smiling.

"Yeah, well, now I know to take your advice about books."

"But you didn't trust me about books when I was just a librarian."

"Okay, you got me there," I said, smiling back at her.

"Can I help you find anything today?" she asked in a very professional tone.

"I think I'll just browse a little bit," I said, sticking my nose up in the air.

She giggled. "Well, just wave if you need help."

"What if I just want to say hi?"

"You can do that too," she said. She blushed almost as easily as I do.

I made myself stay in that row and look at books for another five minutes, but I had no idea what I was looking at. Finally I picked up *The Eye of the Needle,* one of the *Star Wars* books that I had read several times and really liked, and took it up to the checkout desk.

"Did you find what you needed?" Summer asked.

"Yeah. I think this one will be much better."

"It's a pretty good book."

"You've read it?" I asked.

"Well, yeah. Why are you so surprised?"

"I've never known a girl who was into sci-fi." As soon as the words came out of my mouth, I cringed inside. *What a stupid thing to say,* I thought.

"I didn't say I was into sci-fi. I said I had read it."

"Well, you know what I mean." *Great,* I said to myself. *Now you sound like a complete idiot.*

She smiled again, scanned the book into the computer, and stamped the return date. "Will there be anything else?"

"Well, yeah," I said, taking a deep breath. "I'm going to a party tonight and was wondering if you'd like to go with me."

Her smile dropped just a notch.

"You've got a boyfriend, don't you?" I blurted out. "I'm sorry, just forget it. I won't bother you anymore." I felt like crawling under a piece of lint. I reached out to take the book from her.

She didn't let go of it. "No, I don't have a boyfriend. I'm sorry, I guess you just took me by surprise."

"Oh," I said, trying not to look too excited.

"The party's tonight?"

"Yeah. One of the guys at work is having it."

"Well, I don't get off till five," she began.

"I know," I said. "But I don't think the party will start till late. I thought we could meet here, go get dinner, and then go to the party."

"That sounds good," she said. "I'll have to check with my parents, though."

"Well, here," I said, grabbing a piece of paper. "I'll give you my number and you can call me."

"Okay. How are we going to get there?"

I stopped. It had been going so well! I was so surprised she said yes that I hadn't even thought that far ahead. "Ummm...well...um...do you have a bike?"

"A bike?" she asked, raising her eyebrows.

"Yeah. We could meet here and then ride over there together."

"Okay. I guess that would work." She didn't sound too sure.

"And I'd ride back to your house with you," I said quickly. "I wouldn't make you ride all the way back by yourself."

She smiled and blushed again. "I'll call you when I get home. I don't think my parents will have a problem with it."

"Great!" I said. "I'll talk to you later tonight then."

"Bye," she said, waving.

"Bye," I said. I was so happy, I really didn't care when I tripped going down the stairs leaving the high school to get my bike. I took my time on the ride home and just enjoyed the scenery.

When I got to the house, the phone was ringing. I ran to answer it. "Hello?"

"Where have you been?" Gregg demanded.

"I went to town. Where are you?"

"I'm at Roger's."

"Now there's a surprise."

"Don't start, Scott," Gregg warned.

"Okay. So what's up?"

"I was calling to see if you're coming tonight."

"I was planning on it."

"Cool. Do you know how to get here?"

"No."

"Well, everyone else is meeting at the shop at eight. Why don't you just show up there?"

"Sounds good."

"Anything else?"

"No," I said. Then I asked casually, "How'd your weekend go?"

"It was all right. Rocky said I can work with Ray starting on Wednesday, so things should get better. He's such a jackass."

"Ray?" I asked in confusion.

"No, Rocky! He won't let me guide yet. I'm ready, and he admits I've got the skills, but he won't even let me run the supply boats." Gregg was whining. "How am I supposed to make any money? The summer's almost half over already."

"We've still got a couple months left. I'm sure he'll let you start taking the supply boats soon."

"Well, he's got a week."

"What happens in a week?"

"If he doesn't let me start by next Wednesday, I'm going to quit. I need a job that will pay me."

While I was letting those remarks sink in, I heard a loud crash in the background.

"What happened?" I asked. Someone was shouting.

"Roger's roommate just got here. I gotta go. Show up at the shop tonight at eight, okay?"

"Yeah," I said as he hung up.

Summer called around five-thirty to say she could go to the party with me. "I have to be home by midnight."

"That's cool," I said, impressed. I'd figured she'd have to get back at least by eleven. "Where do you want to go to dinner?"

"Um, let's see. Do you like Mexican food? There's a really good place on Main Street, called El Duran."

"Yeah," I said enthusiastically. No need to tell her I had eaten lunch there twice last week. "I know where it is. That sounds great."

"Instead of meeting at the high school, why don't we just meet there?"

"Okay," I said. "When can you be there?"

"I could be there in ten minutes," she said.

"Oh, well, I can't get there that fast. How about we meet in forty-five minutes?"

"Okay. I'll see you then."

"Bye."

"Bye."

I waited for her to hang up first, and then bolted for the shower.

The ride out to town seemed incredibly fast. I felt like I was flying. I was a little disappointed to find her already there and waiting for me.

She was wearing jeans overall shorts and a plain white T-shirt. Her hair was pulled back into a ponytail. She looked great.

"Hi," I said awkwardly.

"Hi," she said. "I didn't know if I should go ahead and get a table."

I looked around. There were only a few other people in the restaurant. "I don't think we'll have to wait for one."

We were seated and given the menus right away. Looking at the menu was a good way to break the tension. Then the server brought us some chips and salsa; I think we spent five minutes just discussing our favorite snack foods.

After that, conversation got a little easier. I asked her a lot of questions about school here because I was nervous about going to such a small school.

"Scott," she said finally, "it's just a high school. We're people. There may not be as many of us, but we're not any different from the kids at your old school. There are all sorts and types."

"I know, but..." I started. "I guess I'm just nervous because I don't know anyone."

"I thought I was someone."

"Oh, no, that's not what I meant," I said quickly.

"I know," she said with a smile. "You'll do just fine."

We talked about our summer jobs. She liked her job as much as I was starting to like mine.

"I've always loved books," she said. "I like the way whole new worlds and people and creatures can just be created and become so real."

I laughed. "You're a daydreamer."

"Well, yeah, a little."

"Are you a romantic too?"

She blinked and shifted a little in her seat.

"I'm only asking because those two terms are usually put together," I said quickly.

"I guess I'm a little bit of a romantic too. My parents must have had some influence on me."

"What do you mean?"

"Well, they got married when they were still in high school and they're still together. They hardly ever fight. They've got all sorts of cute little nicknames for each other, and they're always very affectionate." She laughed. "Every spring, Dad always brings home the first crocus bloom he finds and gives it to Mom because he says that she'll always be his first blossom of spring."

"I'd say growing up with that would have to make you a little bit romantic."

She shrugged. "A little. But they're so into their own romance and having fun together, it's almost like I'm the parent. I set most of my own rules. They want me to be a free spirit, like they are, so they try to give me a lot of space."

"My parents weren't like that."

"Did they get divorced?"

I shook my head and took a sip of Coke. "They were killed in a car accident." I was glad my voice didn't break.

"How old were you when it happened?"

"It's been almost two months."

Her eyes got huge. "Oh, Scott, that's awful. I'm so sorry. I guess I just assumed that it had happened a long time ago. I think I'd be a basket case if I lost both my parents like that."

I tried to smile. "My parents always said not to worry about things you can't change. This is one of them." She didn't say anything. "I *am* a basket case," I admitted. "I can't stop thinking about them, and it still hurts a lot. Especially since Gregg's been such a jerk."

"Who's Gregg?"

"My older brother."

"How's he being such a jerk?"

I told her about the way he had treated Nancy and Rocky. "They both were just doing everything they could to help, and all he did was whine about it or yell at them or just clam up. He's still yelling at Rocky every chance he gets. I have to give Rocky credit for not yelling back."

"It sounds like that's what Gregg needs, though."

"What do you mean?"

"If he's being so awful, he shouldn't get away with it just because your parents passed away. They were your parents too, and you're not being a baby about it."

I sighed and smiled. "You don't know how nice it is to hear somebody say exactly what I've been thinking."

She asked me some more questions about Gregg, and somehow I started rambling about my old neighborhood and the friends I went to school with. Then with a start I realized that I had talked through the entire meal.

"I'm sorry," I said. "Why didn't you just tell me to shut up?"

"Because you sounded like you needed to talk," she said simply.

The server came by with the check. "Excuse me, do you know what time it is?" I asked.

"Seven forty-five," he said.

"Oh, jeez," I said. I turned to Summer. "How fast can you ride?" I asked as I put a twenty on the table.

"How fast do I need to?" she asked with a grin.

"We're supposed to meet at Rugged Rapids in fifteen minutes."

"Wow," she said. "That is fast."

I had been hoping to just take it easy on the way out there and talk, but I guess I had done enough talking during dinner.

We ran out to our bikes, but then she had to laugh at Rocky's beat-up old bike for a few moments before we could start our ride. Comparing it to her slick mountain bike, I had to admit that my bike looked pretty pathetic.

"Does it really work?" she asked between laughs.

"It got me here," I said a little defensively. "You know where Rugged Rapids is, right?"

"Yeah."

"Okay. I'll follow you," I said.

She raised her eyebrows. "I'm not sure that old thing can keep up."

"Trust me."

She only had to stop to wait for me once, and that was at the top of a big hill.

When we rolled into the parking lot, I was relieved to see people still there. I pulled up to a stop in front of Bob's Jeep. "Are we the last ones?"

"No. We're still waiting for Joe and Carol," he said.

"What about Jim and Ray? Aren't they coming?"

"No," Tom said. "They went to Colorado Springs for the night. Somebody's playing a concert down there. I forget who."

"This is Summer," I said, introducing them. "This is Bob. And over in the station wagon are Barb, Lou, Gary, and Tom."

They all waved.

"Nice to meet you, Summer," Bob said. "Did he make you ride your bike all this way?"

"He did," she said, nodding and grinning.

"How about you two leave your bikes here and ride with me," he suggested. "I can give you a ride back when the party's over."

"Thanks, Bob," I said. "That sounds great."

"And here come our slowpokes," Barb called across the parking lot as Carol and Joe pulled in.

"All right, now we can go!" Jim said.

"You could have gone before," Joe said.

"No, we couldn't, because you and Carol are the only two who know how to get to his house, remember?"

"Oh, yeah," Joe said. "Well, then you all had better keep up!" He spun his wheels in the gravel parking lot, leaving the rest of us to follow in a cloud of dust.

As we left, I remember thinking that it might turn out to be my best night here.

Chapter Nine

When we got to Roger's house, there were already at least twenty people there. We walked in, and as I looked around, I realized that Summer and I were easily the two youngest people there.

I was surprised to find that Roger apparently lived with even less furniture than Rocky did. The only piece in the living room was the entertainment center for the stereo and TV, and it was just made of plywood set across cement blocks. Through the doorway to the kitchen, I could see a small table with two chairs. That was the only real furniture I saw. People were sitting around on the floor everywhere.

Bob immediately veered off to the left, but I didn't want to tag after him all night long. Summer and I just stood there for a few seconds before I discovered that I should have just followed Bob.

"Who invited you?"

"Huh?" I looked up at Roger.

"What makes you think you can be here, geek?"

I took an involuntary step backwards, which didn't make me feel very good. When I glanced over and saw the look on Summer's face, I felt even worse.

"Scotty! You made it!" Gregg came charging up. He had a beer in each hand.

"Did you invite the Snot?" Roger asked.

"Well, yeah, of course I did."

"He's a total loser."

"Hey, man, lay off," Gregg said, but there wasn't any anger in his voice. "He's my brother. He may be a geek, but he's cool."

"He better be." Roger turned back to me. "If you get in my way here, Snotty, I'll beat your butt, and not even your big brother will be able to save you." He turned and walked out of the room.

"Sorry, Scott," Gregg said. Then he nudged me. "So are you going to introduce me?"

"Oh, yeah. Gregg, this is Summer. Summer, this is my brother Gregg."

"Glad you came," Gregg said, smiling.

"Thank you. I've heard a lot about you."

"Don't believe anything that's not good," Gregg said. He turned around and surveyed the rest of the room. Then he sighed and turned back to us.

"I'd introduce you, but I don't know many of the people here."

"No problem," I said. "A lot of the staff's here. At least I know them."

"Okay," he said. "Well, there's a keg out in the backyard, and there's rum, vodka, and tequila in the kitchen if you want to do some shots or have mixed drinks."

"Gregg!" Roger hollered from the kitchen. "Get your sorry butt in here!"

"In a minute!"

"Now!" Roger hollered back. "For every minute you're not here, you have to do a shot of my making."

"Oh, man, I gotta go," Gregg said. He leaned over and whispered in my ear, "Not bad! Go for it!" and winked at me. "See ya later," he called over his shoulder.

I turned back to Summer. She was making a face. "What?" I asked.

"I don't know about your brother."

"I used to know a lot about him. I don't seem to anymore." I shrugged. "I guess he's still okay. I mean, he did come and call Roger off."

She shook her head. "Roger."

"What about him?"

"Is he always..." she trailed off.

"A jerk?" I offered. When she nodded, I said, "Actually, he's being pretty nice tonight."

"Tell me you're joking."

"I wish I could." I sighed. "Well, come on. Let's go see where everyone went."

We found Joe and Bob out by the keg. "Hey, guys."

"There you are! Beer?" Bob asked, holding one out towards Summer.

"Okay. Thanks." She took it.

"Sure!" I said, taking one. It was my first real party, and I wanted to look cool. The four of us sat around outside for a while, just chatting. After I had smacked my third mosquito, I suggested we go inside. Summer nodded her head gratefully.

"Before we go, let me get another beer," I said, trying to sound casual. "Want one, Summer?" I asked.

"I'm doing okay, thanks."

Bob peered at her. "I've had three beers so far, and you're not even halfway done with your first one!"

"I don't really like beer a whole lot," she said, blushing.

"Oh, hey, that's okay," Joe said quickly. "We could mix you up a rum and Coke or something."

"No, that's okay," she said. "I don't really drink that much."

"Oh," Bob said, thinking it over. "Well, you know you don't have to drink that if you don't want to. We could get you just a Coke."

She smiled. "That would be really nice."

We went into the house and stopped in the kitchen to get her a Coke. The house was packed. There were at least twice as many people as there had been earlier. Joe and Bob disappeared into the crowd.

"Why didn't you tell me you didn't want a beer?" I asked her in a low tone.

"I don't know. I didn't want, you know, to seem..."

"Like a geek like me?" I asked.

"You're drinking beer."

"Yeah, but I'm still a geek, at least according to Roger and Gregg."

"I don't think you're a geek."

"Thank you," I said. "I've never thought I was either. And I certainly wouldn't call you one."

We found Barb, Carol, Gary, and Tom sitting on the floor in the living room. "Hey, guys!"

"Hi!" Barb said. "Where are Joe and Bob?"

"I don't know," I said, looking around. "Somehow we managed to lose them between here and the kitchen."

Gary arched an eyebrow at me. "I think that's all of ten feet, Scott. If you lose people that quickly, I don't know if you're capable of being a guide."

I laughed. "Well, I guess it's a good thing I wasn't planning on it—not yet, at least."

Tom shook his head. "You should start thinking about it, Scott. You've got a good feel for the river."

"Well, yeah," I said. "It's easy when there are people there to tell you what to do. Besides, I'm too young."

Tom shrugged. "I'd keep the option open, if I were you. You might be young, but you listen well and learn quick. I bet you could run supply rafts by the end of the summer if you wanted. At the beginning of next season, easy."

"We'll see," I said.

"What do you do, Summer?" Barb asked.

"I work at the library."

"Cool," she said, bobbing her head. "Have you ever been rafting?"

"Oh yes. Last summer I worked as a volunteer for another company. They took me on about two trips a week."

"You didn't tell me that," I said.

"You didn't ask," she said. "Besides, I didn't want to talk about a rival rafting company."

We laughed. Someone walking by accidentally kicked Summer. She scooted over closer to me. We smiled at each other. The night was going just fine.

We stayed with that group for a while. Joe and Bob had wandered off somewhere and didn't come back to the living room. Gary and Carol stood up to make a run to the keg.

"Refills, anyone? Scott?"

"No thanks," I said, "I'm doing all right."

Summer leaned over and looked into my cup. "Looks pretty empty to me."

"Yeah, it is. But I don't really want another one."

She gave me an understanding look and didn't push the issue.

The party continued to get louder and more crowded. We had to stand up because we all kept getting stepped on. Even standing we were kind of squashed together.

"Wow," I said to Summer, "I didn't know there were this many people in Buena Vista."

She gave me a tired smile. "It's getting really crowded."

"Think we ought to take off?"

"Yeah," she said, looking around. "I have the feeling this party's going to get broken up pretty soon."

I looked around too. People were pretty much shoulder to shoulder everywhere. A layer of smoke hung in the air. You had to shout to be heard over the stereo and all the other conversations going on.

"Come on," I said. "Let's get out of here." I put my hand on the small of her back and started to guide her to the front door.

Halfway there, I thought I heard my name being called over the noise.

I turned around and saw Gregg and Roger. Gregg's eyes were bloodshot, and he was swaying, one arm around a girl who had been rafting that weekend. I tried to remember her name and couldn't. "Yo, dude, you're not leaving already?"

Before I could say anything, Summer quickly said, "Oh, no, we're just going outside where it's quiet. And, you know, private." She smiled at me and my heart skipped a beat.

"Whoa! Be careful, Scott!" Gregg said, wagging a finger at me. "Be sure to practice safe sex."

"Thanks," I mumbled, feeling the blush go all the way up my neck to my forehead in about half a second.

We got out the front door and I turned to Summer. She started laughing. "If only you could have seen your face!"

"I can't believe you said that!"

She shrugged. "This way you didn't lose face leaving the party early, and I got to get out of all that smoke. We both win."

I shook my head. "You sure are cool."

"I know," she said with a toss of her head. "That's why you like me."

"You're right."

We started walking back to Rugged Rapids to get our bikes. It was really cool because we were able to walk alongside the river most of the way.

"Well, thanks," she said.

"For what?"

"For getting me out of there. I know a lot of guys who would have stayed to party."

I shrugged. "First off, I wouldn't just bail on you like that. Secondly," I sighed, "it's not really my kind of scene anyway."

"I know," she said, and reached out and squeezed my hand. She didn't let go of it either.

"What?" I said. I was so shocked she was holding my hand, I completely missed what she had just said.

"The smoke was really beginning to bother me," she repeated.

"Yeah, me too. I hate cigarettes."

"And it's even worse when it mixes with the other smoke."

"What other smoke?" I asked.

"The Mary Jane."

I stopped. "People were smoking pot in there?"

She giggled. "You couldn't tell?"

"I told you, it's not really my kind of fun." We started walking again. "So how do you know there was pot there?"

"My parents sometimes smoke it on weekends."

I had to stop again. "Your parents do?"

"Yeah. I told you they were hippies. Sometimes I think they just smoke it because the government tells them they can't."

"Wow." I couldn't imagine living in a house where parents were smoking pot, especially right in front of their children.

"I haven't exactly had the typical childhood," she said. "It's kind of weird when you feel like you've let your parents down because you're on the honor roll every year and you've never been in serious trouble."

"You sound exactly like me, except I was doing what my parents expected of me. They really didn't give me any other choice."

"Gregg was pretty stoned tonight."

"Gregg? My brother Gregg?"

She nodded.

For a moment, I thought I might need to sit down. I knew he had done drugs before, but Mom and Dad had tried to convince him to quit. In fact, he had promised he would. He was breaking a promise to them.

"How could you tell?"

She shrugged. "His eyes were all bloodshot."

"That could have just been all the smoke. And drinking."

"Yeah. But he was holding a joint."

"Seriously?"

"Seriously." She looked at me. "Why does that bother you?"

"Gregg and my dad fought a lot for about a year. Gregg wanted to go out and party, and Dad kept putting restrictions on him. They mostly fought about the drinking, but I know Dad found some pot in his room once. They had a huge blowout over that. Then, about a month later, one of Gregg's best friends committed suicide. He was high when he did it. Gregg swore to my parents he'd never get high again."

We were quiet for a while, just walking along. We were still holding hands.

"I can't believe how bright it is outside," I said looking for a new topic of conversation. We were in the middle of nowhere, there weren't any lights visible even in the distance, and yet I could see the ground and bushes clearly in front of me.

She nodded. "Wait till next week. When there's a full moon, it casts shadows."

"Why didn't it look this bright in California?"

"Because there's so much man-made light around, it kind of counteracts the moon. I'm sure if you got away from all the city lights, it would be just as bright."

I must have been staring at her.

"Sorry," she said quickly.

"For what?"

"For giving such a bookish answer."

"What wrong with that? That's where the answers come from. Besides, you're not the only one who likes books. I go to the library during summer vacation. In fact, I think that's how we met."

She laughed.

We reached Rugged Rapids. We unlocked our bikes and rode back to her house. Neither of us said much on the ride. I don't know if she was just all talked out, or if she was trying to figure out how to say good night, like I was.

"Well," she said, dismounting in the driveway. "This is where I live."

I smiled. "So this is where I can meet you next time, right?"

"Yeah." She smiled back. "Thanks for inviting me tonight. I had a lot of fun."

I shook my head. "You drank something you didn't want, you were stuck in a loud, smoky room with people you didn't know, and I made you ride your bike or walk everywhere we went. I'm not sure I believe you had fun."

She laughed. "Well, if you want to convince me I had a bad time, I guess you can try."

I swallowed hard and took a deep breath. "Would you like to go see a movie sometime?"

"Yeah, I would."

"Um, I guess you'll have to call me. I don't have your number, and I might forget it on the way home."

"Okay, then I'll give you a call." She shifted from one foot to the other.

"Okay." I couldn't think of anything else to say, but I didn't want to leave yet.

"Well," she said finally, "I guess I ought to go inside."

"Okay," I said again as she started walking to the door. When she got to the porch, I said, "Hey, Summer?"

"Yeah?" She turned around.

"Call me soon, okay?"

Her face lit up in a smile. "Okay. Good night." And she disappeared inside.

Chapter Ten

I sat straight up in bed, trying to figure out what had awakened me. It was still dark outside. Then I heard muttering coming from the living room. I could tell it was Gregg's voice. It must have been the front door slamming shut that woke me.

"Get off me!" he suddenly shouted. I threw the blankets back and scrambled out of bed.

"Keep your voice down," Rocky hissed back at him.

"Don' tell me wha' to do," Gregg slurred.

I got to the bedroom door. Rocky had an arm around Gregg, helping him get across the room.

"Believe me, young man, I'm tired of telling you what to do." Rocky's voice was controlled. "I'm about ready to try beating you into doing what you're supposed to do."

"Jush try it," Gregg said, but he was mumbling and his voice was quieter. He pushed at Rocky's hand. "Get off me!" he whined.

"No. I don't have the strength to pick you back up off the floor."

"Need some help?" I asked.

They both looked up at me, Rocky more quickly than Gregg.

"I think we're okay," Rocky said easily.

"Yesh! Come ge' him off me, Ssscott."

I went out to the living room and took Gregg by the other arm.

"Thanks," Gregg mumbled. "We don' nee' you," he said, trying to wave the arm that Rocky was still holding to support him.

We managed to get him to our room, and he fell back on the bed. Rocky retreated to the door and watched me take his shirt and shoes off and get him under the covers. I felt very uncomfortable, because the whole time, Gregg was going on and on about what a jerk Rocky was and how happy he was going to be to leave.

"I swear...Schott...if he...if he jush once more...I am so out of here...I am going to jush fly away...forever...and I'll be so happy...and he won' care.... I'll take you," he said, his eyes focusing for just a minute, "I'll take you an' we'll go away...and we'll be a family again...jus' us...jus'...." He drifted off.

I looked up and the doorway was empty, but there was light shining from down the hall. I turned out the bedroom light and wandered into the kitchen. Rocky was sitting at the table, feet propped up against the wall.

I filled the kettle with water and got two mugs out of the cabinet. "Raspberry or lemon?"

"Hmm?" Rocky looked up at me.

"Raspberry or lemon tea?"

"Lemon, please," he said quietly. He just watched me get stuff out, then he said, "Am I really as awful as he says I am?"

I looked up in surprise. I had never had an adult honestly ask me my opinion of him. But Rocky was really concerned.

"No," I said, shaking my head. "He said pretty much the same things about my dad the year they fought so much."

Rocky nodded. "Okay, then. Maybe I'm not a complete failure, if your dad got the same reaction. I'm just not sure. I've never been a parent before. I had no idea what you two would be like—what living with you would be like."

"We didn't know what you were going to be like either."

"I know," he said. "That's why I tried to give you guys some space and tried not to crowd you. I figured it would take some time to get to know each other and get adjusted." He shook his head. "At this rate, I don't know if I'll ever be able to adjust to Gregg." He looked up to the ceiling. "I'm so sorry, Stephen. I had no idea I had put you through such hell."

I felt a chill go over me. Stephen was my father. "What do you mean?"

Rocky looked at me.

"You promised you'd tell me sometime. This seems like a good time."

He bowed his head for a minute before looking up at me. "You know your grandfather, my father, left us when your father was pretty young, right?"

"I think Dad said he was about thirteen when Grandpa took off."

"Yep. And I was about one. Your dad got thrown into the role of head of the family. He tried to take care of Mom and me. I practically worshipped Stephen when I was little, but then I started to resent him when I was older. I got pretty wild, did a lot of things that I bet Gregg has done or at least tried to do. I didn't like being told what to do, but when I got into trouble, I just took it for granted that Stephen would be there to bail me out."

He took a deep breath. "And he was. He got angry every time, but he always helped. He'd yell and preach, and then he'd yell some more. We had some awful fights. But no matter what, he was there for me." Rocky stopped.

"Until?" I prompted.

"Until you were born."

I must have had a strange expression on my face, because Rocky quickly said, "Now don't go thinking this was your fault. This was all my doing, understand?"

I nodded.

"I came to visit once when you were little. I don't think you were even a year old. Your mom and dad were nice, and acted happy to see me, but they knew. Especially your dad. He knew the only reason I had come to visit was to borrow money. I had borrowed a lot of money from your dad…more money than you can imagine. I don't know why he kept giving it to me, why he kept bailing me out of trouble.

"Anyway, I was there for a visit, and your parents were outside on the porch. I went upstairs and took a couple of hits of speed. You started crying in the next room. I still don't know if I woke you up or not, but I thought I should take you outside to your parents. I picked you up and started downstairs. I hadn't taken two steps before I tripped. I let go of you to stop myself from falling, and you fell down nearly a full flight of stairs. I thought I had killed you. Your mother wouldn't let me anywhere near you, so I couldn't see how badly you were hurt. She was screaming hysterically and you were crying. I'm sure my babbling made no sense to either of them. Stephen threw me out of the house."

Rocky took a ragged breath. "But first he wrote me a check for two thousand dollars and told me he never wanted to see me again." He grimaced. "It took me five years before I was finally clean—of drugs, drinking, and smoking. I had to put it all behind me, so I even left my name. I started going by Rocky, to remind me of what I owed Stephen. He always said I had a rock-hard skull that nothing could get through." He shook his head and laughed, but it wasn't a happy laugh; it sounded almost angry. "Everything I've started since then, including the rafting company, I've done with the intent of making enough money to pay him back. And I mean *everything*, not just the two thousand. I thought it would be wonderful if I could give him the money in time to send you to college. Instead, I can't even afford to pay you a salary for the work you're doing." He buried his face in his hands.

The kitchen was still. I didn't know what to say. *It wasn't your fault, it happened a long time ago, brothers should forgive each other, you're doing the best you can.* A thousand other thoughts ran through my head, but none of them seemed right. I felt terrible.

After a little bit, Rocky looked up. "How about that tea?"

"Sure!" I said, relieved to have something to do. I picked up the kettle and suddenly realized I had never turned the burner on. I told Rocky, and he chuckled.

"What an awful night," he said.

"What happened?" I asked.

"Roger had a party," he began.

"Yeah, I know."

Rocky stopped. "You were there?"

"For a while."

He opened his mouth to say something, but then he seemed to change his mind. "The cops called me around one o'clock to come bail Gregg out."

"Oh, no," I groaned. "What happened?"

"The party must have gotten pretty wild, because a neighbor called the police in Buena Vista," Rocky said. "It took me almost two hours to get things straightened out."

"Why did it take so long?" I asked. "The one time Dad had to bail him out, it only took like forty-five minutes, and that was in L.A."

"It probably would have only taken me twenty minutes if I had only had to bail out one person."

I had a sinking sensation in my stomach. "How many people did you have to bail out?"

"Six. Half of my staff was at the station."

The kettle started to whistle. I got up and poured the water, and then handed Rocky his cup.

"Who else other than Gregg?"

"Barb, Lou, Gary, Tom, and, of course, Roger."

"You bailed Roger out too?"

"He's an employee, Scott. Besides, he doesn't have any family here to bail him out. His uncle's in Chicago, and his cousin moved to South Dakota two years ago." He sighed and muttered almost to himself, "Not that he appreciated me bailing him out."

"What are you going to do?"

"I don't even know. Part of me was hurt that I hadn't been told of the party. The other part of me wanted to fire them all on the spot and just leave them there." He laughed. "It's finally happened. I've become an old man who thinks people need to behave responsibly. I would have hated me too when I was Gregg's age."

"Maybe if my dad had slammed you a little earlier, you would have straightened up sooner."

He looked at me.

"Sorry," I said quickly. "I didn't mean to say that out loud."

He shook his head and laughed bitterly. "You're too damn smart for your own good." He finished his tea. "I told them all to meet me at the barn tomorrow, I mean today, at seven. So I'd better go get what little sleep I can."

I looked at the clock and was shocked to see it was almost four. "Should I go too?"

"No, that won't be necessary. You weren't there." He started to get up.

"Not when the cops came," I agreed.

He winced and sat back down. "You shouldn't have reminded me."

"Sorry."

"Were you drinking too?"

"I had a couple of beers."

"I tried not to have too many ground rules because I didn't want you to forget them."

"I didn't forget." I looked him in the eye.

"You broke the rule on purpose?"

I shrugged. "I knew the chance I was running, but I didn't think I was doing anything really stupid or dangerous. I didn't get drunk, I didn't get in a fight or get busted by the cops, and I never got in a car with anyone who had been drinking."

"Did you smoke any pot?"

"No."

Rocky nodded and got up again. "I'm too tired to think of what to do with you right now. We'll talk tomorrow night. Until then, consider yourself grounded to the house." He hesitated, then added, "Tell Gregg he's grounded too. I'll let him sleep in tomorrow, and the three of us will talk tomorrow night."

I nodded. "Good night, Uncle Dave," I said as he left the kitchen.

"Sleep well, Scott," he said, disappearing down the hall.

When Gregg finally got up, I was sitting at the kitchen table where Rocky had been. Gregg had the blanket wrapped around him and was dragging his feet. He looked like death warmed over.

"Morning," I said loudly, even though it was half past noon.

He grunted and sat down on the other chair. Almost immediately he laid his head down on the table.

"Breakfast?" I asked. "Sausage, scrambled eggs, hot oatmeal?"

"Oh, shut up before you make me puke."

"You'll probably feel better after you do."

He raised his head and looked at me with bloodshot eyes. "Why are you so flipping happy?"

"Well, let's see. First, I didn't have near as much to drink as you did, so I'm not hungover. Second, I didn't spend two hours in the middle of the night at the police station. And...oh yeah...I wasn't out as late as you were."

Gregg frowned. "I remember. You left early, you and that chick. Where did you go?"

"Nowhere. We walked back to the shop, picked up our bikes, and rode back to her house."

"What was her name?"

"Summer," I said.

"That's right. She's okay. Pretty cute, even."

"Thanks. Who were you there with?"

"Debbie."

"Did she finally break up with her boyfriend?"

"Nope. She just ditched him for the night."

"How's the Buena Vista Police Department?" I asked casually.

Gregg frowned at me. "Why don't you go get busted for something and find out for yourself? Oh, that's right, I almost forgot. You're too perfect to get in trouble."

"You promised Mom and Dad—"

"Shut up, Scott," Gregg said softly but firmly.

We sat there quietly for a while. After a few minutes, Gregg got up and shuffled toward the phone.

"Who are you calling?"

"Roger. I need to know if he's coming to pick me up or if he expects me to walk over there."

"Oh, I forgot to tell you. You can't go."

"What do you mean I can't go?"

"We're both grounded. We have to stay here."

He just looked at me for a minute. Then he laughed. "Funny, Scotty, very funny."

"I'm serious. We're grounded till we talk to Rocky later tonight."

"Well, he's on something stronger than I was last night if he really thinks I'm going to stay here. Grounded," he snorted. "I'm almost eighteen. He's not our dad."

"No, but he's got custody," I said quietly. "And you haven't exactly been cooperating."

"Whose side are you on? Man, I can't believe that you're sticking up for that bozo. Get a life and quit brownnosing."

"I can't believe you won't give him a chance. He's giving us more freedom than Mom and Dad ever did, but you're still throwing a fit about it."

"You don't get it, do you? He is nothing to me! Just because some judge tells me I have to come stay with an uncle I've never seen, it doesn't mean that I have to love the guy, or do every stupid little thing he says."

"It's not a stupid thing, and I never said you had to love him. But just because some judge says we have to stay here doesn't mean we shouldn't try to get along with him either."

"Scott, you are such a suck-up!"

"I am not!" I slammed my glass down on the table. "I'm just trying to be an adult and deal with the situation, instead of kicking and screaming like some three year old who can't get his way!"

Gregg turned and started out of the room. I got up and followed him. "Just what has he done? Huh? What has he done that's been so awful?"

Gregg shook his head and kept walking to our room.

"Tell me, Gregg, 'cause I'd really like to know. I'd really like to know why you are so bent on making our lives hell! Why do you have to pitch such a fit every time Rocky says or does anything? Dad would have grounded you too, and you know it!"

Gregg spun around. "He is not Dad!" he yelled. I could see the tears glistening in his eyes.

"I never said he was," I said. Suddenly there was a lump in my throat. "And neither did he."

"He doesn't have to and neither do you. He's trying to act like he's our dad, and you're letting him!"

"I'm trying to let him be our uncle!"

"Dad didn't think he was good enough to be our uncle."

"He left us in his custody."

"Only because he and Mom forgot! They forgot to take care of us. They were so busy having fun and spending money, they forgot to make any plans for us. They left us with nothing but a stupid jackass uncle, and you want me to be happy about it!"

Gregg slammed the door in my face. I stood there for a few minutes, not quite sure what to do.

The phone rang.

I turned to answer it, then just stopped, leaned against the wall, and waited.

After the fourth ring, Gregg opened the door and stormed past me, muttering curses all the way. I went into our room and stretched out on my bed. I didn't have to be kicked out of our room just because he was throwing a fit.

I couldn't hear what he said, but the conversation only lasted five minutes. He came back to our room, grabbed his towel without even glancing my way, and went to the bathroom.

Ten minutes later, he came out minus the towel, which I was sure he had left in a pile on the bathroom floor. He opened his top dresser drawer and pulled out four T-shirts. He opened the second drawer and grabbed some shorts and some jeans. From the third drawer, he pulled out a few pairs of underwear.

Then he dragged his duffel bag out from under the bed and began stuffing his clothes into it.

"Gregg," I said, just as a car honked out front.

He grabbed the duffel bag and a box of stuff from the top of his dresser and went to the bathroom. I followed and asked him what he was doing while he threw his toothbrush, toothpaste, and shampoo in the bag. He ignored me and zipped it shut.

"Come on, Gregg," I said louder, as I followed him into the living room.

He opened the front door, and I saw Roger's truck out front. "Gregg, man, don't do this," I said. He reached behind me and grabbed his jacket off the sofa.

"See ya," he said, and he pulled the door shut.

I jumped when the door slammed. Rocky hardly ever made any noise when he came home, let alone slammed the front door. I marked the page in my book and left it on my bed.

"Gregg, Scott, come on out here," he called.

I stepped out into the living room. He was sitting on the couch. "Where's Gregg?"

I lifted my shoulders. "I...I don't know."

"You don't know? Or you won't tell me?"

"I'm pretty sure he's at Roger's."

"How sure?"

"Roger picked him up around one today," I admitted.

"Did you tell him he was grounded?"

I nodded.

"But he went anyway?"

I nodded again.

"Oh, God, is this going to get ugly," Rocky groaned and ran a hand through his hair. He looked at me. "Roger didn't come to the meeting this morning. I've cleaned out his locker."

I just looked at Rocky.

"When he comes in tomorrow, I'll let him know he's fired."

"Oh," I said, nodding and trying not to gloat.

"Did you stick around today?"

"Yeah."

Rocky sighed. "Well, I was going to ground you each for a week. But since you stayed and Gregg didn't, I'll give you time off for good behavior."

"How much time off?"

He smiled wearily. "Starting now."

I smiled back. "Cool."

Rocky stayed home with me that night. We cooked spaghetti together, then played chess out on the front porch. I gave him a hard time for acting like such an old man.

"I am old," he said. "What's your excuse?"

"Working with senior citizens is my favorite charity," I said, and he laughed.

"Where's Laura?" I asked casually.

His hand froze above his rook and he looked at me. "I don't know. Why?"

"Just wondering."

Without saying anything, he finished his move.

"It is her number that you left for us to call if we needed to reach you, right?"

He fidgeted. "No."

I was confused. I was so sure I had it all figured out. "Whose number is it?"

"The Double Diamond." He was staring at the chessboard.

The Double Diamond was a bar in town. I didn't know what to say.

Rocky cleared his throat but didn't look up. "I've been helping them close up on the nights when they need me. Unfortunately, they haven't needed me much lately."

I looked at the top of his head. "Money's that tight?"

He shrugged. "It's always been tight, especially at the beginning of the season. If we can make it another two, maybe three weeks, we'll be just fine."

I could tell "just fine" was an optimistic exaggeration. "Why didn't you just tell us?"

"You were disappointed enough in me. And I didn't want you worrying any more than you already were."

"You were too proud," I said flatly.

He sighed and finally looked up at me. "Yeah. I guess so. Forgive me?"

"Don't worry. It must run in the family."

He grinned. "Just one of the many Baxter traits."

"What are some of the other ones?" I asked.

We spent the rest of the evening sharing stories about my dad. Rocky knew him growing up, I knew him grown-up, and we both knew him as head of the household. By the time we said good night, we both knew my father a little better.

Chapter Eleven

Gregg didn't come home at all Tuesday night, and while neither Rocky nor I was surprised, neither of us was happy about it either. We ate breakfast quietly and headed over to the office.

When we pulled into the parking lot, Roger's truck was already there. I could see Roger and Gregg walking down the trail to the barn. They were about halfway down to the river. Rocky got out of the truck, muttered "Show time," and headed for the raft barn. I followed, partly because I thought I might need to help keep Gregg from blowing his top, but mostly because I wanted to see Roger finally get what he deserved.

We were walking faster than they were, but we were still twenty feet outside of the barn when they went inside. Even so, we could hear Roger's "What the hell is this?" from where we were.

Roger turned to face us as we entered the staff room. "What is this?" he asked, holding up a garbage bag and pointing to his open, empty locker.

"You're fired, Roger," Rocky said simply.

"I'm what?"

"You're fired," Rocky repeated. I could tell he really didn't like saying it.

"For what?" Roger asked indignantly, dropping the bag.

"For several reasons. I've told you at least four times you were on your last chance. Between the party and not showing up for the meeting yesterday, your last chance is gone."

"This is crap. You can't fire me just because I threw a party."

"No, but I can fire you for abusing illegal substances and not reporting for work."

"Like you've never thrown a party," Roger sneered. "You've become such a hypocrite."

"I never said I hadn't thrown parties in the past. But you know I've worked hard to get clean. And I told everyone on staff that I expect them to stay clean during the season. In fact, I have a contract that you signed stating you understood you could be fired if you didn't stay clean."

"You know, Rocky, you used to be real cool. But you just gave in to the system and became a stuck-up old turd." He shook his head. "Not that I care. It's not like there aren't three other companies who want me to come guide for them. When will I get my check?" he asked, picking up the garbage bag that contained his personal belongings.

"It's waiting for you up in the office, minus the bail money, of course."

"Of course," Roger mocked. "Nice knowing you, loser." And he walked out of the barn.

Gregg stood up. He pulled some clothes out of his locker, grabbed his life jacket off the hook, and started to follow Roger. Rocky stepped directly in front of the door. "Sit down, Gregg."

Gregg looked him in the eye. I hadn't realized that Rocky was only a couple of inches taller than my brother. "No."

"We have some things to discuss."

"I have nothing to say to you."

"Fine. Then I guess this will just be a lecture." Gregg still didn't say anything. Rocky sighed. "Did Scott tell you that you were grounded yesterday?"

"Of course he did. Scotty always does what he's supposed to do," he said, glaring at me.

"But you decided to leave anyway."

"You don't own me."

"No, but I do have custody. That means that I am legally responsible for you, and that you have to do as I say in my house."

"Fine. Then I won't stay in your house."

"That's not an option."

"Oh, yes it is."

"Gregg, you're almost ready to take the supply boats. I'd like to give you your own boat to guide when you turn eighteen. Until then, you need to keep working with the other guides. If you're not living with me, I see no reason to continue your free training."

"I'll go work somewhere else."

"You won't get hired without the proper certification," Rocky warned.

"I didn't say I was going to be a guide. I never wanted this job, remember? This was what *you* decided I had to do. You've been trying to control us and make us think and act like you since the day we got here."

"Gregg, that's not true. The reason I've asked you to work for me—" Rocky began.

"Oh, you've never *asked* us anything," Gregg cut in. "You've told us everything and never once asked for our opinions or thoughts. Well it's my turn now. I'm not going to be grounded, I'm not going to be your damn guide, and there's no way I'm going to keep living with you. Now get out of my way."

He threw his life jacket on the floor and started for the door. At first

Rocky didn't move, and I thought Gregg was going to try to go through him. At the last second, Rocky stepped aside and Gregg strode through the door.

I stood there for a few seconds, just staring at Rocky. Finally I said, "You're just going to let him go?"

Rocky shook his head. "I don't have a choice."

"What do you mean, you don't have a choice? Go get him! Go tell him that he's not grounded and can still stay with you! Tell him he doesn't have to work for you!"

"I can't do that."

"You can, you just won't! Gregg's right!" I cried. "You don't care. It doesn't matter to you. You've never cared about how we feel or what we want! You've never cared at all!"

"Scott," Rocky started, but I was bolting out the door after Gregg and Roger.

I ran all the way back up the trail, but the truck was pulling out when I got to the parking lot. "Gregg!" I yelled after them, "Gregg, wait for me! I'm coming too, Gregg!"

"Scott!" Rocky called. I turned around. He was only fifteen feet behind me. He must have run too.

"Scott, don't do this." He came up to me and tried to put a hand on my shoulder.

I shoved him away. "Don't touch me. He's my brother, the only real family I've got left, and you let him go, you drove him away!"

"No, Scott," he said.

"Yes!" I shouted at him. "Yes, you did! You don't care and you drove him away! And now I'm all alone!" I turned and ran as fast as I could.

The tears blinded me, and I kept tripping on the blurry ground, but I kept going. I ran and ran, but when I got to Rocky's house, no one was there. Gregg's dresser was completely empty. All of his stuff was gone. He was gone.

A few hours later, after I had started and stopped crying three or four times, I was still trying to figure out what to do. I knew where Roger lived; I could pack up and follow Gregg. But Roger didn't like me and I certainly didn't like him. I could go over and try to get Gregg to come back, but he wouldn't listen to me if Roger was around. I wasn't sure he would listen even if he were alone.

Then the phone rang. At first I didn't answer it, because I thought it would be Rocky. It stopped ringing after the fourth ring, and then a minute later, it started ringing again. I decided to answer it. It might not be Rocky, and if it was, I could just hang up on him.

"Hello," I said, and even I could hear the sullenness in my voice.

"Scott?"

"Nancy?"

"Yes. Thanks for the letter. I tried to call you several times but there was no answer." She hesitated. "Are you okay? You sound kind of funny."

"I've had a really bad day," I said.

"Do you want to talk about it?" she asked.

"Well, yeah, actually I do." But once I said that, I didn't know where to start. I was quiet.

"So," she prompted. "What's been going on since you wrote?"

Haltingly, I told her everything, starting with Rocky bringing Gregg home, to me finding Gregg's stuff all gone. I sort of left out the fact that I had been crying before she called.

She listened to the whole thing without saying much. She interrupted a couple of times to ask questions when I got ahead of myself, but that was all. When I finished, it was her turn to be quiet.

I couldn't stand the silence. "What? What are you thinking?"

She sighed. "I'm trying to figure out why you got so mad at Rocky. You were mad at Gregg to begin with, but it doesn't sound like you yelled at him as much as you yelled at Rocky."

"But Rocky didn't do anything to get Gregg to stay."

"Didn't he tell him to stay? Didn't he try to tell him that leaving wasn't an option?"

"Well, yeah," I said.

"What else could he do?" she asked. "What did you want him to do?"

"I don't know," I said, "something. My dad never let him just walk out like that."

"Did you want him to give Gregg everything he wanted?"

"No," I said slowly.

"It sounds like Gregg was leaving because Roger was, not because of anything Rocky said to him today, right?"

"Yeah," I said, starting to see what she was getting at. "I guess there was no way to get Gregg to stay."

She sighed. "I'm just guessing, but it doesn't sound like he would have stayed even if Rocky had let him off of being grounded, promised to promote him to guide, and given him a pay raise all at once."

I shook my head. "The only way Gregg would have stayed would have been if Roger stayed too."

We were both quiet. After a while I cleared my throat. "I bet you're thinking that I should be mad at Gregg instead of Rocky."

She didn't say anything.

"And you're probably right."

She laughed softly. "I'm not here to tell you how to feel. I'm just here to listen, remember?"

"I am mad at Gregg," I said. "I know that. But I'm mad at Rocky too. He really didn't try to work with Gregg at all."

"Did he treat you guys differently?"

"No," I began.

"Then why aren't you off with Gregg if Rocky's so awful?"

"He's not awful. But Gregg and I...he's my brother. He's all I've got left."

"What about Rocky?"

"Well, yeah, I've got him now...but Gregg...he's..." I struggled. She didn't say anything, just let me keep going. Finally I blurted out, "Gregg and I grew up together. We've always been together. He's my brother. He's...he's the only tie I've got to my mom and dad."

"I know, Scott," she said gently.

"I can't believe he left me like that." I felt dangerously close to tears again. I put my hand over my eyes and racked my brain frantically for a new topic of conversation.

Before I could come up with one, she said, "He wasn't leaving you. He was leaving Rocky. And for him, that's a big difference."

"It doesn't feel like it."

"I wish I could do something to help, Scott."

"Just calling was a help, Nancy."

"Well, unfortunately, I've got to go. Is there a good time that I could plan on calling you again?"

I told her that I was usually home in the evenings, and that Monday and Tuesday were my days off. She said she'd try to call next week, but she told me I could call her collect if I needed to. I thanked her again and then we said good-bye.

About fifteen minutes after I got off the phone with Nancy, the phone rang again. This time I answered right away. "Hello?"

"Um, yeah, is Scott there?"

I started to grin. "Yeah, Summer, it's me."

"I was just calling to see..." she faltered and trailed off.

"I don't suppose you've got today off, do you?" I asked hopefully.

"Well, yeah, actually I do."

"Want to go do something? I've got to get out of the house. And I really need to talk to someone," I added.

"Sure," she said. "Why don't you just come over and we'll figure it out from here."

"See you in about half an hour," I said.

"Bye."

"Bye."

I hurried through my shower and rode away from the house as fast as I could. I felt a weight lift off my shoulders as soon as I was out of the front yard. Just getting out of the house made me feel free.

Summer was waiting on the front porch when I came around the corner. She stood up and walked over to her bike as I coasted into her driveway.

"Hey," I said. "How are you doing?"

"Okay," she said. "How are you?"

"Better. I'm really glad you called."

"Well, where to?"

"Is there a park or something nearby? Someplace we can just sit and hang out for a while?"

She nodded. "Follow me."

We ended up at the playground of the elementary school. We propped our bikes up against a tree and I followed her over to the swings.

"So," she said, sitting down. "What's going on?"

For the second time that day, I told my story. This time, because of Nancy's help, I was able to tell it a little more calmly.

"By now you're probably thinking I'm a big baby with a really messed-up family."

"No," she said, shaking her head and swinging higher. "I'm thinking more about Gregg being a big messed-up baby. But we won't go into that. You've had a rough day already."

We just sat in the swings quietly for a few minutes with our feet occasionally dragging on the gravel.

Suddenly she laughed. "Well, I guess I made the right decision about leaving early on Monday, huh?"

"Yeah, you did." I pushed off with my feet and started to swing again. "Gregg was pretty impressed with you."

She looked over at me doubtfully. "Yeah, right."

"The only thing he didn't like about you was that we left early. But I think he's just jealous."

She smiled and blushed a little. I let my swing slow down.

"Hey, do you want to go to the Dairy Delight? They've got a two-for-one sale on banana splits right now."

"That sounds great. Let's go." She jumped off the swing.

I dragged my feet to stop the swing and spun around in an awkward circle.

She laughed. I stood up and we walked over to our bikes. This time, I took her hand.

We spent the rest of the afternoon together, just hanging out and talking about everything from movies to parents, from the afterlife to aliens. I really didn't want to go back to Rocky's, even though I knew I had no other choice.

We rode to her house at five because she had to be home for dinner. I got her phone number, and we made plans to go see a movie Sunday night.

I took my time riding home, hoping Rocky had gone to Laura's. As I neared the house, I could see someone standing on the front porch. He was home. I cut around to the back of the house as soon as I saw him.

Putting my bike in the shed as quietly as I could, I stalled for time. I kept hoping maybe he hadn't seen or heard me and would just leave. I thought I had pulled it off, because he wasn't on the porch when I came around to the front.

I had only taken a few steps into the living room when Rocky came out of the kitchen. I tried to hold on to my anger, but it almost completely disappeared when I saw the relief flood his face.

"Scott," he said with tentative smile. "I'm glad you're here."

I shrugged. "I don't really have any other place to be."

His smile faltered just a little. "Well, I hope you're hungry. Dinner will be ready pretty soon."

I walked past him into the kitchen and started getting dishes out. He had fixed pork chops, stuffing, corn on the cob, and a fresh salad. There was a pie in a box sitting on the counter too. It was a bribe dinner if I had ever seen one.

I had decided to be polite, but not outwardly friendly. I wasn't going to start any conversations. I'd answer questions, but I wasn't going to just chat with him like nothing was wrong.

After a few minutes, Rocky said, "Missed you on the river today."

"Thanks."

"What did you do?"

"Went into town."

He waited, then asked, "Did you go shopping?"

"No. Summer and I just went to the elementary school playground and hung out for a while. Then we went and had banana splits, and we hung out some more."

"Summer's the one who works at the library?"

I nodded.

He grinned. "So you were successful when you returned the book."

"Yeah. I took her to Roger's party with me," I said, going for the dig. I succeeded.

Rocky's grin disappeared. The silence drew out and became very uncomfortable.

Finally I couldn't stand it. "How was the river today?"

"Fine," he said in a flat voice. That was it.

The silence stretched out again.

I felt guilty. Rocky had been trying to smooth things over and be nice, and I had just messed everything up again. The silence was pretty painful, but I couldn't make myself say anything.

Neither of us said a word as we finished the meal. I got up to clear the table. Rocky helped, and we had the kitchen clean in less than five minutes. I started to leave the kitchen.

"Game of chess?" Rocky asked tentatively.

"Sure," I said unenthusiastically. "I'll set up the board. Front porch?"

"Yeah," he said. "I'll be there in a minute."

When he came out, I told him he could go first.

The first five or six moves were made in complete silence. Then he said, "I dropped by Roger's after work today."

"Oh?" I tried to keep my voice neutral.

"I was hoping that after having the day to cool down, Gregg and I could sit down and talk."

"What happened?"

"Roger opened the door. He refused to let me in, refused to go get Gregg, and told me that if I wasn't off his property within three minutes, he would call the cops and file trespassing and harassment charges against me."

I groaned. "They won't even try to be reasonable."

Rocky looked kind of surprised, but he said, "No, they won't." He paused, then said, "I called a lawyer before you got home."

"About what?"

"About changing custody."

I didn't say anything.

"I know Gregg would rather somebody else have custody of him. And I don't want to keep custody of him if he's not living here. I can't be responsible for someone I don't even see."

I nodded. My stomach was churning.

"I didn't get much information today. The lawyer's supposed to call me back tomorrow. I'll let you know all the details as I get them. If you don't want to stay here, I'm not going to force you to, as long as the person you ask to take custody is a responsible individual."

"And who decides they're responsible?"

"I would. I'd want to meet them before I'd let you go live with them."

We made a few more moves in silence. My mind was spinning. I could get out of here. I could go back to California and live with Nancy. I could go back to my friends, to the way of life I knew and loved. But I was starting to like it here too. I couldn't believe Rocky was just going to let me go like that, just kick me out.

As if he had read my mind, he said slowly, "I'd really like it if you stayed. I've enjoyed getting to know you, and you've made me realize how much I have missed having family around." He hesitated. "I guess I messed up by leaving you and Gregg alone so much when you first got here, but I didn't know what else to do. I've been living alone so long, and I've never had kids around. I didn't know if we were going to get along. I didn't want you and Gregg thinking I was trying to take your father's place. I didn't want you thinking I sent for you just because I had to. Now I've discovered that I like you...and Gregg too. He's a lot like I used to be. I can tell you," he said, shaking his head, "it scares me to see myself reacting the way your father reacted to me."

I tried to absorb everything he was saying.

Rocky sighed. "You don't have to decide right now. I'd like you to take your time and think about it. But understand this. This is a one-time deal. If you do decide to stay, my rules have to stand. You don't threaten to leave me every time we disagree."

I looked up at him. "And you can't threaten to kick me out if we disagree either."

He looked me in the eye. "I wouldn't ever kick you out."

"Isn't that what you're doing now?"

He sat back, blinking with confusion. "No, no! I'm not kicking you out. I don't want you taking it that way." He shook his head. "I just know Gregg wants nothing to do with me. I don't know if you feel the same way. If you do, then I don't want to make your life miserable. I'm trying to give you options." He sighed. "I'm trying to be fair."

"Life isn't fair," I said. He looked up at me. "You're stuck with me," I said, and as he started to smile, I added, "checkmate."

For a second he stared at the board in disbelief. Then he laughed. We decided to finish another game before going to bed. He won, easily.

We walked back into the house. He was halfway to his room when he stopped. "Scott?"

"Yeah?"

In a hoarse voice, he said, "There are times when you must let the people you care about make decisions that might hurt them."

I cleared my throat before asking, "You really care about Gregg?"

"Of course. Otherwise, neither of you would be here." When I didn't answer immediately, he continued, "I could have told the courts I wasn't able to take you."

As he turned to go into his room, I said, "Uncle Dave, I'm sorry about this morning."

"Me too, Scott. Now let's just let it go. And," he said, dropping me a wink, "let's stick with Rocky."

I nodded.

"Sleep well."

"You too."

Chapter Twelve

The rest of the week would have been great, except that I kept worrying about Gregg. I called several times, but no one answered, and there wasn't an answering machine. I went to Roger's house twice, but no one was home. Both times I left a note stuck in the front door, asking Gregg to call me, but he never did.

Meanwhile, work was going even better. I hadn't really been aware of the tension between the staff members before, but now that Roger and Gregg were gone, everyone seemed to open up a whole lot more, smiling and joking with each other.

According to Tom, Roger wasn't really boasting when he had said that other companies wanted him. He got hired on with another company that Thursday. Gregg didn't. Neither Joe nor Lou seemed to think Roger would be able to stay with the other company for long. The company had called Rocky for references, and while Rocky tried to make the situation look better than it was, it still looked bad. Roger was hired, but he was also told that it was on a trial basis. One mistake and he'd be gone. I wondered if he was tired of hearing that. I tried not to think about them, but every time I took my life jacket off the hook and saw Gregg's hanging there next to mine, I couldn't help it.

The rafting itself was awesome. I got to go on one half-day trip each day that week. On Friday, I didn't go until the afternoon trip. The clouds were piling up and rolling in as we launched, and by the time we pulled out, the temperature had dropped. It hadn't rained yet, but I could feel the electricity in the air, and the clouds kept getting lower. Fortunately, the rain held off for the river run.

On the drive back to the office, it started to rain. It was impressive. The water poured out of the sky like someone had slit the clouds open and let everything fall out at once. Lightning flashed across the mountaintops. Thunder cracked above us and then echoed off the canyon walls. The bus windshield wipers were going nonstop, and it was hard to see more than twenty feet in front of us. The ride was quiet and subdued, as if everyone on the bus felt the pressure of the storm.

The storm raged on through Friday night. Rocky stayed home, and I was glad he did. Otherwise, I wouldn't have been able to find the candles when the power went out. The rain slacked off a little around seven-thirty, so we grilled some burgers outside, staying as far under the eaves of the house as we could.

The storm came back full force as we were finishing the dishes. There was hardly any time at all between the flashes of lightning and the thunder. The thunder was so close and loud, it rattled the window panes. After a really vicious crack of thunder, one of Rocky's framed pictures fell off the wall and the glass cracked.

I went to bed around ten, during another lull in the storm. I was awakened twice more during the night, probably around one and four, by other thunderstorms as they rolled across the sky. The rain was almost constant, but it seemed like I could feel the old house crouch down and settle in for the night, keeping Rocky and me warm and dry.

When I went into the kitchen the next morning, the house was quiet and gray. It was still raining outside. Rocky had left a note on the kitchen table.

Too much rain last night, forecasting continued T-storms today. Canceling trips. Enjoy the extra day off! I'll be at the shop if you need me.

Rocky

Initially, the note made me smile to myself. I could use the day off. I could call Gregg and see if we could get together, I could call Summer and see if she wanted to go to the movie tonight instead. I could read, I could finish my laundry, I could take a nap....

As it turned out, pretty much the only thing I could do was read or take a nap. The phone lines were down. Every time I picked up the receiver, I heard nothing but static. The power was still out, so I couldn't do my laundry. It was still raining, so I didn't want to ride my bike anywhere. The day was long and slow.

The rain finally tapered off to a very light drizzle sometime in the early afternoon. I watched it for five minutes before I decided that I would just chance it.

I rode over to Roger's, and by the time I got there I was dripping wet. I had to keep wiping my wet hair back from my forehead so it wouldn't drip in my eyes. The trip turned out to be a waste of time. No one was home.

At first I was frustrated because I didn't have any paper to leave a note. But then I decided that it would be useless anyway. Gregg hadn't responded to me all week. Might as well accept the fact that he didn't want me around anymore.

I just stood there in the rain, straddling the bike, while I tried to figure out what to do. Finally I decided I didn't want to go home, so I started for town. Maybe I would get lucky and Summer would be at the library.

The drizzle didn't really increase, but riding along the highway made it feel like it had. I rode with my head down as much as I could, trying to keep the rain out of my eyes. I had just started thinking about how I was going to look like a drowned rat by the time I got there when I heard my name called. I pulled on the brakes and slid along the road. I still don't know how I managed to keep the bike upright, but luck was on my side for a change.

I looked across the road, and there was Summer on her bike, facing the opposite direction. She was drenched too, but she was grinning from ear to ear. She looked great.

We waited for a car to pass, then she walked her bike over to me.

"Hey," she said a little breathlessly. "Where are you going?"

"I was going to go check the library and see if you were working."

Somehow her smile got even bigger. "Really?"

"Really."

"Why didn't you just call?"

"Our phone's out."

"Ohhh!" she said, nodding.

"What?"

"I've been trying to call all day, and all I've gotten is a busy signal. I thought you were talking to your girlfriend or something."

"But then I would have been on the phone with you," I said.

She blushed. "Oh." This time she barely whispered it.

I grinned. This was great. "So why were you calling?"

"I wanted to know if you wanted to catch the matinee show today. I kind of figured you wouldn't be on the river in this mess."

"I'd love to see a movie," I said, "but the power's been out all day."

"Not in town," she said.

"Cool. Let's go."

We went into the theater, ignoring the frowns we got from the ticket taker when we dripped on the carpet. I bought a huge bucket of popcorn and the biggest soda they had for us to share, and Summer got a couple of candy bars.

When we came out of the theater, the weather was absolutely beautiful. The clouds were virtually gone, and the sky was starting to turn a light violet in the last of the twilight. The sweet scent of the rain hung in the air, and the birds were calling to each other everywhere.

"So," I said. "Now I bet I have to take you home."

"Not yet, unless you want to," she said. "My parents went to a barbecue with some of their friends. I don't have to be home till midnight."

"A barbecue? With all that rain?"

She shrugged. "Maybe it's indoors. Anyway, it looks like the rain is over for tonight."

"Well," I said, grinning, "what do you want to do now?"

"How about we go grab dinner?"

"Okay," I said slowly. "But after all that popcorn, I'm not that hungry."

"No wonder, you ate most of it," she said. "Anyway, I've kind of got a craving for some McDonald's fries," she confessed.

"Let's go," I said. "I'm sure by the time we get there, I'll be hungry again."

When we got to McDonald's, she insisted on buying, because I had paid for the movies. I didn't argue a whole lot, because I was running short on cash. We managed to stretch dinner into nearly an hour and a half. We started with just one order of fries, then went back to get another one with an order of Chicken McNuggets. Then we split a sundae, but ended up going back for another one in a different flavor because we ate the first one so fast. I'm sure the people who were working there thought we were absolutely crazy, but I didn't care. We were having a great time.

We stepped outside into the darkness. "Now what?" I asked.

She took a deep breath and turned herself in a slow circle. "I'm glad most of the clouds left. There's supposed to be a full moon tonight."

"So I'll get to see full shadows, huh?"

She nodded. "Almost as clear as day. So let's ride back up to Rugged Rapids."

"And do what?"

"Leave our bikes there and walk along the river."

I shrugged. "Okay."

It wasn't raining at all as we rode out of town. We left our bikes propped up against the office building and walked down toward the river. There was a light coming from the raft barn.

"That's weird," I said, pointing it out to Summer. "Let's see who's here."

We walked into the barn. Rocky was sitting in the middle of one of the rafts, yanking on a rope and muttering to himself.

"Hey, Rocky," I said. "What's up?"

"Hey, Scott," he said, without turning around. He gave another tug on the rope, grunted with satisfaction, and then turned to face me. "What are..." he stopped short when he saw Summer, and he gave her a huge grin.

"Well, hello," he said. "I don't believe we've met."

Summer smiled back. "I'm Summer," she said simply.

"And you're as pretty as your name," Rocky said. "And intelligent if you're smart enough to choose Scott." He winked at her. "What have the two of you been up to?"

"We went to a movie and then got something to eat," I said, trying not to blush. "What are you doing?"

"Oh." He waved his hand in the general direction of the rafts. "Just some routine maintenance. Making sure that the ropes aren't fraying and that any patches we have are still sealed tight."

"You haven't been doing this all day, have you?" I asked.

"Oh, no. I was at the shop for several hours, working out the refunds and rain checks for today, paying bills, and working out the budget. I only got to start all this fun stuff a couple of hours ago."

"Need any help?" Summer asked.

"No. Thank you, though. This is dull stuff. Besides, I'm almost done. I would have been done a lot earlier if it wasn't so boring. I keep falling asleep," Rocky said.

Summer smiled.

"So where are you off to now?" he asked.

"Oh, we're just going to take a walk."

"By the river?"

"Yeah," I said.

"Be careful," he warned. "With all that rain last night and today, there may have been some flash flooding or erosion. Parts of the riverbank that you're used to may have washed away."

"We'll be careful, Rocky," I said as we turned to leave.

"Oh, and Scott...don't stay out too late."

"Don't worry," Summer said with grin. "He has to have me home by midnight."

"Then I expect you in by twelve-thirty," Rocky said to me.

I nodded. "Good night."

"Good night. And it was nice meeting you, Summer. You'll have to come over for dinner some night."

"Thank you. I'd like that."

We stepped back into the darkness.

"So that's your uncle," she said.

"Yep. That's him."

"He seems pretty nice," she said slowly. "And you didn't seem too angry with him."

"No, I'm not very angry anymore. At least, not at him."

"Now who are you mad at?"

"You make it sound like I'm always mad."

"I didn't mean that," she began.

"I know. I'm just being difficult." I sighed. "I know that the fight was mostly Gregg's fault. He's been gone three days now. He hasn't called or dropped by to let me know what's going on, and he's ignored my messages."

"Give him some time. I'm sure he'll come around."

"I hope so," I said doubtfully. "Although part of me is thinking that I don't want him coming back if he's going to be such an idiotic jerk."

"Just try not to let your anger build up too much. You don't want to be completely pissed at him when he finally does come back."

I laughed. "You sound like Nancy, our neighbor in California. When we left home, she told me to look out after Gregg, even though I'm younger and he won't want my help."

"Well then, I hope you listen to both of us," Summer said.

I reached out and took her hand. "I'll think about it," I said.

She raised an eyebrow at me. "You might want to do more than think about it."

We had reached the river. The moon came out from behind a cloud and reflected off the river. I could easily see the rocks and bushes around us.

"Well," I said, "do we want to go upstream or downstream?"

"Upstream," she said immediately.

I laughed. "Why?"

"I like to go against the current."

"We're walking, Summer, we're not going to be in it."

"I know, but it's the idea of the thing."

"We'll be going downstream when we come back," I warned.

"I know." She looked at me. "Do you want to go downstream from here?"

"Not really."

"Then why are you giving me such a hard time about going upstream?" she demanded.

"Because you got so defensive."

She put her hands on her hips and I laughed again. "You're fun to pick on." I took her hand again. "Come on. Let's go."

We walked upstream for almost an hour. I couldn't believe how beautiful it was. The moon was casting full shadows everywhere, and we could see everything in detail. There were still quite a few clouds, and every time the wind blew a cloud in front of the moon, it became as dark as any regular night. It was like being in a black-and-white movie. I told Summer she was right about the full moon and that I was very impressed with the river at night. She tossed her head and told me I should just get used to her being right.

I pretended to try to push her in the river. She screamed and grabbed on to me, and almost pulled me off balance. The only way I could save both of us from falling in was to pull her close to me. She looked up at me, and without really thinking, I leaned down and kissed her on the lips.

At first she kissed me back, but then she took a step away from me. She looked confused and a little scared. "Um..." she began nervously.

I grabbed her hand before she got too far away. "It's time to start heading back, right?"

She nodded. We didn't talk much on the way back. I didn't know what to say. About halfway back, Summer stumbled on a tree root and let go of my hand to catch her balance. Then she put both hands in her pockets. I was miserable.

Following the turn of the river, we could soon see the Rugged Rapids buildings. There was still a light on in the raft barn.

"I thought Rocky said he was almost done," Summer said.

"Yeah, he did. Either he had more to do than he thought, or he's waiting to make sure we made it back okay." I looked at her. "Did we?"

She shrugged. "I think so."

The light in the raft barn winked out. "He must have been working," I said.

Summer stopped. "Scott?"

"What?" I stopped too, my heart pounding. Maybe I hadn't messed up as badly with her as I thought I had.

"Isn't that a raft?"

I turned in the direction she was pointing. There was a raft about forty feet away from us, waiting on the bank of the river. "Yeah, it is. Let's go check it out." As we started walking towards the raft, the moon slipped behind another bank of clouds.

It was an oar raft, but the oars weren't in their locks yet. I felt a sinking sensation when I got close enough to make out the Rugged Rapid logo on the raft. "Something's wrong," I said to Summer.

A voice came out of the darkness. "No, nothing's wrong. Everything is just right."

"What are you doing here, Roger?" I asked.

"None of your business, snot-face," he said. I heard a girl giggle.

The moon shone out from behind the clouds briefly, just long enough for me to see Roger standing there with Debbie and Stacey.

"Where's Gregg?" I asked as the moon hid again.

"I'm over here, Scott," he said from my right.

I turned and saw him standing a few feet away from me, holding the oars. "What are you doing?" I asked him.

He opened his mouth, but Roger cut him off. "I already told you, it's none of your business!" He shoved me.

"Roger, knock it off," Gregg said, but he sounded tired. He handed Roger the oars. "Here."

Roger took the oars and headed to the raft. Gregg turned to me.

"Now you're stealing rafts?" I asked in disbelief.

"We're not stealing it," Gregg said. "We're just borrowing it. We're going to do a midnight run."

"Gregg, that's stupid."

"With a full moon, we'll be able to see just fine," he said. "It'll be really cool. Why don't you come with us?"

I ignored his question. "Why haven't you called?"

"I don't have anything to say to Rocky."

"*Me*, you moron! Why haven't you called *me?* I've left messages. I've tried to call, but you're never home. What have you been doing?" I could hear my voice rising. Summer took a step closer to me and put her hand on my shoulder. I took a deep breath.

"I'm sorry, Scott. I've been busy. I'll give you a call this weekend, okay?"

"Gregg!" Roger called from the raft.

"Come on, Scott, come with us."

I hesitated, and looked over at Summer. She shook her head ever so slightly. "I can't," I said. "I've got to get Summer home."

Gregg looked at her for a second. "Okay."

Roger came up. "Come on, guys, let's get going."

I shook my head. "We've got to get going." I turned to leave. "Call me, Gregg."

I hadn't taken three steps before I was grabbed from behind in a huge bear hug and lifted off the ground. "Hey!" I yelled.

"Roger, what the hell are you doing?" I heard Gregg ask.

"Grab her, quick!" Roger yelled in my ear.

Gregg just stood there looking confused.

"Now!" screamed Roger. "Don't let her get away!"

I heard Summer's cry and a thump as Gregg tripped her in order to catch her. I struggled, trying to wriggle out of Roger's iron hold on me. If I had ever had any doubt as to whether he was a strong paddler, it was resolved. I couldn't move his arms at all. I managed to kick him really hard once, and I was glad to hear a pained grunt. But then he increased the pressure across my chest. I could barely breathe.

"Knock it off," he growled in my ear.

I could hear Gregg struggling with Summer behind us. The raft was in the water. Debbie was already in it, and Stacey was holding the bowline. Roger stopped right in front of the raft.

"Throw her in," he said over his shoulder.

Gregg walked past us and dumped Summer in the raft. Then he took the line from Stacey and she climbed over Summer. Roger waded out a few steps into the river before dumping me into the front of the raft. I scrambled up as quickly as I could, but Roger was already next to me in the raft, and Gregg had given us one good shove as he hopped in.

We were on board for the midnight run.

Chapter Thirteen

Roger and I stood up at the same time.

"Where do you think you're going?" he asked, pushing me back down.

"I'm going to the back to make sure Summer's okay."

"I'll send your little girlfriend up to you," he said mockingly. He moved back to the seat and took the oars.

"Ow!" Gregg yelled suddenly.

"Don't touch me again, you stupid jerk!" Summer said.

"You better watch it or I'll throw you off," Gregg warned.

"Then why go to all this trouble to throw me on?" she asked. She stood up and moved to the front of the raft with me, stepping carefully over the oar.

She sat down next to me on the pontoon and leaned in close. I put an arm around her. "Are you okay?" I asked, keeping my voice low.

"Yeah," she muttered. "I can't tell if I'm more angry or scared right now."

"Me too," I said. "Gregg didn't hurt you?"

"I scraped my knee pretty good when he tripped me. That's why I just kicked him."

"Will you please tell me why we had to bring them along?" Gregg asked Roger.

"Yeah," one of the girls said in a pouty voice. "Why do we have the kiddies with us?"

"Because otherwise, Mr. Goody-Two-Shoes here would have gone straight home to tell Rocky what was going on. We would have been met at the pullout by the Bureau of Land Management and a bunch of cops."

"Scott wouldn't have snitched," Gregg said. "I got him out of that habit by the time he was six."

"It wasn't worth the chance," Roger said. "Besides, this way he'll go down with us if he does decide to tell."

"Right, like I'd get in trouble for being kidnapped," I snorted.

Roger looked at me with an innocent expression on his face. "You weren't kidnapped! You agreed to meet us here. This was all planned. And I've got three other witnesses to prove it."

"They'd never believe you."

"It'd be four witnesses against two. And you two would look like you were just trying to cover your backsides."

I shook my head. It wasn't worth arguing with him. Rocky would believe me any day of the week before he'd believe Roger.

Next to me, Summer sighed.

"What's wrong?"

"My parents are going to be really worried when I'm not home on time."

"I'm sorry," I said. I felt along the equipment line, searching for the spare life jacket. It wasn't there.

"Hey, Scott!"

I turned around. Gregg was leaning toward me, holding out his life jacket. "Put this on," he said.

I took it from him and turned to Summer. "Here," I said, helping her put it on.

"Scott! That's for you!" Gregg exclaimed.

"Yeah, right," I said, "I'm not wearing a jacket when she doesn't have one."

"What about you?" Summer asked, looking up at me.

I shrugged. "It's my fault you got mixed up in this. I don't want anything to happen to you."

I cinched up the last clip as tight as it could get. She smiled at me and then kissed me softly on the cheek. "Thank you," she said quietly.

I gave her a tired smile. "You're welcome."

"Come on, Roger," Gregg was saying. "Give him your life jacket."

"Why?"

"Because we made them come with us."

"So? Just because they stuck their noses where they don't belong doesn't make it my problem."

"Roger, come on. They didn't have a chance to get jackets of their own, and we didn't get any for them. Give him yours."

"Little brother will be fine, Gregg. It's not like I haven't run this river thousands of times. Nothing's going to happen." He laughed. "None of us needs a jacket tonight."

"Then give him yours!"

"No," he began.

One of the girls began undoing her jacket. "Here. He can have mine."

"No, Stacey, put that back on," Gregg said.

"No, Stacey," Roger said at the same time. He gave a disgusted sigh and put the oars up. "I'll give him mine if he's too much of a wuss to ride without one." He tossed it in my general direction, and I just barely managed to catch it before it went overboard.

We floated on in silence for a while. Debbie had crawled forward and was sitting on Roger's lap. Stacey and Gregg were in the back, out of sight. I was glad they were. It was embarrassing enough just thinking about what was going on behind us.

Summer and I sat facing forward. I was afraid to touch her, afraid that she'd get upset again. So we just rode in silence, watching the moon throw its light and cast shadows in the canyon, listening to the water lap against the side of the raft. Branches and other debris floated past us in the current. Since Roger wasn't doing anything with the oars, the boat just wandered and spun lazy circles in the river without any purpose.

After a little bit, Summer inched closer to me. I took a deep breath and reached out for her hand. She squeezed gently and smiled. Maybe the raft ride wouldn't be too bad after all.

"So when was the last time you did Brown's Canyon?" I asked her, keeping my voice low.

"This summer."

"Really? When?"

"A few weeks before I met you. I go a couple of times every year."

"You didn't sound that enthusiastic about rafting when I asked you before. Why didn't you tell me you're a pro?"

"No, no," she laughed. "I'm not a pro. It's just not really a big deal when I go, since I've been so many times," she said, then she laughed. "This is a big deal, though. I've never gone through Brown's Canyon like this."

"Me either. I thought the canyon was impressive in the daylight. It's really fantastic with the moonlight."

The canyon had an almost ghostlike quality to it. Although the moonlight allowed us to see some things clearly, part of the riverbank seemed to disappear into an inky blackness. The normal chatter of people and birds was replaced only with the sounds of our breathing.

We could hear the static of the first rapid. Summer squeezed my hand briefly. She looked a little nervous.

"We'll be fine," I whispered to her. "Roger's really good at guiding."

"How often have you ridden with him?" she asked.

"Only once," I admitted. "But Rocky was always impressed with his rafting skills. It was his people skills that got him in trouble."

As if to prove my point, Roger said, "Get off me, babe. It's time to rock and roll." He took the oars and with three quick strokes he headed the nose of the raft downstream and moved us more toward the right side of the river.

"Time for the first rapid," Roger said. "And Snotty, what's its name?"

"Canyon Doors, followed immediately by Pinball," I said by rote.

"Very good. Too bad you couldn't have spent more time on my raft. I could have taught you much more than Rocky ever could."

I shook my head and whispered to Summer, "If I had spent more time with him, I would have quit before Gregg did."

She nodded in agreement.

We slid through Canyon Doors quickly and went into Pinball right where we wanted to be. It was so smooth and easy, I couldn't believe it. The tricky sleeper rocks and holes were now so far underwater they were nothing more than standing waves and we cruised through like a roller coaster. This was my first time on an oar boat, and it definitely reacted differently from a paddle boat. It felt strange not to have to worry about paddling. All I had to do was stay in the raft. And the way Roger guided it, staying in was easy.

Stacey and Debbie were screaming in the back, shrieking every time they got wet. Gregg was laughing, whether at them or at the ride I couldn't tell. Roger, Summer, and I were quiet, just enjoying the river. About halfway through the rapid, the moon went behind a cloud just for a few seconds. Without the full moonlight, it was difficult to make out the individual waves and virtually impossible to see the dark rocks. I looked up at the sky to see how many other clouds we would have to worry about, but the narrow canyon walls limited our view of the sky. I hoped that the moon would stay with us for the rest of our ride.

When we got out of Pinball, I could feel Summer relax next to me.

"That was fun," she said. "It's so bright out, it's not real different from running it in cloudy weather." She laughed. "Maybe this will be worth getting grounded for a month."

"Don't say that," I said quickly. "I'll go crazy if I don't get to see you."

She looked at me. "You don't think you'll be grounded too?"

I thought about Rocky telling me to be home at twelve-thirty. "I probably will," I sighed. "But I don't think it will be for a month."

She shrugged. "I probably won't get grounded for a full month either. Then again," she added ruefully, "my parents might ground me for two months instead. I can never tell how they are going to react."

"I could always tell how my parents were going to react. But Rocky's not my parent." I paused and then I grinned just a little. "If we were talking about my parents, we'd be looking at a minimum sentence of two months hard labor. Dishes, laundry, yard work, and general housecleaning without pay."

She laughed.

The next two rapids were quick and easy too. Everything was going just fine. Roger asked Debbie to come sit next to him again, since we were going into a little stretch without rapids now. Once again we drifted in silence. The moon ducked behind a large cloud.

Suddenly Summer sat up straight.

"What?" I asked.

"Do you hear something?"

I listened. "It sounds like there's a rapid ahead."

She looked at me. "There's not another one for a while, right?"

I shook my head. "No. We go around this bend and then have almost another mile or so before the next one." So where's that noise coming from? I wondered.

We sat still. The raft drifted aimlessly, doing slow turns. The roar of the river got louder.

"Hey, Gregg," I called to the back of the raft. "Do you hear something? It sounds like a rapid."

"Scott," he groaned. "You know there's not another rapid yet."

"No, really, listen for a minute."

We got quiet again. I glanced up at the sky. The moon was still behind the clouds.

Then Gregg said, "You might be right. What do you think, Rog?"

"What?" he asked irritably. I could tell he hadn't been listening.

"It sounds like there's a rapid coming up," I said.

"Snotty, Snotty, clearly you're not done with your training. The next rapid is Big Drop, and that's not for another mile."

"I know, but—" I began.

"You're just being paranoid. You're spooked because it's a midnight run and your adrenaline is pumping. No big deal."

I bit my tongue and listened helplessly to the river noise change into river thunder as the raft continued to drift.

"Scott," Summer said nervously, "I think the river's moving faster now."

I shook my head. *The water doesn't move faster until you are actually in the rapid*, I thought. *But there has to be a rapid coming up around the bend.* "Hang on," I said. "We don't want to get thrown out tonight."

She shook her head and grabbed the oar frame.

We got to the blind turn in the canyon. The raft had drifted again, and we were on the right side of the river, going down broadside. As we cleared the turn, the roar of the river seemed to triple in volume. The rapid churned and thundered in front of us. We had less than thirty feet before we'd be in it.

"Damn!" Roger yelled. "Get off me, get off me!" he hollered at Debbie.

She scrambled, trying to get to the back of the raft. Twenty feet to the tongue.

The rapid was directly in front of us, but I couldn't see what was there. The moon was still behind the cloud. Roger was fumbling with the oars. One of them got stuck on something and wouldn't swing out. Ten feet.

Finally he freed the oars, and swung them out. He put all he had into powerful strokes...One...two...three.... Too far! The raft turned wildly—first we were broadside to the rapid, then nose first, then leading with the other side.

The standing wave in front of us was bigger than any I had ever seen. The first wave took us, and the side of the raft went up so high I was sure we were going to flip. We slammed down on the other side, and water sprayed into the raft. I was vaguely aware that there were no more screams from the back of the raft. The second wave took us up even higher. All I could hear was the thunderous crashing of the rapid. It was angry, and we were in its grasp. The side of the raft kept going up, higher and higher. It was over my head, and I was falling.

We had flipped.

Chapter Fourteen

I came up gasping for air, and another huge wave crashed down, choking me. Coughing and spluttering, I tried to keep my head above the water. The cold water kept sucking me down in spite of the life jacket. The moon came out of the clouds just in time for me to see the rock that was right in front of me. I tried to get my feet up in front of me, but I didn't quite make it. My shoulder and chest slammed into the rock and I bounced off.

The waves on the other side of the rock were smaller. I spotted the raft just a few feet in front of me and to my right. Someone was clinging to it. I tried to get over to it, but it was moving faster than I was. Another big wave crashed down over the raft, and when it was gone, so was the person. I hugged my jacket and felt sick. I was so worried about Gregg and Roger in the river without life jackets that I didn't see the next rock until it was too late again. This time my feet were up, but the impact jarred my knees.

The water smoothed out just a little, but I could see some more big waves in front of me. I started trying to swim to the side. Maybe I could get to shore before I hit the next stretch.

Suddenly someone grabbed me from behind and pulled me under. I started choking on the water again. I clawed my way to the top of the water, trying to shove whoever it was away.

"Help!" Gregg shouted over the rapid. "Help me!"

"Okay!" I said. I could hear the fear in his voice. "Let's kick over to the side."

He pushed me under again, and I kicked him pretty hard. He was thrashing around. "Lean back!" I tried to yell over the water. "Just try to float! I'll help you!"

He stopped struggling quite so much, and we were both able to keep our heads above water.

We were making progress, but it was slow and painful. He kept dunking me from time to time. The life jacket was not designed to support two people. We couldn't make it to the shore before the next set of waves. Unfortunately, as we edged closer and closer to the shore, there were more rocks near the surface. We kept bouncing off them.

I managed to get to the left of a particularly big rock, but somehow Gregg smashed into it. I heard a muffled cry, and his grip on my arm started to relax. Frantically I reached out and grabbed his hand just as he let go. I shifted my hold until I had his arm just under the armpit. That was better because I could hold him up easier, but it was worse because I kept going under even more often.

The last section of the waves smoothed out, and we started kicking to the shore again. Gregg was whimpering. I asked him repeatedly what was wrong but got no answer.

We made it to the shore. We climbed out, and Gregg would have fallen with the first step if I hadn't caught him. He couldn't put his weight down on one foot. I helped him farther up the shore till we were clear of the water, and then we both sank down into the sand.

I don't know how long we sat there. It took me forever to get my breathing back to normal. I could feel a couple of places where I had hit rocks, and I knew that in a few hours they'd be really sore. Gregg wasn't moving or making a sound. He was bent almost double with his head between his knees.

I watched the river, hoping to see someone. The moon had broken free of the clouds again, and I could see up and down the riverbank fairly well. I could even see most of the bank on the other side of the river. I didn't see anyone moving.

I had no idea what had happened to Summer. I didn't know where anyone else was. I didn't know what to do, and I was too tired and hurt to do much anyway. Thinking about what might have happened to her and the others made me sick to my stomach. All I wanted to do was go look for Summer, but Gregg still wasn't moving. At least he had quit whimpering.

"Why'd you let go of the raft?" I finally asked Gregg.

"Huh?"

"Why'd you let go?"

"I never had hold of it."

"You didn't?"

"No."

"Oh." *It must have been Roger,* I thought. *Oh, please let everyone be okay.*

He started shaking. "Gregg?" He didn't answer. "Gregg? Gregg, what's wrong?" He was really shaking. I started to panic. What if he had hit his head and was having a seizure or something? I didn't have a clue how to help him.

"Gregg?" I said louder. I reached out and touched his arm. He jumped and tried to move away from me. At least he wasn't having a seizure.

"Come on, Gregg, try to relax," I said soothingly. "We're okay. It's going to be okay, Gregg. Calm down."

"No, it's not," Gregg cried. His head was still down and his voice was muffled. "I almost died in there! I couldn't breathe, I couldn't move. Nothing was working. You saved me, Scott, but I almost took you down with me!" He drew a quivering breath. "And you weren't even supposed to be with us. You didn't want to come and I nearly killed you!"

"Okay, Gregg, okay, calm down." He was rapidly approaching hysterics. I had to reassure him before he completely panicked. "I'm okay. We're both okay. Nobody died. Relax. It's over," I said. I scooted over closer to him and put my arm around him, leaning my head against his. I felt like crying too. "We're going to be all right, Gregg. Really. It's okay."

Slowly his shaking started to taper off. I stayed next to him, but I lifted my head to watch the river some more. I wondered where Summer, Roger, and the other girls were, praying everyone really was okay, or at least not any worse off than Gregg and I were.

Finally Gregg lifted his head and wiped the tears from his face with his hands. When he looked at me, though, the tears started again. "I'm so sorry, Scotty. I didn't mean to hurt you. You're all I've got left."

We hugged each other for a few minutes, then he kind of pushed back. "Are you sure you're okay?" He took my chin in his hand and turned my face side to side, looking at me just like Mom used to after an accident.

"Yeah," I said. "I'm freaked out and a little wet, and I'm really worried about Summer, but other than that, I'm okay. I think we ought to start moving, to see if we can find anyone else. You ready to do some walking?"

He shook his head. "I'm really spooked," he said with a wry smile. I smiled back. "I don't think I can do any searching tonight. I hurt my ankle."

"How bad is it?"

"I smashed it pretty good on one of the rocks, I guess. In the river it hurt so bad I thought my foot had been ripped off. When we first stood up, I almost wished it had been."

I scooted down by his feet. There were some dark shadows on his white socks.

"I'm going to take your Teva off," I said. He sucked in his breath as I pulled on the velcro to undo the straps. When I tilted his foot a little to get it off him, he yelled so loud it echoed off the canyon walls. I barely got his sock down three inches before he stopped me.

"Just leave it, Scott," he moaned.

"Yeah, but we need to see how bad it is," I said.

"And do what? We don't have any supplies. And it's not like you can run and call help."

"Maybe that's exactly what I should do," I said slowly.

"Scott, we're at least three miles into the canyon. There's no way."

"I could make it," I said stubbornly.

"Scott," he said, "please don't leave me alone."

I looked at him. "No. I won't do that."

We sat there for a few minutes. The wind had kicked up, and we both began to shiver. I stood up and started to wander around. I looked and listened, but all I could see was the river and clouds, and all I could hear was the rapid in the distance.

"Scott," Gregg said, "you said you wouldn't leave me."

"I won't," I said, "I'll be right back."

By the light of the moon, I wandered back upriver a little way. Most of the shore was sand and brush grass. Farther back, though, I saw some large rocks. There was no sign of anyone else. I turned and went back to Gregg.

"If I help you, do you think you can hop a bit?"

"Why?" he asked warily.

"I think we'd be warmer if we were out of the wind. There are some big rocks that we can kind of get under, if you can make it."

"I'll try," he said, trying to get up.

I reached out and gave him a hand up. It took us a while to get to the rocks. We had to stop often, even though it wasn't very far. Both of us were exhausted, and I had a hard time supporting his weight. We were quiet the whole way, and when we finally made it, we slumped down under a boulder.

After a few minutes, I turned to Gregg. "See? Isn't this warmer?"

He nodded, and then he began to cry again. It was starting to scare me. This wasn't the Gregg I knew. I had never seen him cry so much.

"Gregg," I said, putting my arm around him again, "don't, man. It will be okay. We'll sleep here tonight, and—"

"No," he broke in. "It's not...I just...Oh, God, Scott, I miss them so much!"

I was so startled that I almost asked Who? before I realized he meant Mom and Dad. "Hey, I do too. It's okay to miss them. I mean, we *have* to miss them."

"I thought for a while that I should die, too, just so I wouldn't miss them." He took a deep breath. "But after tonight...I don't want to die, Scott. I don't want to die!"

"No!" I said, scared. "No, you can't want to die! You can't leave me. I couldn't take it!"

"Yes, you could. You've always been able to deal with anything. You've always known all the answers and you've always been able to do the right things."

"Gregg, that's not true," I began.

"Yes, it is, Scott. And it's a good thing, it really is." He sighed. "I wish I was more like you."

I was struck dumb. Gregg had never wanted to be like me. I was his favorite thing to make fun of. He always picked on me. Why would he want to be like me?

"I sometimes think I hate Mom and Dad," he mumbled.

I looked at him. "Why?"

"Because they left us," he said, continuing before I could defend them. "Oh, I know it wasn't their fault, but...then...in a way, it was. I mean, I keep wondering if Dad was drinking that night. We know neither of them had their seat belts on. Why couldn't they have been more careful, even if it was just for our sake?"

I couldn't answer. I had asked myself the same questions every night since they died.

"And then they leave us with someone we don't even know—"

I jumped in. "Yeah, but now we have the chance to get to know him," I said. "It's kind of like they gave us a gift."

"Well, they can take it right back. I want our family back, Scott. I want you and Mom and Dad."

"Rocky's part of our family too," I said.

"No, he's not. If he were our family, he would have been around for Thanksgiving and birthdays. He would have been our uncle."

I started to tell Gregg about the things that Rocky and I had talked about, but I knew I couldn't. That would have to be between Gregg and Rocky.

"You're all I've got, Scott. And I almost lost you too."

"I almost lost you too," I said, hugging him. "But now we know we can't lose each other, right?"

"Right," he agreed. He took a deep shaky breath. "I'm so tired."

"Me too."

I took off the life jacket and spread it out so we could both use it as a pillow. We curled up as best we could on the cold sand in the overhang of the boulder and Gregg quickly fell asleep. I got up at least five or six times, thinking I had heard a voice calling for us, but it must have been the wind. I lay awake for a long time, listening and hoping to hear the others. I couldn't get my mind off Summer. My head was aching and my stomach hurt, but finally I drifted off to sleep.

Chapter Fifteen

The next morning, I woke up suddenly. I couldn't remember where I was. I could hear the rumble of the rapid nearby, and for a minute I thought I was on a two-day trip. Then my eyes focused on the rock above my head, and the memories of last night came thundering back.

I turned quickly to Gregg. He was sound asleep. In fact, he was breathing so slowly that at first I thought he wasn't breathing at all. I sat up and looked at his foot and winced. The sock was dry and crusted with blood. I hadn't thought about the sock drying into the wound last night, or I would have made him take it off anyway.

The sky was a pale blue. The sun couldn't be up very far. I guessed that it was close to six o'clock. We had a few more hours before the tours would start going. *Maybe Rocky has sent someone out to look for us,* I thought. *But no. He's probably thinking I'm off with Roger and Gregg.*

I stretched, reaching up as far as I could. I was stiff and sore all over. My right shoulder was particularly tender, and when I pulled up my sweatshirt, I understood why. There was a dark violet bruise about the size of an orange covering the front of my shoulder. I touched it gently, and decided that that was something I didn't want to do again. I pulled up my pants legs and I could see three more bruises on the front of my legs. One of them was pretty big, but none of them was as dark as the bruise on my shoulder.

Slowly I stood up and wandered down to the river's edge. I splashed my face with the cold water, moving my right arm carefully. I rinsed my mouth out and felt a little better. Then I took the time to examine the new rapid that had left us stranded for the night.

The roughest water was on the right side, exactly where we had entered the rapid. It started with a huge hole, followed by tall standing waves and then a nasty rock field. The left side of the rapid, in contrast, was almost nothing but small standing waves for the whole length of the rapid.

In daylight, had we known the rapid was there, we would never have flipped. In fact, if Roger hadn't disregarded the river static, we probably would have been all right. Of course, if it weren't for Roger, we wouldn't be in this mess anyway.

Thinking of Roger made me wonder where Summer was. I hoped she was okay. Maybe she had been able to get out of the river with Stacey or

Debbie. I felt guilty and angry knowing she might have spent the night in the canyon alone. I didn't want to think about her being hurt.

I don't know how long I stood there just watching the river, but when I turned to go, for some reason I hesitated. I looked over my shoulder. I wasn't too far from the boulder where we had slept. If Gregg woke up and called for me, I would hear him. I sat down on a rock and continued to watch the river.

A few minutes later, an oar raft rounded the bend. The raft was well in the center of the river, and the oarsman quickly moved it to the left. I assumed that it must be a private boat, since commercial trips didn't usually leave this early. I stood up to call and flag them down, when I spotted the Rugged Rapids logo on the front. Then I recognized Rocky at the oars.

"Rocky!" I screamed. "Rocky, over here! River right, river right!" I hollered.

The passenger in the back waved to me. They had heard. The nose of the raft turned slightly, and Rocky began rowing with powerful strokes to the right side of the river.

They were going to be landing close to where Gregg and I had landed last night, maybe a little more downriver. I hurried over to our boulder. Gregg was sitting up slowly.

"What's going on?" he asked.

"Come on!" I said happily, pulling him up. "Rocky's here!"

Gregg hopped over to a rock and sat down on it.

"Come on, Gregg, let's go!"

He shook his head. I started to argue when I heard Rocky call my name.

I turned and started to jog downriver toward the raft. I met Rocky about halfway there. He wrapped me in a big bear hug, lifted me off my feet, and swung me around.

"Are you okay?" he asked, finally, pushing me back so he could look at me.

"Good first-aid technique, Rocky," Jim said from behind him. "Swing him around and then ask if he's okay."

I grinned, trying to ignore the pain in my shoulder. "Yeah, I'm okay. But Gregg's pretty banged up."

"Gregg's here too? Where is he?"

"Back by that big boulder," I said, turning to lead the way.

Gregg had gotten up and was hopping after me. He wasn't very far away.

Rocky went running up to him, but Gregg held his arm out stiffly in front of him, preventing the hug. "I'm a little off balance right now," he said, wobbling a little.

"Well, let me help you," Rocky said, moving to put his arm around him.

Gregg kind of pushed him away. Defensively he said, "I've got it." He started limping along.

"No, you don't," Jim said, coming up. "You need to stay off that foot. Here, Rocky, let's make him an arm chair and carry him down."

Rocky and Jim clasped wrists, and Gregg, muttering that he was okay the whole time, gingerly sat down on it and let them carry him to the raft. I started to follow, then turned and ran back to the boulder to get the life jacket.

I reached the raft just as Jim and Rocky were getting Gregg settled in it.

Jim tugged gently at the sock, and Gregg clenched his teeth. "Nope," Jim said, shaking his head. "I think we ought to just leave it on for the doctor to deal with. Best we can do now is splint it."

Rocky nodded in agreement. "Let's get a space blanket around him too."

I spied Rocky's water jug clipped to the frame. "Rocky," I said with a suddenly dry mouth. "Can I have some water?"

"Sure." He unclipped it and tossed it to me.

I upended it and started gulping it down as fast as I could.

"Whoa, slow down there," Jim said, reaching out and taking it from me. "We need to save some for Gregg and the rest of us."

"What are you guys doing down here so early?" I asked, climbing into the raft. "Not that I'm complaining or anything."

Rocky sighed. "When you didn't get back at twelve-thirty, I was pretty angry. By three o'clock, though, I was really worried. I couldn't remember Summer's last name, so I couldn't call her house. I waited another hour, and then I headed to the office to see if your bike was still there. It was, along with Summer's. I was sure something was wrong, so I went inside to call the police. The office was trashed."

I looked at Gregg. He lowered his head and intently studied his hands.

"After I called the cops, I called Roger's house on a hunch to see if you had gone there. His roommate answered and said that Gregg and Roger hadn't returned from their midnight run yet. When I checked the raft barn, I found a raft missing and Gregg's life jacket gone. I figured you were with them, Scott. I just couldn't figure out why you had left your jacket."

He paused looking from me to Gregg. Neither of us said anything. I could wait to tell him that I hadn't come willingly on this trip; Gregg was in enough trouble as it was. If I waited till everyone was found and things had settled down, maybe Rocky wouldn't take it out on Gregg too much.

"Midnight runs can be fun," he said slowly, "but they're really stupid to do right after heavy rains."

Gregg nodded, but he still didn't say anything.

"Well," Rocky said, "let's go see if we can't find Summer and Roger." He stopped. "Where'd you leave your life jacket?" he asked Gregg.

"Here," I said, and tossed the jacket to Gregg.

Rocky looked at me. "Where's yours?"

"Don't have it."

Rocky made a face at me. "I don't mean *yours,* I mean the one you were using last night."

"I was using Gregg's."

Rocky turned back to Gregg. "Where's the one you were using?"

Gregg shook his head.

Rocky's eyes widened.

"You weren't using one?"

Hunching even further under the blanket, Gregg shook his head again.

"Of all the stupid, asinine things to do! Gregg, how could you be such a moron!" Rocky exploded. "What were you thinking? Do you realize you could have been killed? You never ever go rafting without a jacket! You know that!"

"Yeah, thanks for reminding me," Gregg said in an unsteady voice. He dashed a hand across his eyes, trying to hide the sudden tears.

Rocky's face softened just a little. He turned to me and said, "You know where we keep the spare."

"Yeah," I said, reaching down and unclipping it from the frame. I put it on and adjusted the straps so it fit snugly.

"Well, let's go get Summer and Roger," Rocky said again. "Maybe we'll get really lucky and find the raft in one piece too." He nodded to Jim, who had been standing on the shore holding our bowline. Jim gave us a shove and jumped in, stowing the bowline immediately.

"We also need to be looking for Stacey and Debbie," I said, watching Gregg carefully. He had started shaking just a little, but not as much as last night.

"Stacey and Debbie?" Rocky asked, frowning. "Who are they?"

"They're the ones who went with us a couple of weeks ago on the multiday trip."

Rocky grunted. "Did anybody else go without a life jacket?"

"Just Roger," I said. "He and Gregg gave their jackets to Summer and me."

Jim looked at me. "I take it you weren't on the original passenger list?"

"You could say that," I said with a weak smile.

Rocky muttered something, but all I could make out was "Roger," "stupid," and "trust."

On river left, just below Big Drop, we found Summer and Debbie. They were both sitting on the boulders, watching the river, the same way I had been, except they were pretty far back from the riverbank. Debbie started shouting and waving when we came into view. I didn't know my heart could jump so high into my throat. I hopped out of the raft before we were all the way on the shore and ran up to Summer.

She had dark smudges under her eyes and her face was pale. She tried to smile at me, but I could tell she was in a lot of pain. She turned to one side, stopping me before I got to her.

"I think I've broken my wrist," she said. She was holding her left arm close in to her body.

Jim came up behind me carrying the first aid kit. "Let's take a look," he said. He reached out and gently took her left hand. She gasped and turned a shade whiter. I held her right elbow, steadying her.

"Well, I think it's a pretty good guess that it's broken," he said, surveying it critically. "All we can do right now is splint you up, to try to keep it still." He looked at her. "But it's still gonna hurt going through the rapids."

"I know," she said.

Jim looked over at Debbie as he dug through the first aid kit. "How are you?"

She shrugged. "I'm not hurt like her, if that's what you mean."

"That's what I mean," he said.

"Good," Rocky said, coming up from behind her. "Why don't you head on down to the raft then?"

"I'm not ever getting in another raft!" she said. "I thought I was going to die!"

"It's a lot safer in the daylight," Rocky said dryly. "And it's the only way out of the canyon from here."

"No way. Uh-uh. You don't understand. I nearly died!" And she burst into tears.

"I do understand," Rocky said, putting his hands on her shoulders. "It's a terrifying experience. But the only way we can get you out of here and to a hospital is to get you on this raft."

She looked at him, tears still rolling down her face. "He said we'd be okay. He said he knew the river and it wasn't dangerous. He said it'd be fun!"

"Roger? Is that what he said?"

She nodded.

Rocky sighed. "The river is always dangerous. And the river changes, especially when there's a lot of rain."

"Then I'm not getting back on it!" she said, backing up quickly.

"Now, Debbie, it's the only way back. And as long as you recognize that the river is dangerous and you respect that, you'll do just fine."

Her bottom lip quivered. "Do you promise we won't flip over?"

"I can't do that. I can almost guarantee, but I can't promise. I've got two hurt passengers with me now, so you know I'm going to be extremely careful."

"This can't be the only way out," she insisted.

"No," Rocky admitted. "You could try to walk. But from here in the canyon, it's going to be almost a ten-mile hike to the nearest road. And we don't have any supplies for you. The river will be much faster."

"Come on, Debbie," I added. "I've been rafting this section of the river with Rocky lots of times. He knows what he's doing."

Debbie still hesitated.

"We need to get going," I pressed. "We need to find Stacey and Roger, and we need to get Gregg and Summer to the hospital as quickly as possible."

"Okay," she said finally. "Okay."

We walked back to the raft. She stopped a few feet away from it. "I don't want to ride with Gregg," she said.

I didn't understand, but I didn't want to stick around here any longer. "Fine. Summer and I will get in the back with him. You and Jim can ride up front."

I helped Summer climb to the back of the raft without hitting her wrist on anything. She sat down across from Gregg, tucked in as close to the frame as she could get. That left me at the very end of the raft, without a whole lot to hang on to. But they were hurt; it was more important they be secure in the raft. Jim tossed me another space blanket, and I helped Summer get it around her shoulders.

Even though I had been terrified last night, afraid that I might actually die, I was looking forward to rafting today. I guess the river had finally gotten into me completely, heart and soul.

I turned to Summer as we shoved off again. She was pale and trembling a little. I inched closer to her. "Are you sure you're okay?"

She nodded. I could tell she was close to tears. "I was so afraid we'd have to wait till nine or ten, when the other trips come through. I hope we find Stacey and Roger soon."

"Me too."

"Brrrr." Her teeth were chattering. "I'm freezing."

I scooted even closer to her and put my arm around her. She leaned into me and rested her head on my shoulder. Her shivering shook me too.

"Is Debbie really okay?"

"Yeah, but I'm glad you all showed up. I was going to kill her if she didn't quit whining. That's all she was doing—whining about how scared and awful she felt. As if I hadn't been through the same thing! That and her boyfriend. She's paranoid about what her boyfriend's going to say."

"It must've been awful, being in the river for so long," I said. "I had a hard time just swimming through the new rapid, let alone getting through Big Drop too."

"Oh," she said, "I didn't swim through Big Drop. I started walking downriver, hoping that maybe I'd find the rest of the group, or maybe even the raft and we'd be able to get going again." She sighed. "All I found was Debbie. And she was too terrified even to walk along the river. She was afraid she was going to fall in. I couldn't just leave her."

I gave her half a hug. "I'm sorry about the whole thing." I kissed her on the forehead. "I'm glad you're okay."

"You don't have anything to apologize for," she said, glaring at Gregg. "It wasn't your fault we got thrown into the raft."

Gregg didn't even raise his head to look at her. All the good feelings from our long talk last night seemed to have disappeared. He owed everybody lots of apologies, and he wasn't giving any. All he was doing was sulking like he was the one who had been done wrong.

"Excuse me," Rocky said over his shoulder from the cockpit. "Did you say you were thrown in?"

"That's exactly what I said. Bozo here grabbed me and the other jerk grabbed Scott and they threw us into the raft!" Her voice was full of rage. "At least this one gave us his life jacket."

"And he talked Roger into giving us his too," I added.

She looked at me, and I could almost hear her ask me "What are you doing?" but she didn't.

Rocky didn't say anything else. We hit the next rapid, Squeeze Play, and he did everything he could to pick out a smooth run. Even so, Gregg and Summer got bounced around quite a bit.

Suddenly Jim called out, "River right, Rocky, river right!"

Rocky began pulling us to the right, and I stood up, scanning the beach for what Jim had seen.

The raft was pinned up against some rocks in the shallow water. Only one oar was still with it, and that one was split in half, hanging at a crazy angle. One of the tubes had ruptured and was flat, but the rest were pretty well intact.

Gregg and Summer stayed on the raft, following Rocky's instructions. Debbie was too scared to stay there, so she got out with us. Jim gave her the bowline and had her anchor the raft to a tree and stay with it.

Rocky, Jim, and I waded out into the river to get the raft. Rocky pulled the broken oar off and tossed it up onto the beach. We struggled for a few minutes, but we finally got the raft up on the rocks and out of the river so we could drain the water from the bottom. Then we picked it up and carried it to the beach.

"Go ahead and open the valves to start deflating," Rocky said. "Open the floor valves first."

I went around the raft, opening the valves. Jim took the bowline and tied it to a nearby tree, then came back to help me. Rocky made a couple of trips back to the river and returned carrying some good-sized rocks. He set them in the bottom of the raft.

I looked at him. "We're not taking it with us?"

He shook his head. "We don't have the room, especially if we find Stacey and Roger. And we don't have the time to completely deflate it, pack it, and secure it to the raft. I'll send someone to pick it up later today."

"I think it's pretty well anchored, Rocky," Jim said.

Rocky nodded. "Let's get going and see if we can find the last two renegades." He looked tired, almost defeated.

Jim quickly stowed the bowline and pushed us off shore.

We went through the next two rapids without seeing anyone. Right before we got to the third one, I heard someone yelling. I looked around. There was Stacey, on the right bank.

It was too late for us to stop to get her, so we went through the rapid and pulled in on the right side as quickly as we could. Jim tried to get Debbie to hold the raft again, but she took off up the riverbank after Stacey. I climbed out and took the bowline from Jim.

"Go ahead. I'll tie off."

He nodded, picked up the first aid kit, and trotted after Debbie. Rocky moved to the back of the raft.

"How are you two doing?"

"Okay," Summer said with forced optimism. Gregg didn't answer.

"Gregg? Are you going to make it?"

"Yeah," he said lifelessly.

"I'm trying to get us the fastest, smoothest ride out of here. I know you're both in a lot of pain."

"Thanks for your help, Rocky," Summer said.

"Well, you know what this means now," he said.

"What?"

"Instead of me cooking a nice dinner for you and Scott..."

Summer laughed. "Scott and I will have to cook a nice one for you," she finished.

"Hey," I said, wading in to stand by the back of the raft. "That's not fair. I've been doing most of the cooking so far anyway."

"Yeah, but I just saved your tail," he said.

"Good point," I said. "So what can you cook?" I asked Summer.

"I can pretty much make toast and boil water," she said.

I groaned. "I'm going to get stuck with the whole thing again!"

Rocky leaned forward and pretended to whisper to Summer, even though he made sure I could hear. "Let him do all the work. He's a good cook."

Summer laughed.

Gregg ignored the whole conversation and just stared at the far side of the canyon.

"I wonder what the problem is," Rocky began, looking up the trail. "We really need to get going to find—Oh, God," Rocky said, breaking off. He hopped out of the raft and was halfway up the hill before I could even see what he was reacting to.

Jim was carrying Stacey to the raft, and Debbie was carrying his first aid kit. Stacey was unconscious.

"What happened?" Rocky asked, moving to take Stacey from him.

Jim shook his head ever so slightly and kept moving to the raft. "I can't find any broken bones or bruises, but that doesn't mean it's not internal bleeding. I'm pretty sure it's shock, since she was able to call for help like that. Most likely the relief of being found just overwhelmed her and she passed out. We still need to get her to the hospital, though, and quickly."

Debbie had started crying again, a silent stream of tears. I don't think she even realized she was crying. It was kind of spooky.

"Do we have any more blankets?"

Rocky shook his head. "I didn't even think to grab another first aid kit."

"Here," Summer said. "Stacey needs it more than I do."

Jim looked at her closely before nodding and taking it from her.

"I'll try to stay close and keep you warm," I said in a low voice, but Jim's grin and sudden coughing fit told me he had heard as well.

As Jim got Stacey settled into the raft, I untied the bowline again and coiled it up. He came to take it from me.

"Go ahead and get in the back, Scott," he said.

"Is she going to be okay?" I asked.

"We'll know as soon as we get to the hospital, but it needs to be quickly. We need to get you all to the hospital. I might have missed other injuries on any one of you."

"Do you think we'll find Roger?" I asked very quietly.

Jim looked at me for a minute. "He didn't have a jacket?"

I shook my head.

Looking at the ground, he said, "I don't know, Scott. We've already come a few miles downriver from where you flipped. Swimming that far through those rapids without a jacket..." He hesitated. "I'm not saying it can't be done..." His words trailed off again.

"But it doesn't look good," I said for him, barely whispering.

"No," he said, "it sure doesn't."

"Let's go, Scott," Rocky called from the raft.

I climbed to the back of the raft and sat down next to Summer.

"You okay?" she asked.

I put my arm around her but didn't answer. After a minute, she leaned her head against my shoulder. Jim shoved us off.

The rest of the trip was the quietest rafting I ever experienced. With each passing rapid, the tension in our group increased.

When we reached the last rapid, I looked across the raft to Gregg. His dull eyes met mine. I could tell he already knew. In his heart, he knew.

Ray was waiting for us at the pullout. Rocky ushered us all quickly on to the bus. I helped Summer climb in and silently followed her. There was virtually no talking among any of us. There had been no sign of Roger.

Jim stayed by the raft. He would wait until arrangements could be made to come pick it up. Rocky quietly asked Ray to drive us to the hospital in Salida. As we drove, Rocky gave Ray instructions. First, Rocky Mountain Search and Rescue needed to be notified. Laura and Ray would have to reschedule a couple of the trips, and Ray would take Rocky's trip down the Gorge. Two of the first-year guides would go to pick up the damaged raft.

Debbie was still crying off and on. Stacey had opened her eyes, but she answered only direct questions, and then in a soft voice that was hard to hear.

Rocky went to the back of the bus and talked to Stacey and then Debbie quietly for a few minutes. Then he came up to Summer and me. He sat down in the bench right behind us.

"Summer, I need to get your parents' names and their phone number so I can call and let them know where you are while you get checked out by the doctor."

She turned around and told him quietly.

Rocky leaned back in his seat and looked at Gregg, who was sitting across the aisle and a couple of benches in front of us. Slowly he shook his head.

"He'll be okay," I said.

"Good," Rocky said shortly. "I want him in one piece when I kill him."

I didn't quite know how to take that, so I turned back around and we rode the rest of the way to the hospital in silence.

The group got split up in the emergency room. My exam didn't take very long. The doctor only found several bruises and scrapes, most of which I had already identified. The worst bruise was on my shoulder, and he thought it was possible that I might have a small fracture. He sent me for X rays, but they came back all right.

I wandered back to the waiting room, looking for Rocky. He wasn't there, but a cop was.

"Scott Baxter?"

"Yeah?"

"I'm Deputy Harris. I need to ask you a few questions about last night. If you'll just come with me?"

"Okay," I said, and followed him to a room down the hall.

We sat down and he took out a little pad of paper.

"What happened?"

I laughed nervously. "This will take a while."

"That's fine."

So I told him. Everything. The fact that we hadn't found Roger made it a little easier to keep the vindictive tone out of my voice when I talked about him and the fact that Gregg was sulking so much made it a lot easier to tell the truth about his role, without sugarcoating it for the cop.

When I finished, the deputy asked a few more questions, mostly just rephrasing what I had said to make sure he had it right. Then he stood up, shook my hand, and gave me his card in case I remembered anything else that he should know.

"What about Roger?" I asked.

"We're keeping in touch with Search and Rescue. Hopefully we'll be able to find him."

I nodded. "What's going to happen now?"

He shrugged. "I can't say for sure until I talk to the other members of this trip. Right now though, my guess is that Roger and Gregg will be charged with theft, breaking and entering, trespassing, and possibly several other counts as well, including kidnapping."

My mouth got dry. He was talking about my brother like he was a criminal.

"This is pretty serious," I said weakly.

"Yeah," he said. "It most definitely is."

I walked back to the waiting room, and this time Rocky was there.

"Hey," I asked, "where did you go off to?"

"I had to go speak to the cops. I think they'll want to talk to you too."

"They already did."

Rocky nodded. "Did you tell them everything?"

"Yes."

"Even about Gregg?" he asked, arching an eyebrow.

"What's that supposed to mean?"

"I just know that you've been in the habit of covering up for him. I was curious if you were still doing it."

"There's nothing wrong with helping a brother," I said defensively.

"There is if it means he never learns how to help himself." I started to say something, but then he added softly, "Believe me, I know."

I sighed. "I told them everything."

"Good."

"You don't have to sound so smug about it."

"What?"

"I know you don't like Gregg, but that doesn't mean you should be happy that he's going to get busted for this."

"I do like Gregg, and I'm not happy that he's in trouble—"

"Yeah, right, whatever."

"Scott—" he began, but then the doctor came out.

"Mr. Baxter?"

Rocky stood up. "Yes?"

"Your son's going to be okay. He's got a pretty nasty fracture and an infection. We're giving him a lot of antibiotics to try to stop the infection from spreading. We'll need to keep him here tonight for observation, but he should be all right. He's resting now, if you'd like to see him."

I looked at Rocky for a second, waiting for him to say something, then turned to the doctor. "He's not Gregg's father. He's our uncle. And I'd like to see my brother."

Rocky looked like I had kicked him. The doctor looked surprised but then he nodded and said, "Third door on your left."

I started to walk down the hall.

"Just a minute, Scott." I turned around. Deputy Harris was there. "I'm afraid I need to speak to Gregg alone for a few minutes before anyone else sees him."

I stalked back to the waiting room and threw myself into a chair. Rocky followed me, but he didn't say anything. I refused to look at him.

A few minutes later, Summer came into the room. Her left arm was in a cast.

She grinned weakly at us. "Dr. Jim called it right. I've got several little fractures in my wrist." She turned to Rocky. "Were you able to reach my parents?"

"Yeah, I was. They should be here pretty soon."

Almost as soon as the words were out of his mouth, the double doors opened, and a couple rushed in. The woman immediately ran over and swept Summer into a hug.

"Oh, baby, are you all right?"

"Yeah, Mom, I'm okay," Summer said. She looked exactly like her mom.

Her dad came up. He was tall and lean, and his hair was a little darker than Summer's. She had his blue eyes, though. "Hey, now, save one of those hugs for me."

He gave her a big hug and patted her on the back. Then he stepped back and looked at her. "We were furious last night when you were late."

"Until about one," her mother added quickly. "Then we knew something was wrong. But we didn't know who to call. We were worried sick about you."

"Um, Mom, Dad, this is Scott," Summer said, turning to me.

"Hi," I said. "Sorry we missed curfew."

"But it wasn't his fault," Rocky said, before they could say anything.

Deputy Harris came back. "Summer Greene?"

"Yeah?"

"I need to ask you a few questions. Will you come with me, please?"

"Wait a minute," Mr. Greene said. "I'd like to come with her."

"And you are?"

"Her father."

Deputy Harris nodded and led them down the hall.

Mrs. Greene turned to us. "Do you know where the doctor is? I'd like to find out from him what I need to watch for. Summer will just tell me she's fine and that the cast will melt off by itself when it's ready."

Rocky stood up. "I can help you find him." As he walked toward the hall with her, he called over his shoulder, "Scott, you can probably go see Gregg now."

I got up and walked down the hall. I knocked softly before I went in.

Gregg was lying on the bed. His leg was in a cast, suspended from a contraption on the ceiling.

"Hey," I said softly.

Apparently he didn't hear me. "Hey," I said again, louder.

"Go away."

I stopped short. "What?"

"You heard me."

"Why?"

"You got me busted. I don't need you around."

"Excuse me?"

"That deputy that was just in here," he said, staring straight at the ceiling. "When I told him that we all just went for fun, he said you had a different story. He said that based on your story, I'll be charged with kidnapping, theft, breaking and entering, and who knows what else. I think you've done enough for today. Why don't you just leave me alone?"

"What did you expect me to do?"

"You didn't have to bust me!"

"Yeah, I did, because the only other thing I could have done was lie and get busted for something I didn't do!"

"You were on the raft too."

"Not by choice."

"Oh, like you really fought that hard. You know you wanted to go with us."

"I did not! I kicked and twisted and tried to get away from Roger. Besides," I said, "you can't tell me that Summer didn't fight you."

"Oh, she fought me all right. Fought harder than you could have. You're such a wimp."

I shook my head in disbelief. "Let me get this straight. You break into our uncle's office, trash the place, steal his raft, kidnap me and my girlfriend, and *you're* mad at *me?*"

He didn't answer, just stared at the ceiling.

"Gregg, what is your problem? You act like the world owes you a favor or something. Like you should just get to do whatever you want and ignore reality, while the rest of us have to struggle through everything! You owe everybody—Summer, Rocky, me, everybody—an apology. And you're acting like we did you wrong!"

"I do not owe—" he began.

I cut him off. "Rocky has done nothing wrong. He's given us all he can, and all you do is spit in his face! You better apologize to him when he comes in here."

"Thanks for the lecture, *Dad,*" he said, sarcastically.

"Dad is not here!" I exploded. "I wish he was so he could kick your sorry butt back into shape! Get it together, Gregg. It's time for you to grow up." I turned and pulled the door open to leave.

As I stepped through the door, I kept listening, waiting for him to call me back into the room. All I heard was the door shutting behind me.

169

Chapter Sixteen

ummer and her parents left around ten. Debbie and Stacey had to stay overnight for observation. Their boyfriends showed up, but they didn't stay very long. I couldn't blame them.

Deputy Harris came out to talk to Rocky again around eleven. While they had a hushed conversation in a corner of the room, I played a game of solitaire and tried to hear what they were saying.

"Scott?"

I looked up into Rocky's face. He looked defeated. "We need to talk."

"Sure," I said, collecting the cards from my game. I was losing anyway. "What's up?"

"Gregg's not going to be coming home for a couple of days," Rocky said as he pulled a chair up close to mine.

"Why?" I asked, alarmed. "What's wrong with him? I thought they just needed to keep him for observation for a night."

"No, no, he's fine. He'll just be here tonight."

"I don't understand."

"You and Summer won't be charged, based on what the two of you, Stacey, and Debbie all reported. Roger and Gregg, however, face several charges." He paused and took a deep breath. "Gregg is under arrest, and there is a warrant out for Roger right now."

For a few seconds I just looked at him. "What does that mean?"

"It means that tomorrow, when Gregg's released from the hospital, he'll be taken to the station and formally charged."

I swallowed. "How long will he have to stay in jail?"

"The arraignment won't be until Tuesday, so he'll have to stay at least Monday night."

"At least?" I asked. "Why would he have to stay longer?"

"The only way he will be released is if someone posts bail." He was looking at the wall behind me.

It took a minute for me to recognize what he was implying. He was thinking about leaving Gregg in jail!

I started to shout, "That's—" then I stopped abruptly.

"That's what?" Rocky asked.

Slumping down in my chair, I muttered, "That's exactly what Dad said he'd do the next time Gregg got busted."

Rocky looked at me hopefully. "Your dad threatened to leave him there?"

I nodded. "He said he only allowed one major screwup from each son."

"That makes me feel a little better," Rocky sighed. "I wish I could say that was the only reason I'm thinking he'll be there for two nights. It's also going to take me a couple of days to get the money together."

I bowed my head. "We sure have wrecked your summer."

Rocky tried to laugh. "I'm sure nephews cause problems for uncles on a regular basis. You and Gregg have just been making up for lost time."

Looking back up at him, I said gratefully, "You're pretty cool, Rocky."

He shook his head and ran his fingers through his hair. "I thought learning how to manage a rafting company was hard. It's nothing compared to learning how to deal with you two." He took a deep breath. "I should go see if Gregg's awake. We have a lot to talk about."

"Do you want me to come with you?"

"No," he said, standing up. "Gregg and I need to work on our communication. I can't think of a better time for us to start."

"Okay." I shrugged.

I watched him walk down the hall, stopping to talk to the nurse on his way. Before he opened Gregg's door, he actually stopped and stood up straighter, pulling his shoulders back.

I stayed in the waiting room for twenty minutes, playing three games of solitaire. Then an orderly came in and started mopping the floor. I was dying to know what was going on anyway, so I used getting out of the orderly's way as an excuse to go stand outside Gregg's room.

The door was open a few inches. Just as I was raising my hand to knock, I heard Rocky.

"Ignoring me is not going to make this go away, Gregg. I need to know if you have anything to say."

I put my hand down and turned so I was leaning against the wall.

Rocky waited a few moments before he said, "Sulking like this is not going to make me want to find bail money any faster. Maybe I should just leave you there, like your father said he would."

"You are not my father!" Gregg exploded. I jumped. I was outside the room, but it sounded almost like he had yelled in my ear.

"No, Gregg, I'm not. I've said that before and I'll say it again. I'm not your father. I'm your father's brother, I'm your uncle, I'm someone who cares about you. That's all I am."

"You don't care about me." Gregg's voice was sulky and muffled. I could almost see him turning his head into the pillow.

"If I didn't care—" Rocky began.

"You wouldn't be here," Gregg finished in a very sarcastic voice. "Yes, you would. You're required to be here."

"Actually, Gregg, I'm not. I could have dropped you and Scott off here and gone back to the shop for the day. I have a lot that needs to be taken care of—keeping up the daily trips, bringing a damaged raft in from the canyon, cleaning up my vandalized office, filling out police reports. I'm here because I care. I..." Rocky's voice broke. "I don't want to spend the rest of my life without family. I loved and missed your father, and I'll never get a chance to tell him that. I don't want to lose my nephews too."

Standing outside, I swallowed. Rocky had kept his emotions from us for so long, we couldn't tell if he felt anything. At that moment I didn't have to see his face to know that he was hurting.

There was no answer from Gregg. In my mind, I screamed at him to give Rocky a chance, just a small one. I was tired of being in the middle. I was tired of having to pick sides. I was tired of watching the only family I had spend all their energy fighting.

It was quiet for so long that I risked a quick peek through the door opening. Rocky was standing next to Gregg's bed. Tentatively, he reached out with one hand and brushed Gregg's hair back.

Gregg jerked his head to the other side.

Rocky sighed and bowed his head. "Well, I hope you'll think about what I've said. You'll have at least a couple of nights to think about it. Since you don't seem to want me here, I'll leave now, and I won't bother you tomorrow either. But I will come see you on Tuesday. I'll be there for the arraignment. Maybe you'll feel like talking then."

I pulled my head back from the door and walked quickly back to the waiting room.

After waiting almost ten minutes for Rocky, I started to get fidgety. I wondered if I should go back. Maybe Gregg had finally given in. Or, more likely, they were involved in another shouting match.

Just as I was starting to get up, Rocky came in from a different hallway. He looked totally composed and in control again.

"Where did you go?" I asked.

"I had to talk to Deputy Harris again," he said, "and fill out some paperwork for the hospital. Are you ready to go home? It's almost two o'clock."

Eagerly, I nodded.

"Let's go."

On the way out, I casually asked him how the talk with Gregg had gone.

"It was pretty typical," he said.

"What did you tell him?" I asked.

"Nothing he hasn't heard before."

"Like what?"

Rocky looked at me, amused. "Why?"

"You were in there for a long time," I said.

"We had a lot to cover."

"So what did he say?"

He shook his head. "Hardly anything."

"But—"

"Scott," Rocky stopped and turned to me. "I really think this needs to stay between me and Gregg. That's why I asked you to wait while I talked to him alone. It's really none of your business."

"He's my brother," I said hotly. "That makes it my business."

Rocky reached out to put an arm lightly around my shoulders. "Yes, he's your brother, but that doesn't mean you need to know everything between us."

Annoyed, I ducked out from under his arm. "I might be able to help."

"This is for Gregg and me to deal with," Rocky said firmly. He looked around the parking lot. "Now where did Laura leave my truck?" he muttered to himself. We found it a few seconds later and drove home in silence. The vibration of the truck made me sleepy.

As soon as we got home, I went straight for the shower. The hot water beating down on me felt wonderful on all my sore muscles. I stayed in until the water started to get cold.

Rocky made us some hamburgers and salad. We ate in silence. I was still angry, both at him and Gregg, and I didn't know what to do about either of them.

When we finished the dishes, he turned to me. "Chess?"

I shook my head. His smile faded. "I'm sorry, Rocky. All I want to do right now is curl up in bed and sleep forever."

"Of course," he said quickly. "You've been acting so normal today, I almost forgot you were with them last night." He paused. "I have a lot of things to do tomorrow, to try to straighten things out." He looked at me. "I want you to stay home and take it easy tomorrow and Tuesday."

"Okay," I said, trying to keep my eyes open.

"Go on, you're falling asleep right here."

I didn't argue. I managed to brush my teeth, but that was about it. I stretched out on top of the blankets, telling myself I'd get up and change in a few minutes.

When I woke up the next morning, the sun was streaming in the window. I was under the comforter from the couch, and my shoes and shirt were off. I couldn't help smiling a little. Rocky may not have had anyone living with him for a long period of time, but he was very attentive and caring when people were here.

When I tried to roll out of bed, I gasped in pain. My shoulder was throbbing, and the rest of my body had stiffened up. I hurt all over. I slowly lifted myself off the bed, stumbled to the bathroom, and got in the shower. The first few minutes, the pressure of the water caused even more pain. I stayed in anyway, and soon the warmth made my body relax and loosen up. I used all the hot water in the tank again.

I settled down on the couch to read. I woke up almost three hours later, absolutely starving. I made lunch and then called Summer.

Her mother answered and said she was sleeping. I asked her to leave a message for Summer to call me, and she promised she would.

In my bedroom, I tried to reorganize the clothes in my drawers and straighten things up. I guess I wanted things to look good for Gregg when he came back. Then I picked up my book to read again. I think I got through four chapters before I fell asleep again.

This time when I woke up, it was already dark out. As I stumbled out of my bedroom, rubbing my eyes, I heard Rocky's chuckle. I squinted at him in the glare of the living room lights.

"What's so funny?" I demanded.

He raised his eyebrows. "Nothing, nothing. Are you hungry?"

I nodded, and put my hand on top of my head. I could feel my hair sticking up all over in every direction. I didn't care.

Rocky made dinner, and then we played a couple of games of chess. He beat me both times. By the second game I could barely focus on the board.

"Why don't you go to bed?" Rocky suggested.

Ignoring the idea, I asked, "What's the plan for tomorrow?"

"The arraignment is scheduled for three. I'll go in and work tomorrow morning, and then go down to the courthouse."

"What about me?"

"You take tomorrow off again."

"Can I come to the courthouse with you?"

Rocky looked at me for a long moment. "I don't know," he said slowly. "I don't want to keep you away from Gregg, but I really think he and I need time alone to sort things out." His tone indicated it was my choice.

I frowned at the chessboard. I wanted to see Gregg; I needed to make sure he was okay. But I knew Gregg didn't want me around right now. And as much as I hated to admit it, Rocky was right. I couldn't help him and Gregg get along. They had to figure it out themselves.

Sighing, I said, "I guess I'll stay here and cook a welcome-home dinner." I picked up my bishop and moved it.

Rocky looked at the board for a minute and then looked at me. "Why don't you go to bed?" he repeated.

I shook my head stubbornly. "I slept all day."

"Well, of course you did. You went through a very exhausting and traumatic experience." Slowly and deliberately, he took my bishop with his pawn, showing me how stupid my move had been. "Now go on, go to bed."

I was too tired to argue. I slept until nearly ten the next morning.

After hanging around the house for a while, I started getting bored. I went outside and sat on the old tire swing for a little while. I kept thinking about Rocky and Gregg, though, and that made me mad again. So I went back inside, trying to find something else to occupy my mind.

I wandered around the house for a while, then decided to just walk down to the office. At least that would get me out of the house.

When I got to the office, I saw my bike still propped up against the wall, right next to Summer's. For a minute I thought about it, but then I shook my head. There was no way I was going to be able to ride all the way into town and back again.

Instead, I walked into the office. Bob and Joe were sitting by the register, talking. When they saw me, they both got up and came over, asking me how I was.

"I'm okay," I said with an embarrassed smile. When Joe moved to put his hand on my shoulder, I practically jumped away from him. "Just a lot of banged-up, tender parts right now." I pulled my shirt collar aside and they admired the bruise.

"So what's the new rapid like?" Joe asked.

"I can't believe you were the first to ever run that rapid. Man, that is so cool!" Bob exclaimed.

"I think it would have been a little cooler in the daylight," I said dryly. "It's right off the blind curve before Big Drop," I continued, and described the hole and the rocks and the length of the rapid.

"Cool. I can't wait to see it," Joe said.

"Me too!" Bob said. "Hey, do you think they'll name it 'Baxter's Bend'?"

"Or maybe 'Midnight Run'?" Joe suggested.

"I have no idea what they'll decide to name it," I said tiredly. "Have they found Roger yet?"

Both of them shook their heads quietly. There was an uncomfortable silence.

"Hey, is the morning paper here?"

They exchanged looks. "No. Why?"

"I was wondering if there would be anything about it in the paper. I don't suppose either of you would be willing to take me into town?" I asked, smiling hopefully.

After a little arguing and some pleading, I got Joe to drop me off by McDonald's.

"How are you going to get home?" he asked as I got out.

I shrugged. "I'll either call Rocky or I'll walk," I said.

"Before you walk, call the office. There will probably be someone there who can come get you."

"Thanks, Joe."

"No problem," he said, driving off.

I hesitated before I walked over to the pay phone and called Summer. She hadn't called back last night. I didn't know if that meant she was mad at me or not. I was afraid her parents might be mad at me too. She answered on the second ring. "Hello?"

Nervously, I asked, "Hey, Summer, how are you feeling?"

"Scott!" she said, and I could hear the smile in her voice. "I'm feeling much better, thank you. How about you?"

"I'm doing all right."

"Sorry I didn't call last night," she said quickly. "I slept through most of the day, and by the time Mom gave me your message, I thought it was too late to call."

"That's okay." I grinned to myself. She wasn't mad at me. "Um, listen, the reason I was calling was to see if you could get out of the house for a bit, or if you're really grounded for a month."

She laughed. "After I explained everything twice, they decided not to ground me. Well, sort of. Mom says I have to take it easy and stick around the house for a few days. She's even taking a couple of days off to stay home with me."

"Oh," I said.

"Besides," she said, "there's no way I'd be up for a bike ride."

"I hear you there," I said as a car passed by.

"What?"

"I hear you," I repeated.

"Where are you?"

"McDonald's."

"Hang on a second," she said.

"Sure," I said, but she was already gone.

"Scott?" she said a few seconds later.

"Right here," I said.

There was an annoying beep in my ear, and the operator said, "Thirty seconds."

"Come over," Summer said quickly.

"What?"

"Come on over for lunch."

"It's okay?"

"I just asked my mom," she said.

"Okay. I'll see you in a few minutes," I said. "Bye."

"Bye," she said, and the operator disconnected us.

I hoped she would be waiting on the front porch, but she met me halfway down the street instead.

"Hey," I said, hugging her carefully.

"Hey," she said back, grinning.

I got on her right side so we could hold hands. "How's the wrist, really?"

She shrugged. "I'm on painkillers, so I'm okay. It's just annoying, having only one hand."

"I bet," I said. "When do I get to sign the cast?"

She laughed. "As soon as we find a good pen."

Mrs. Greene had made us tuna salad sandwiches, brownies, and lemonade. She stayed in the kitchen for a few minutes, then she went outside to work in her garden.

"She's pretty cool," I said after she left.

Summer kind of nodded. "She's a parent. She can be cool when she wants to be, but she can also be a complete pain in the neck. Sunday night she didn't want to let me out of her sight. She was convinced that I was going to pass out from pain or exhaustion or a brain injury or something. I had to chase her out of the bathroom so I could shower in private."

I laughed. "She was just worried about her little girl."

"Yeah, I know," Summer sighed. "But I'm not a little girl anymore."

We took our time eating lunch, talking about a lot of things. Summer mentioned she heard that Roger and Gregg were being charged and wanted to know if it was true.

"Yeah," I said, "but I really don't want to talk about it right now."

"Okay." She shrugged.

"It's not that I don't want to talk to you," I began.

"Scott, it's okay. I'm not offended."

"Are you sure?"

She laughed. "Yes. Now stop it."

So we talked about other things for a while. Then Mrs. Greene came back into the kitchen. "Okay," she said briskly. "Summer, you need to take your medicine and go lie down for a nap."

"Mother!" Summer exclaimed, turning crimson.

"The doctor said you needed to get plenty of rest. Besides, that medicine puts you to sleep anyway. Scott, I'll give you a ride home."

"Thank you, Mrs. Greene," I said, watching Summer. She looked really tired. "You don't have to do that."

"No," she said, smiling agreeably, "but I'm going to anyway."

Summer shook her head. "There's no arguing with her today, Scott. I'm sorry." Then she looked at her mother. "I'm coming with you."

"No, Summer. Just stay here and rest."

"And trust you not to say anything embarrassing to him? No way!" She turned around and padded down the hall, returning a few seconds later with a pair of shoes.

On the drive back, Mrs. Greene asked how everyone else from our midnight run was doing. I told her briefly about Gregg, skipping over the arrest, and then about Debbie and Stacey.

"What about your brother's friend?" she asked when I finished.

"Roger," Summer said.

"He hasn't been found yet."

"Oh, how awful," Mrs. Greene said, shuddering. I could tell she was thinking that it could have been Summer who was still missing.

I asked her to drop me off at the office, saying I had forgotten something. I made Summer promise to call me later that night. Mrs. Greene and I loaded Summer's bike into their car. As they pulled out of the parking lot, I wandered into the office.

"Hey, Scott!" Bob called when I came in. "Rocky left about an hour and a half ago to get Gregg. He was kind of mad when he found out Joe took you into town."

"Thanks for the warning," I said. "See you tomorrow."

The sky was overcast and it was threatening to storm again, but I didn't hurry. I walked slowly back to the house, wondering how I was going to deal with Gregg and Rocky. I knew I couldn't play middleman any more. They were going to have to learn to deal with each other.

I loved them both. It came as a surprise to realize that I loved Rocky, but I did. And no matter how much my brother pitched a fit and ticked me off, I still loved him.

Gregg needed to realize that just because Mom and Dad had died, it didn't mean our family had died. Life went on, and he needed to go on, too, with our family. And Rocky needed to know that just being an uncle didn't automatically mean we would love and respect him.

The question was, how was I going to get them to sit down with each other long enough to make them realize that all we had left was each other? How was I going to get them to stop tearing our family apart?

There was a light on in the living room, and the window was open. I could hear Rocky and Gregg before I got very close to the house.

"This sucks!" Gregg complained.

I sighed. Apparently Rocky's conversation hadn't gone as planned.

"It's not that bad," Rocky said.

"Your TV doesn't even get any good stations."

"That will leave you with plenty of free time for other things."

"Like what? I'm stuck on this stupid couch."

"Like reading up on the rivers and procedures. And learning to play chess."

I stopped just short of the front porch and stared in the window in disbelief.

"I'm not sure I want to learn how to play chess," Gregg said.

"Why not?"

"It's a boring game."

Rocky laughed. "I bet you'll find it a lot more exciting than watching static on the TV."

Rocky and Gregg were leaning over the chessboard. With the light behind them, all I could really see were the silhouettes of their faces. I had never realized that they had the same profile, but they did.

"Just set your side of the board up the same way I'm setting my side up."

"Why do you get to be black?"

"Because it's my chessboard."

"I want to be black."

"Tough."

I had to smile. They were bickering, but it finally had a friendly tone to it. The chances of them ever agreeing without bickering probably didn't exist. I wondered what Rocky had said to Gregg, but I knew he would probably never tell me. I decided it didn't matter, not if we were all going to stay together.

I opened the front door. "Hey!"

"Scott, you were supposed to stay home and take it easy today," Rocky began.

"I know. I'm sorry."

"Go ahead, Rocky, ground him," Gregg said.

"What if I just make him cook dinner instead?" Rocky asked.

"I guess that will work," Gregg said.

My family. It felt good.

The End

Rafting Guide Drowns

Buena Vista, CO (AP)—The Arkansas River claimed another victim Monday afternoon when the body of 21-year-old Roger Anderson was found.

Authorities say Anderson was part of a group who made a "midnight run" down the Arkansas. They were flipped at a new rapid which had been formed by a flashflood earlier in the day. Although Anderson was an experienced guide, he was not wearing a life jacket at the time of the accident.

Other members of the group will be charged with negligent